MARRIED TO THE MOP

Books by Barbara Colley

MAID FOR MURDER

DEATH TIDIES UP

POLISHED OFF

WIPED OUT

MARRIED TO THE MOP

Published by Kensington Publishing Corporation

A Charlotte LaRue Mystery

MARRIED TO THE MOP

Barbara Colley

KENSINGTON BOOKS
www.kensingtonbooks.com

KENSINGTON BOOKS are published by

Kensington Publishing Corp.
850 Third Avenue
New York, NY 10022

All Kensington titles, imprints, and distributed lines are available at special quantity discounts for bulk purchases for sales promotions, premiums, fund-raising, educational or institutional use.

Special book excerpts or customized printings can also be created to fit specific needs. For details, write or phone the office of the Kensington Special Sales Manager: Kensington Publishing Corp., 850 Third Avenue, New York, NY 10022. Attn: Special Sales Department. Phone: 1-800-221-2647.

Library of Congress Card Catalogue Number: 2005924282
ISBN 0-7582-0764-6

First Printing: January 2006
10 9 8 7 6 5 4 3 2 1

Printed in the United States of America

For Captain Charles Colley,
Captain Keith Taylor,
and the rest of our brave soldiers
serving all over the world.

ACKNOWLEDGMENTS

I would like to express my sincere appreciation to all who so generously gave me advice and information while I was writing this book: Detective Mitch Weatherly with the New Orleans Police Department; my dear friend, Linda Fielding; and those wonderful friends who are equally wonderful writers—Rexanne Becnel, Jessica Ferguson, Marie Goodwin, and Karen Young.

I also want to thank Evan Marshall and John Scognamiglio. Their support and advice is invaluable.

Any mistakes made or liberties taken in the name of fiction are solely my own.

Chapter 1

"Is this Charlotte LaRue with Maid-for-a-Day?"

Charlotte barely suppressed an impatient groan. Why, oh, why had she answered the phone? She should have ignored it, or, at the very least, she should have checked the caller I.D. before answering it.

Besides, today was Sunday, for Pete's sake; she didn't work on Sundays. She figured that if even the good Lord Himself had seen fit to rest one day a week, then who was she to question His wisdom?

But ignoring a ringing phone had never been easy for her. She had always been just a bit superstitious that the very call that she ignored would be an emergency call informing her that something had happened to a member of her family.

So, now that you know it's not, just hang up the receiver.

The temptation was strong, but she just couldn't do it. With an impatient sigh, she finally said, "Yes, this is Charlotte."

"Charlotte, my name is Emily Rossi, and I need your help."

Charlotte sighed again and drummed her fingers on the desktop. The one thing she didn't need was another customer. As it was, she had more work than she could handle. Besides, any minute now her family would be coming through the door expecting Sunday lunch, and she still needed to carve the roast and put the food on the table.

Be nice, Charlotte, her conscience chided. *Hear the woman out. You can always say no.*

Charlotte took a deep breath. "What kind of help do you need, Ms. Rossi?"

"Just the general stuff, you know—dusting, vacuuming, mopping."

Charlotte glanced down at the envelope in front of her on her desk. The return address on the envelope belonged to Cheré Warner, one of her full-time employees. She'd received the envelope Friday, but hadn't opened it yet, and, in fact, had put off opening it, dreading the contents, since she was fairly certain that it contained Cheré's resignation letter.

Charlotte tapped the envelope with her forefinger. Then there was Nadia. In addition to being her nephew Daniel's wife, Nadia was also another full-time employee. Any day now Charlotte expected to get a resignation letter from Nadia as well. Not that Charlotte blamed either of the women for her decision.

Cheré had been slowly but surely working her way through college. She'd graduated from Tulane in December and had been actively seeking other employment that fit her business degree.

Nadia was still on maternity leave, but she'd been dropping hints about staying home with her new baby permanently instead of returning to work. And why not? As a well-respected attorney, Daniel made more than enough money to support his new family.

Charlotte had figured that she and Janet Davis, her only part-time employee, could pinch-hit for a while, filling in for Cheré and Nadia until she found replacements for the two women. Anticipating the resignations, she'd gone ahead and placed an ad in the newspaper in hopes of hiring another full-time employee. As a result, she'd already received several résumés that looked good. Even so, she still had to interview them and . . .

"Ms. Rossi, I'm really sorry. Right now I'm booked solid and am shorthanded. I just can't take on any new clients."

A frustrated sound from Emily Rossi whispered through the phone line. "Not even temporary ones?" she asked. "I'm not looking for full-time, permanent help," she hastened to add. "Only temporary help, just a few days until Jennifer—she's my regular maid—can work again. My friend Bitsy—Bitsy Duhe—says you're the best in the city. She's had a family emergency—Jennifer, not Bitsy—and she isn't sure when she can come back to work."

When Emily Rossi paused, Charlotte frowned. Either the poor woman was on the verge of a nervous breakdown or she was as scatterbrained as Bitsy.

"Sorry," Emily finally said. "I'm probably not making sense. It's just that I'm at my wits' end, and Bitsy, bless her old heart, assured me that not only were you the best, but you were trustworthy and—and discreet."

Discreet? Charlotte had to bite her bottom lip to keep from laughing out loud. She supposed she should be flattered, and she would have been had the compliment come from anyone but Bitsy. Bitsy Duhe was the worst gossip in all of New Orleans and didn't know the meaning of the word *discreet.*

"You see," Emily continued, "my husband and I are giving a Mardi Gras party Friday night. We thought that would be the best time since the Endymion Parade and Ball is Saturday evening, and of course no one wants to miss Endymion. Of all times for Jennifer to take off, this is the worst. Not that she can help it," Emily hastened to add. "Believe me, I understand about family emergencies. I've had a few of my own. Anyway, I only need you to come in on Thursday, half a day on Friday before the party, then clean up on Saturday and possibly Sunday after the party. Hopefully Jennifer will be back by the following Monday. And before you say no, I'm prepared to offer you two hundred dollars a day for all four days. Even the half day," she added.

Charlotte blinked and her breath caught in her lungs. Two hundred dollars a day? Emily Rossi had to be desperate indeed to offer that kind of money. Talk about an offer hard to refuse.

After Charlotte remembered to breathe again, she once more glanced down at the letter on her desk. "Ah, you did say 'temporary'?"

"Yes, just those four days. Really, just three and a half days," she added quickly. "Eight hundred total. So, do you think you can do it?"

Charlotte's mind raced. *If*, as she suspected, the letter on the desk was Cheré's resignation and *if* Cheré gave the requisite two weeks' notice, then Charlotte figured that she could do it. She'd already resigned herself to the fact that once Cheré left, she'd have to give up her own two days off each week until she could find a replacement. Working for Emily Rossi just meant giving them up earlier than she had planned.

Taking the temporary job would also mean that she'd have to work for almost two weeks straight, but it wouldn't be the first time she'd done so and she was sure it wouldn't be the last. Besides, she could use part of the money to finally buy paint for her house. The outside of the century-old Victorian double was beginning to look a bit shabby, and she'd been intending to repaint it now for the past two years. Any money left over could be added to her retirement account.

"Hello? Ms. LaRue? Are you still there?"

Emily Rossi's words were barely above a whisper, and the desperation in her tone tugged at Charlotte's heart. She'd been desperate a time or two in her life as well and knew how it felt.

"I'm still here, Ms. Rossi." Charlotte swallowed hard. So much for just saying no. She'd always been a sucker for a sob story. *Yeah, and the money ain't bad either.* Ignoring the irritating voice in her head and telling herself that the money was *not* the only reason she was going to accept the offer, she said, "Okay, Ms. Rossi, what's your address? And what time would you like for me to be there on Thursday?"

"You'll do it? Oh, thank you, thank you! And please, just call me Emily."

"Okay, Emily, but only if you call me Charlotte. Now, what's that address?"

You're such a hypocrite, Charlotte. Again Charlotte ignored the pesky voice and scribbled down the address and time. After once again reassuring the poor woman that she would be there on Thursday morning, she hung up the receiver.

Charlotte stared at the small stack of file folders she'd placed on the corner of her desk. Good thing she'd run that help-wanted ad, she decided. Now all she had to do was find a time to interview the prospects she'd chosen from the responses she'd received.

Two hundred dollars a day. Unbidden, Emily Rossi's offer came to mind again, and Charlotte's gaze slid over to the envelope from Cheré. Ignoring the letter wasn't going to make it go away. With a sigh, Charlotte picked up a letter opener and the envelope, slid the tip of the opener beneath the flap, and ripped it open.

Maybe she was being a bit of a hypocrite about the money, but so what? For more years than Charlotte wanted to count, she had worked in the exclusive, historic Garden District, one of the wealthiest neighborhoods in New Orleans. Her regular clients paid her well, but this was the first time that she'd ever been offered that much money just to clean someone's house. With a shake of her head, she pulled out the one-page letter from inside the envelope and began reading.

Just as she had thought, Cheré was giving notice, but only one week's notice. According to the letter, she'd been hired by an accounting firm in Atlanta and would be reporting to work in two weeks. When Charlotte read the last two lines of the neatly typed letter, her throat grew tight and tears blurred her vision.

I love you, Charlotte, and I'll miss you. You've been like a mother to me, and I'll never forget all that you've done for me.

Though Charlotte had often thought of Cheré as family, until now she had never realized that the bright, energetic young woman had considered her family as well.

Outside, a car door slammed.

Charlotte's gaze flew to the window. "Oh, no," she whispered. They were here and she wasn't ready. Charlotte dropped the letter and hurried to the front window. Peeking out of the window, all she saw though was her neighbor across the street.

"Whew! False alarm, Sweety Boy," Charlotte told the little green parakeet inside the birdcage next to the window.

The parakeet squawked and chirped as he sidled over to

the edge of the cage. Charlotte smiled. "Yeah, yeah, what do you care, you little scamp?"

Turning away from the cage, she hurried back to the kitchen. For years she and her sister, Madeline, had taken turns hosting the family for lunch after church services on Sunday morning; it was a tradition that they had started when their children were young, and surprisingly enough, even now that their children were all adults, everyone usually showed up.

The family was growing by leaps and bounds, she thought with a smile as she grabbed two hot pads. From the oven she removed the huge roast she'd baked earlier that morning before she went to church, and carried it over to the kitchen counter. With her son Hank's recent marriage to Carol, her nephew Daniel's marriage to Nadia, and her niece Judith's ongoing relationship with Billy Wilson, an NOPD patrolman, not to mention Daniel and Nadia's two little ones, her sister, Madeline, and herself, the body count was up to ten.

Charlotte gingerly peeled back the foil from the steaming roast. Using an electric knife, she began slicing it. Everyone in the family had a partner now, everyone but Madeline . . . and everyone but her.

Unbidden, bittersweet memories of the past tugged at her emotions. She'd been engaged once, but thanks to Vietnam, the love of her life had not come home alive. But she'd had one night with him, the night before he'd left, and she would forever be grateful for it. Without that one night she wouldn't have the precious gift of her son, Hank, who had proved to be the joy of her life.

A commotion at the front door jerked Charlotte back to the present.

"Mom?" a deep voice called out.

"Speak of the devil and he shall appear," Charlotte murmured. And from the sounds of things, everyone else was following close behind.

"In the kitchen, son," she called out.

Minutes later, the women were scurrying around setting out the food on the kitchen table buffet-style. From the living room, Charlotte could hear the rumble of male voices where the men had congregated. Charlotte would have loved to be a fly on the wall to hear what they were talking about.

With Hank being a doctor, Daniel a lawyer, and Billy a policeman, Charlotte couldn't help but wonder just what the three men had in common to talk about.

Then she heard the distinct sound of the television, and she rolled her eyes when she recognized the voice of a well-known sports announcer followed by the roar of a crowd.

Of course. What else? She had all but forgotten that today was Super Bowl Sunday. Too bad the New Orleans Saints hadn't made it to the Super Bowl, she thought. At least this year they had made it to the playoffs though, but only by the skin of their teeth.

At that moment Nadia's four-year-old son, Davy, burst into the kitchen. "Aunt Chardy! Mommy! Daddy Danol says I can eat in the living room with the guys and watch football."

Charlotte smiled at the little boy. "Of course you can, honey. After all, you're one of the guys too."

Nadia laughed as she swung baby Daniella, the newest member of the family, up onto her shoulder to burp her. "Guess that means us girls have to stay holed up in the kitchen."

"Mommy! Girls don't play football."

Nadia smiled at her little son indulgently.

Judith walked over to Davy and knelt down in front of him. "Girls may not play football," she said tapping him on the nose with her forefinger, "but this girl likes to watch it."

Davy placed his hands on his hips and frowned. "Aunt Jude, I know you a police 'tective, but Daddy Danol says it's a guy thing."

Judith laughed. "That's *de*-tective, you little scamp, but even girls like football too," she said as she stood.

The little boy puffed up his chest. "Daddy Danol says one day I can play football too."

"Humph! We'll see about that," Nadia and Madeline said at the same time. Then everyone laughed, and even though Charlotte was sure that Davy didn't quite understand why they were laughing, he laughed too.

Nadia smiled at her little son. "Sweetheart, I think Aunt Chardy is ready for everyone to come into the kitchen for blessings and lunch. Would you like to go tell the guys it's time to eat?"

Davy's face brightened, and with an excited yelp he ran out of the kitchen.

Minutes later, everyone gathered around the kitchen table. Charlotte smiled and nodded at Hank. "Would you say the blessings, son?"

Hank grinned. "Sure, Mom." He wrapped his arm around Carol and pulled her close to his side. "Before I do though, Carol and I have an announcement to make." His gaze held Charlotte's and a mischievous look glimmered in his eyes. "Mom, how would you like to be a grandmother?"

Charlotte took a quick, sharp breath and tears stung her eyes as she glanced from Hank's smug expression to Carol's beaming face and back to Hank. "For true?" she exclaimed, her heart pounding with joy.

Both Hank and Carol laughed and nodded. "Yes, ma'am," Hank responded with pride. "Carol is pregnant."

Suddenly, cheers, laughter, and heartfelt words of congratulations erupted around the table as everyone took turns hugging Hank, Carol, and Charlotte.

A few minutes later, when everyone had quieted down again, Hank said, "Now, if everyone would bow their heads . . ."

Long after everyone had finished eating, had cheered for their favorite Super Bowl team, then went home, Charlotte wandered around in a daze.

"Finally," she whispered, savoring the warm feeling within while she stared out of the front window at the sun sinking behind her neighbor's oak tree. After so many years of longing to be a grandmother, she was finally going to have a grandchild.

On Tuesday morning, after she'd brushed her teeth, Charlotte stared at her image in the mirror above the sink as she applied her makeup. A grandmother. She was going to be a grandmother.

Charlotte tilted her head and narrowed her eyes. Did she look like a grandmother? She reached up and smoothed makeup across her forehead. Thanks to good genes, there were only a few wrinkles there. Her finger slid down to trace the ones near the outside corners of her eyes. Only a few there too.

After a finishing touch of lipstick, she picked up the hairbrush and began brushing her hair. Again, thanks to good genes, what little bit of gray she had blended with the honey-brown color.

Charlotte frowned when several strands refused to be tamed into submission. Her usual short, no-nonsense style had grown out a bit longer than she liked. She'd have to add a note to her to-do list to call her hairdresser for an appointment. Meanwhile . . . She picked up a can of hair spray and aimed the spray at the errant strands, then using her hair pick, she held the wayward strands down until the spray dried.

Finally satisfied and deciding that she was being silly about the whole appearance thing, she rolled her eyes and left the room. Who cared whether she looked like a grandmother or not? Certainly not the baby. That baby wouldn't care what she looked like as long as it got lots of love and affection from her. Besides, she had work to do, and standing around worrying about her looks wouldn't get it done.

Outside was a cold, drizzly day as Charlotte climbed in her van and drove to Bitsy Duhe's home. Bitsy's home was a very old, raised-cottage-style Greek Revival and was located on the same street where famed vampire novelist Anne Rice had once lived before she moved to California.

As usual, Bitsy, with her gray-blue hair and dressed in one of her many flowered dresses, was standing on the front gallery waiting for Charlotte to arrive.

Charlotte unloaded her supply carrier and vacuum cleaner, locked and slammed the rear door of the van, then trudged up the narrow sidewalk toward the porch. "Good morning," she called out to the tiny birdlike woman as she climbed the steps. "And where is your sweater?" she added. "Aren't you cold?"

"Oh, Charlotte, I'm too excited to be cold. You'll never guess what's happened." In true Bitsy fashion she rushed on without giving Charlotte a chance to answer. "Bradley has made arrangements for me to fly to California and stay with him for two whole weeks."

Charlotte figured that if she stopped on the porch to talk they would both end up catching a chill, so she headed straight for the front door, knowing that Bitsy would follow. Only when they were both inside did she respond. "Bitsy, that's wonderful news." She set the vacuum cleaner down in the center hallway. "When do you leave?"

Bitsy grinned from ear to ear. "Day after tomorrow. Can you believe it? In just two days I'll be in sunny California, and I've got a million things to do before then."

Charlotte was truly glad that Bitsy was going to visit her son, especially after the last time Bradley had paid a visit to his mother. At least now Bitsy didn't still think that her son was trying to put her away into a retirement home.

Bitsy frowned. "One of the things on my list is to get that girl you use to do my hair. What's her name again?"

"Valerie."

Bitsy nodded. "Before you leave I need you to write down her name and phone number. I want the works this time—a haircut and a permanent." She patted her blue-gray hair. "And I suppose a little color wouldn't hurt either. . . ." With a thoughtful frown she turned her hand palm up, curled her fingers, and stared at her fingernails. "And maybe even a manicure."

For the remainder of the day, as Charlotte cleaned, Bitsy followed her around, chattering about her upcoming trip and all of the things that she hoped to see and do. Charlotte's only reprieve was when the phone rang and when Bitsy's soap operas came on.

By the time Charlotte was ready to pack up and leave that afternoon, she could feel the beginnings of a headache coming on.

"Now you won't forget to check on my house for me, will you?" Bitsy asked her for what Charlotte figured was the umpteenth time.

"No, ma'am," Charlotte reassured her as she knelt down to rearrange her cleaning supplies in the supply carrier.

"You do still have that key I gave you and the security code, don't you?"

Charlotte nodded. "And I have Bradley's phone number and his cell phone number on my notepad," she added, anticipating Bitsy's next question. Charlotte stood. "By the way, I want to thank you for referring me to Emily Rossi and for the kind things you said about me to her."

Bitsy waved a dismissing hand. "No problem. Everything I said is true." Suddenly her face collapsed into a frown and she slowly shook her head. "That Emily is such a nice young woman," she said. "And I'm glad that you agreed to work for her. She hasn't had an easy life, you know. Her parents died when she was young, and she was raised by her grandmother. Then, when Emily was a senior in high school, poor Thelma—Thelma was her grandmother—anyway, Thelma passed away, God rest her soul, and Emily came to stay with me. It was the least I could do what with Thelma and me being best friends and neighbors for all those years. Why, even after Emily graduated and went off to college, she still came back and stayed with me during holidays and the summers."

A sad little smile pulled at Bitsy's lips. "Why, she's been like a daughter to me—at least she used to be. Of course I don't see her near as often as I used to, not since she married Robert."

Charlotte suddenly went stone still. Then she swallowed hard and a feeling of foreboding came over her. "Robert? Emily's husband's name is Robert?" she asked Bitsy. "*The* Robert Rossi?"

Bitsy nodded, and a sudden chill settled in Charlotte's stomach.

Chapter 2

"Now, Charlotte, just get that look off your face. You shouldn't believe everything that you hear about the man. I know what people say about Robert," Bitsy continued, "about him being a Mafia don and all and about him being so much older than Emily. Of course he is almost fifteen years older, but so what? My late husband, rest his soul, was ten years older than me."

Bitsy waved her hand. "And that other business—you know—that gossip about Robert's first wife and children disappearing."

Though Charlotte knew she would regret asking, the words just popped out. " 'Disappearing'? I don't remember anything about that."

Bitsy sniffed as if it were no concern at all. "Well, there's two versions. Some say she ran around on Robert, got pregnant by her lover, then took the two kids and ran away to South America with him. Of course others say that Robert had her and the baby murdered and stashed his two children away in a boarding school. But that's all just a bunch of mean-spirited gossip—a bunch of hooey, if you ask me. Besides which, Emily is a sweet, kindhearted person, and she wouldn't have married

Robert if she thought for one moment that he'd done half of what he's been accused of doing."

Charlotte shuddered. She couldn't believe that she hadn't made the connection when she'd first talked to Emily, couldn't believe that she'd actually accepted a job working for the Mafia. It was well-known that Robert Rossi was one of the wealthiest, most ruthless mafiosi in the country.

And what if Bitsy was wrong? What if the rumors were true and he had murdered his first wife? After all, he had been the primary suspect in the murder of Roberto Rossi, his own father, and that wasn't just gossip. In fact, it had been all over the television news and in the newspapers for weeks. Even the national media had picked it up. Of course, in the end, the courts had been unable to prove Robert's guilt and he'd been acquitted.

Charlotte shuddered again. Emily might be sweet and kind, but according to everything she'd ever heard about Robert, he was anything but. Regardless of Bitsy's rose-colored opinion of Emily, Charlotte figured that either Emily was blind, deaf, and dumb, or she just flat-out didn't have good sense for marrying Robert Rossi in the first place. Charlotte also figured that she'd just made a huge mistake agreeing to work for Emily.

"Besides," Bitsy went on, "nothing was ever proven about his father's murder. As for his wife and children, you and I both know that anything could have happened. Just because they disappeared doesn't mean he had them killed."

A shiver ran up Charlotte's spine. *If it looks like a duck and quacks like a duck, then it probably is a duck.*

"But I guess I should warn you of one thing," Bitsy said.

What now? Charlotte wondered.

"Because of the ugly rumors connected with the family, there will probably be bodyguards all over the place. Don't be surprised if you get frisked before you're allowed inside the house. Humph!" Bitsy made a face. "Why, last time I visited Emily, they even frisked me." She suddenly chuckled. "Can you imagine anyone thinking that I could be some kind of hit woman?"

Only if your mouth counts as a lethal weapon.

Charlotte winced and was immediately sorry for the unkind thought. Bitsy was a terrible gossip but she was also a lonely old lady who had nothing better to do with her time.

"Thanks for the warning," Charlotte said with a forced smile. Since she figured she'd had enough gossip and enough of Bitsy for one day, she picked up her supply carrier and vacuum cleaner, then set out with purposeful steps toward the front door. "Have a good time in California," Charlotte called out over her shoulder as she hurried out. Despite Bitsy's flattering recommendation, Charlotte suddenly wished that the old lady had kept her mouth shut and never mentioned her to Emily Rossi.

Once she got home, Charlotte decided to go ahead and try to set up interview appointments for late Saturday afternoon with the three people that she had chosen as a result of her newspaper ad. Now, more than ever, she needed to hire replacements for Cheré and Nadia.

For the rest of the afternoon though, and during the following day, she tried her best to come up with an excuse that sounded good enough to get her out of the commitment that she'd made to work for the Rossis.

* * *

As Charlotte resignedly climbed into her van on Thursday morning, she murmured, "So be it." Other than outright lying, there was no good reason not to keep her commitment. Besides, the last thing she wanted was to tick off the Mafia, and she would only be working for the Rossis for four days. Surely nothing horrible could happen in four short days?

Thursday-morning traffic was light, and in no time she was searching for the address that Emily Rossi had given her. When Charlotte spotted the house, she smiled and parked the van alongside the curb. She'd driven past the enormous Italianate mansion numerous times and had often wondered who owned it and what it looked like inside. With its four imposing columns and the way the double verandas curved at the ends, the facade reminded her of vanilla ice cream and a wedding cake combined. Each Christmas, when the Preservation Resource Center held its annual Holiday Home Tour, she had always hoped that the beautiful old home would be one of the houses featured on the tour. At least now she knew who it belonged to. And now she also knew why it had never been showcased. No way would a Mafia don open his home to just anyone.

The house was located on a corner lot much larger than most in the Garden District. Behind the main house, toward the back of the property, another building was visible. Charlotte was fairly certain that it had once served as a carriage house, but like many of the old carriage houses, it had been renovated into what looked like another, much smaller home. Possibly a guesthouse, she figured.

A high wrought-iron fence encased the entire property, and the grounds were meticulously groomed. While Charlotte unloaded her supply carrier and vacuum cleaner, she eyed the gate. It was probably locked, she decided. But even if it was locked, she figured that there was either a call box or buzzer of some kind that would alert someone inside that a visitor was at the gate.

Wondering where all of the bodyguards were that Bitsy had mentioned, and with a firm grip on her vacuum cleaner and supply carrier, she approached the gate. Without warning, a man suddenly appeared from behind a huge azalea bush, giving Charlotte a start.

The man stood well over six feet tall and had a face that reminded Charlotte of a growling bulldog. Because of his close-cropped gray hair and wrinkle-lined face, she figured that he was probably in his fifties and estimated that he weighed around two-fifty. At least now she knew the answer to her question about the bodyguards' whereabouts.

"Ah—hello. Good—Good morning," Charlotte stuttered. "My name is Charlotte LaRue and I'm with Maid-for-a-Day."

In a voice that sounded like a grinder he said, "I need to see some identification."

Charlotte set down the vacuum cleaner and supply carrier, then slid the strap of her purse over her shoulder. From inside her purse she pulled out her billfold, slipped out her driver's license, and held it out for the man to see.

The man narrowed his eyes and glanced from the license picture to Charlotte then nodded.

Once Charlotte was inside the gate, he escorted her to the front gallery where another, younger man stepped out from behind one of the columns.

"Sorry, ma'am," the younger man said. "But I have to search you. If you'll just put your arms up, this won't take but a minute."

The sight of the younger man pricked Charlotte's memory.

Something about him seemed familiar, and she wondered if she'd met him before.

As the younger man patted her down, she searched her memory for where and when she could have met him, while she watched the older man inspect her supply carrier and vacuum cleaner.

Charlotte was thankful that Bitsy had given her advance warning about being frisked. Otherwise she would have been outraged. The entire procedure only took a few minutes. Both men were thorough, but they were also courteous and performed the inspections with a detachment that could in no way be construed as personal or invasive. By the time they finished, Charlotte had decided that she was mistaken about knowing the younger bodyguard.

The older man returned to the gate. The younger one went to the front door and gave the door knocker a couple of whacks. While they waited, Charlotte admired the huge Mardi Gras wreath that almost covered the upper half of the entrance door. Rows and rows of shiny purple, gold, and green tinsel had been wrapped around the base of the wreath and were sprinkled with tiny Mardi Gras masks, King Cake babies, and glittering Mardi Gras beads.

The wreath reminded Charlotte that she'd yet to put out her own Mardi Gras decorations. As she tried to decide which day she would decorate, the door swung open.

The bodyguard nodded deferentially at the slim, attractive, dark-haired woman. "Mrs. Rossi, this is Charlotte LaRue, the maid."

"Thank you, Mark."

Emily Rossi had startling sky-blue eyes and looked to be in her mid-thirties. Charlotte could tell that the pale green slacks and matching sweater she wore were expensive, and though her makeup was, for the most part, flawless, it seemed to be caked on pretty thick over her left cheek. Charlotte had to wonder what the younger woman was trying to hide. Maybe a scar, or . . . Charlotte swallowed hard. Or possibly a bruise.

"Charlotte, come in, come in." Emily motioned for Charlotte to come inside. "I'm truly sorry that the guys had to frisk you, but unfortunately it's a necessity that we have to live with. My husband has many enemies who would love nothing better than to . . ." Her voice faded away. She sighed, then, smiled. "Never mind all of that. Next time you come, it shouldn't be necessary. Now"—she motioned for Charlotte to follow her—"why don't we go to the kitchen and we can discuss what needs to be done?"

Charlotte only got a glimpse of the front rooms as she followed Emily down the wide entrance hall back to the kitchen, but a glimpse was all she needed. Over the years she had been in enough of the old mansions in the Garden District to know the difference between elegant and tacky when she saw it, and the furnishings and décor of this house were tacky. She would have thought that with all of the money that the Rossis supposedly had, they could have afforded the best decorator in the country. In Charlotte's opinion, whomever Emily had hired as a decorator should be run out of town on a rail for the mess he or she had made.

Charlotte bit her tongue when an imp of mischief urged her to ask for the name of the decorator. *It's none of your business, so just keep your mouth shut.* Considering that Emily's husband was reportedly a big-time mobster, she decided she'd probably better listen to her inner voice of reason instead.

In the kitchen Emily indicated that Charlotte should sit at the kitchen table, then she seated herself across from Charlotte. "I can't tell you how much I appreciate you helping me out on such short notice," she said. "And I'm going to have to apologize again. It's been a week since the last time Jennifer cleaned, and I'm afraid that even when she did clean, she didn't do a very good job.

"Of course she's young," Emily hastened to add. "Robert was the one who hired the poor thing. She'd been working as a cocktail waitress in a really sleazy bar, and he felt sorry for her."

I'll just bet he did, Charlotte thought, picturing a twenty-something sweet young thing who was hot to trot. Was it possible that Emily was truly that naïve?

Emily grimaced. "Between you and me, I'm kind of hoping Jennifer doesn't come back."

Maybe not so naive after all.

"Anyway," Emily continued, "the whole house needs a good dusting and polishing, vacuuming, and mopping. The kitchen is a mess too. And if you have time, clean sheets on all the beds would be heaven. I've been trying to keep everything straight, but with Robert's mother living with us and the children underfoot, cooking, not to mention the bodyguards who are in and out, well"—she shrugged—"there just aren't enough hours in the day. And now there's this—this party that Robert wants to give."

Just talking about the chores seemed to distress Emily, and Charlotte truly felt sorry for her. Before she thought about it, she reached over and patted Emily's hand. "Now don't you worry about a thing. It will all get donc. So, why don't you show me around so I can get started?"

Emily released a huge sigh and smiled brightly. "We can start here and work our way upstairs."

As Emily gave her a guided tour of the huge mansion, what Charlotte saw only further confirmed her initial impression of the décor of the house. The house itself was a dream and had been beautifully preserved. Charlotte suspected that the exquisite chandeliers, the ornate ceiling medallions, and the Italian marble mantelpiece over the fireplace were original to the house. The colorful ceiling frescoes in the magnificent ballroom also impressed her.

Too bad the furnishings, the eclectic contemporary artwork, and the drapes were so pretentious that they bordered on gaudy, and in Charlotte's opinion, were much too flashy to be tasteful.

In the front parlor, Charlotte had to really work to keep her expression impassive. Of all things, bookcases lined one entire wall. Though they were filled with what she suspected were rare collectibles, bookcases in the formal parlor were unheard of and considered crass.

If possible, the library was even worse. A huge ornate oak desk dominated the center of the room, and facing the desk were two leather Chippendale wing chairs. But what really caught her attention and sent a shiver down her spine was the vast display of some really wicked-looking knives, guns, and swords that hung on one of the walls.

Immediately, the Rossis' children came to mind. Didn't Robert Rossi realize just how dangerous such a collection could be with children around?

"You must take extra care when dusting these."

Emily's voice jerked Charlotte out of her reverie and she glanced over to where the younger woman was standing.

"These are Robert's pride and joy, so please, do be careful when you dust them."

Charlotte stepped closer to the huge glass-enclosed curio cabinet and stared at what could only be authentic Fabergé eggs. "Will I need a key or something to open the case?"

Emily shrugged. "No key. I've tried to get Robert to install a security system for them, but he says that's what he pays the bodyguards for." She shrugged again. "That, and other things."

"They're beautiful," Charlotte murmured. She had seen collections of the eggs before, most under lock and key, but in all of her years of working in Garden District homes, she couldn't remember ever seeing so many in one place. Of course, considering who Robert Rossi was, a thief would be a fool to steal from him.

"Yes, they are beautiful, and several are priceless—one of a kind. I should know." Emily's voice held a note of resentment as she reached up and smoothed her fingers over her cheek.

Though Charlotte didn't totally understand the connection between the eggs and Emily's cheek, she understood enough to suspect that the makeup covered a bruise, not a scar, and the implication fueled a deep-seated fury. In addition to Robert Rossi's obvious sins due to his connection to the Mafia, was he also abusive to his wife?

"Robert counts them every day." Emily grimaced. Then, as if she'd suddenly realized what she was doing, she dropped her hand. With a forced smile, she said, "Never mind that. Why don't we head upstairs?"

The oak banister of the sweeping spiral staircase was definitely original to the house, Charlotte decided, as they climbed the steps to the second floor. The handrail had the look of years of use about it.

"There are five bedroom suites upstairs," Emily told her when they reached the second-floor landing. "And each has its own private bathroom. This is the master bedroom suite." Emily opened the door nearest the staircase.

Charlotte's mouth dropped open when she stepped inside. The huge room reminded her of a turn-of-the-century Victorian whorehouse, and she had to make a concerted effort to close her mouth. The predominately red room with its dark, oversized furniture, flocked wallpaper, bloodred velvet bedspread and matching drapes was claustrophobic and jarring to the senses. And it was hard not to notice the skimpy black-and-red negligée carelessly thrown across the foot rail of the bed. When Emily signaled that they should continue their tour, Charlotte was only too happy to follow her back out into the hallway.

"And this is our son Brandon's room," Emily said as she threw open the next door down the hallway.

Charlotte breathed a sigh of relief when she peeked into Brandon's room. Though the colors of the furnishings varied from Shrek-green to aqua, and there were several large stuffed wild animals strewn about, at least it somewhat resembled a child's room.

After the whorehouse bedroom and the jungle bedroom, Charlotte wasn't quite sure what to expect when Emily opened the third door. "This one belongs to our daughter, Amanda," Emily said.

Charlotte laughed. "I take it that Amanda likes pink."

Emily laughed with her. "Not *just* pink. She insisted on hot pink, and, unfortunately, the bedspread and drapes had to be satin."

"A room fit for a princess," Charlotte murmured.

"Oh, believe me, Amanda is anything but a princess. Around here we call her Demanda."

Emily's tone was dripping with sarcasm. Then she laughed. To Charlotte's ears, the laughter sounded forced, which made her wonder if Amanda was a problem child.

When Emily paused at the last door near the end of the hallway, she said, "This is my mother-in-law's suite." She raised her hand to knock, but before she could do so, the door swung open.

A heavyset elderly lady with snow-white hair stuck her head through the opening and said, "I thought I heard voices out here."

"Charlotte, this is Sophia, my mother-in-law. Mama, this is Charlotte, our new maid."

Sophia narrowed her eyes and gave Charlotte the once-over. "She's older than the other one. Does Robert know that you hired someone new?"

Emily nodded. "Yes, Mama. Don't you remember? Jennifer had a family emergency she had to take care of, and didn't know when she would be able to return to work."

Sophia waved her hand. "Yes, yes, of course I remember. I'm not as addle-brained as some people around here think I am. As for what's her name—the other maid—that girl wouldn't know work if it bit her on the butt."

"Mama!"

"Well, it's true, and you and I both know it."

"Ah—yes—well, I was just showing Charlotte around before she begins cleaning."

Sophia opened the door wider and motioned for them to come inside. "Bring her in and get it over with," she grumbled. "I want to get dressed, and I'm hungry. With all of those men in and out, a body has to dress before they can even eat breakfast around here."

Though her manner was a bit coarse and she was clearly irritated, Charlotte decided that she liked Sophia anyway. Now there was a woman with spunk, she thought.

Out of all of the bedrooms, Sophia's looked the most normal. Though primarily royal blue, Charlotte could clearly tell that Sophia had put her own decorating touches on her room.

Unlike the sterile atmosphere of the other bedrooms, Sophia had added little personal touches here and there: some throw pillows, an overstuffed easy chair facing a wall-mounted plasma TV, doilies, and several framed photographs. When Charlotte spotted the crochet hook and yarn on the side table next to the chair, she figured that Sophia had probably crocheted the doilies herself.

The final bedroom was a guestroom, the colors primarily purple and gold. "This one we call the LSU room," Emily told Charlotte, motioning toward a small collection of LSU pendants hanging on the wall. "You know, purple and gold? LSU colors?"

Charlotte tilted her head to one side. "You went to LSU?"

Emily shook her head. "LSU is Robert's alma mater."

A few minutes later they walked into the kitchen to find a short, muscular man with salt-and-pepper-hair and a ruddy complexion filling a travel mug with coffee. "Just getting a refill, Ms. Rossi."

Emily nodded and smiled. "Anytime, Gus. And by the way, this is Charlotte LaRue. She'll be cleaning for us during the next four days." Emily turned to Charlotte. "Gus is another of our guardian angels."

Stains of scarlet darkened Gus's already-ruddy complexion. With a gruff "Nice to meet'cha," he hurried from the room.

As soon as he left, Emily laughed. "Gus is a sweetheart. I just love teasing him. All total, there are six men who work around the house full-time," Emily continued. "You've already met Mark and Gino—which reminds me. All of the men live out back in the old carriage house. Three years ago Robert had it renovated so the men would have somewhere to bunk.

If you get caught up around here today, maybe you could clean it as well tomorrow."

If Charlotte remembered right, it had been just about three years since Robert's father had been murdered, which meant that there was a good possibility that his father's murder was the reason for all of the bodyguards. But were the bodyguards strictly for show, an attempt to make people think there really was an outside threat, or had Robert Rossi's claims of innocence been true?

Chapter 3

Even knowing that she would probably have to straighten the kitchen again before she left, Charlotte decided to clean it first. She had just finished scrubbing down the stovetop and the oven when Sophia Rossi entered the room.

"Oh, phooey," Sophia grumbled. When Charlotte turned, Sophia made a sweeping motion with her hand. "I was hoping to fix my breakfast before you started cleaning."

Charlotte smiled. "That's okay. I can begin dusting the parlor while you have breakfast."

Sophia nodded. "That's very kind of you. More than I can say for that other maid. Why, that one wouldn't give you the time of day." She paused, narrowed her eyes, and tilted her head to one side. "Are you a believer?"

Surprised by the abrupt change of subject and not quite sure exactly what the older lady meant, Charlotte said, "If you mean am I Christian, then yes—yes, I am."

Sophia beamed. "That's wonderful!" She launched herself at Charlotte, and before Charlotte realized what she intended, the older lady threw her arms around her for a surprisingly strong hug. "Now I'm not alone," Sophia whispered, releasing Charlotte.

"Mama, what are you doing?"

Sophia whirled around to face Emily. "Nothing, dear." Looking a bit flustered, Sophia smoothed the skirt of her dress. "Just getting a bite of breakfast."

Emily sighed. "Now don't go pestering Charlotte. She's got a lot of work to do."

"I wasn't bothering her," Sophia replied with a petulant expression. She turned back to Charlotte. "Was I?" she demanded, a pleading look in her eyes.

Charlotte smiled and shook her head. "No, not at all." Still a bit flustered herself after Sophia's spontaneous affectionate gesture and unwilling to get caught in the middle of the two women, Charlotte said, "Now, if you ladies will excuse me, I think I'll begin dusting in the parlor while Sophia has her breakfast."

Charlotte had just finished dusting the double parlor and was ready to begin on the dining room when Emily walked into the room.

"Just wanted to let you know that Mama has finished breakfast now, in case you want to clean in the kitchen. And, Charlotte"—Emily lowered her gaze to the floor for a moment—"I overheard what Mama was saying to you earlier." She raised her head. "I don't know quite how to say this, but Robert's mother can be a bit fanatic about things, if you know what I mean. She's harmless, but ever since Papa Roberto was murdered, she hasn't been the same."

"I understand," Charlotte said.

Emily sighed. "Poor thing. It wasn't long afterward—after his death—that she claimed she'd had a religious epiphany. Don't get me wrong. I'm a believer too. But Mama, bless her heart, goes to the extreme with it. Robert and his brothers all think she went a little crazy. Of course none of them could ever claim to be believers. But now . . ." Emily shrugged. "I'm afraid she's getting senile as well. Not because of her beliefs," she quickly added. "But you see, before I married Robert, I was a nurse, and I worked in a nursing home. So I do recognize the symptoms. In fact, that's how I met Robert. He was visiting one of his father's old business acquaintances who lived at the home.

"Anyway, just so you know, we don't talk about Mama's condition to Robert. He's mentioned putting her in a nursing home several times, and if he knew just how really bad off she was . . ." Her voice trailed away, and after a moment, she shook her head. "What Mama needs is to be with family, not stuck away in some home."

Emily's eyes suddenly twinkled and a tiny smile pulled at her lips. "I love Mama, but sometimes she says the most outrageous, off-the-wall things. Just says whatever pops into her head without regard for anyone else. But that's what I love the most about her."

Suddenly Emily sobered, and a horrified expression crossed her face. "Oh, Charlotte, I'm so sorry. Here I am going on and on, keeping you from your work."

Before Charlotte had a chance to say anything, Emily backed toward the door. "I'll just get out of your way now, but just remember, please don't mention Mama's little idiosyncrasies to Robert." Then she turned and fled the room.

Back in the kitchen, Charlotte loaded the dirty dishes from Sophia's breakfast into the dishwasher, but she couldn't stop thinking about the look on Emily's face when she'd apologized. Charlotte finally concluded that Emily's panicky reaction had nothing to do with interrupting her. More than likely, Emily had panicked because she'd suddenly realized that she'd said too much. She'd revealed more about her family than she had intended.

How sad, Charlotte thought as she headed upstairs to strip the sheets off of the beds. Unlike Sophia, who was spunky and said what she thought, poor Emily was cowed and afraid of her shadow—classic signs of an abused woman.

By midmorning Charlotte had washed the bedsheets, put them in the dryer, and washed a load of towels and washcloths. She'd cleaned the upstairs bathrooms, dusted and straightened the bedrooms, and all she had left to do upstairs was make up the beds and vacuum.

She was taking the sheets and pillowcases out of the dryer in the laundry room when she heard voices in the kitchen. With her arms full of clean bedding, she passed through the kitchen on her way upstairs. Two men were seated at the breakfast table with Emily. On the table were several sheets of what appeared to be a list of some kind.

All three looked up when Charlotte entered the room, and Emily smiled. "Oh, Charlotte, wait a minute." When Charlotte stopped, Emily motioned for her to come closer. "I want you to meet Mario and Tony—Robert's brothers."

Charlotte stepped closer and nodded at the two men. Both had dark hair, dark eyes, and looked to be in their mid-thirties.

"Nice to meet'cha," the one named Mario said. Then he returned to studying the list on the table. The other brother, Tony, gave her a curt nod, then he too returned his attention to the list.

"We're going over the guest list for the party," Emily explained. "It looks like just about everyone that was invited is going to show up."

The brother named Tony glanced up and gave Emily a frustrated look. "Em, there's no reason for the maid to worry about the guest list."

When Emily's cheeks darkened with embarrassment,

Charlotte decided to save the poor woman the trouble of apologizing . . . again. "Guess I'd better get busy," Charlotte told them. "Nice meeting y'all."

By midafternoon, Charlotte was back in the laundry room folding the towels and washcloths. So many people had been in and out all day that she ignored the sound of the back door opening and closing.

"Who are you?"

Charlotte jumped at the unexpected question, and when she whirled around, a young girl who looked to be around thirteen or fourteen and a boy who was probably a bit younger were standing in the doorway.

"I'm Charlotte, with the maid service," she told the girl. "And who are you?" she asked even though she already knew from the framed photos scattered throughout the house that they were the Rossis' children.

"I'm Amanda Rossi, and this is my brother, Brandon. So what happened to Jennifer, the other maid?"

Charlotte smiled. "Your mother said that Jennifer had a family emergency to take care of."

For several moments more, both children stared at Charlotte, then, without a word, they both turned and headed for the kitchen.

"She's older than Jennifer," Charlotte heard Brandon tell his sister. "I wonder if Daddy knows yet. If he don't, he's gonna be mad."

Unease crawled through Charlotte. Did Robert Rossi know that his wife had hired her, or had Emily done so on her own? Surely he did.

"Daddy's always mad about something," Amanda retorted. "I hate him."

"He is not always mad. You're just being mean."

"Is too always mad. And he's the one who's mean, especially to Mama."

"Is not!"

"Is too!" Amanda argued. "And I'm going to kill *him* just like he killed Papa, if he hurts Mama again."

In the laundry room Charlotte stiffened with shock and a suffocating sensation tightened her throat. *He killed Papa . . . hurts Mama again.* Out of the mouths of babes. Charlotte shivered. The courts couldn't convict Robert, but courts made mistakes. And Emily . . . At least now she knew the reason that Emily's makeup was heavier on one side of her face.

Even so, Charlotte tried telling herself that all teenagers, at one time or another, hated their parents and spoke out of turn. *But not all teenagers threaten to kill a parent.*

"You're a liar!" Brandon shouted. "And I'm gonna tell Daddy what you said."

"If you know what's good for you you'll keep your mouth shut, you little brat."

Since no one else seemed to be paying attention, Charlotte decided that she'd better break up the fight before one or both decided to get physical.

"I'm gonna tell," Brandon yelled defiantly.

Just as Charlotte stepped out of the laundry room, another voice interrupted the two squabbling children.

"And just what are you going to tell?" The voice was male, hard-edged with a cold, disapproving tone. "And what's all the shouting about?" Several moments passed without a sound. "Well?" he demanded. "I'm still waiting for an answer."

"Nothing, Daddy," Amanda said meekly.

Charlotte halted in her tracks. *Uh-oh. Daddy's home.*

"I didn't ask you, Amanda. I asked your brother."

Several more quiet moments passed before Brandon finally spoke up. "N-nothing, Daddy. We were just arguing over the cookies."

Charlotte rolled her eyes, but she had to admire Brandon's fast thinking.

"In case you two haven't noticed, I have guests with me."

"Sorry, Daddy," Amanda mumbled.

"Sorry," Brandon added.

"We'll go to our rooms," Amanda offered.

"Good idea," her father said.

Charlotte stepped back into the laundry room. Ever since she had realized that Emily was married to Robert Rossi, she had dreaded coming face-to-face with the mobster. Since she now realized that there could be some doubt as to whether Robert knew that Emily had hired her, Charlotte dreaded it even more.

Charlotte eyed the basket of folded towels and washcloths and mentally went over the tasks still to be done. With a grimace and a shake of her head, she picked up the laundry basket. There was no getting around it. She still had work to do, and she certainly couldn't hide out in the laundry room for the rest of the day. Besides, all he could do was fire her.

Charlotte entered the kitchen just in time to see the Rossi children, armed with cookies and soft drinks, disappear through the doorway leading to the hall.

Three men were in the kitchen, their attention on the retreating children. Out of the three, there was no mistaking which one was Robert Rossi. For one thing, though shorter than his brothers, Robert shared the same dark hair and dark eyes that his brothers had. But Charlotte would have recognized him anyway because of the many newspaper photos and TV news clips she'd seen when he'd been on trial for the murder of his father.

When Robert turned and saw Charlotte, his eyes narrowed. "You must be Charlotte, the new maid."

Clutching the laundry basket with an iron grip, Charlotte nodded. If he knew who she was, that must mean that he'd okayed Emily hiring her. Feeling a measure of relief, she tried to speak, but the words seemed to stick in her throat.

There had been a few times in Charlotte's life that she had sensed pure evil when coming in contact with certain people, and meeting Robert Rossi was one of those times. It was his eyes, she decided. Though seemingly polite and friendly, there was a cold, soulless look in the depths of Robert Rossi's dark eyes that chilled her to the bone.

"Well, Charlotte, nice to meet you," he said. Stepping aside, he motioned toward the two men with him. "This is Leo Acosta, my attorney, and Porter Anzio, an associate of mine."

The contrast between the two men with Robert was the difference between hot and cold. The attorney, a sharp dresser, had a shrewd, calculating look about him, whereas Robert's so-called associate, though dressed nicely enough, had a hard, mean look about him and was the epitome of a mob enforcer, just like in the movies.

"You don't happen to know where I can find my mother, do you?" Robert asked.

Praying that she could answer, Charlotte cleared her throat, but at the last minute Emily entered the room and saved her.

"Mama asked me to—to tell you th-that she will be down in a minute," Emily said, her voice soft and tentative.

Robert sighed heavily. "Tell her we'll be in the library. And keep those kids quiet. I don't want any interruptions once we get started."

Feeling somewhat like a fifth wheel, Charlotte didn't know

a polite way to exit the room except just to do it. With a nod to Emily, she hurried past her and fled up the stairs.

Once Charlotte had distributed the color-coded towels and washcloths in each bathroom, she ventured back downstairs to return the laundry basket. As she passed through the kitchen, she made a mental note to turn on the dishwasher before she mopped the kitchen.

A few minutes later, Charlotte was ready for the final chore of the day. She always saved mopping the kitchen for last. As she poured pine cleaner in the mop bucket then filled the bucket with warm water, she eyed the mop hanging on the wall in the laundry room. Since it looked to be in fair condition, Charlotte decided to use it instead of the one she always carried in the van.

She took the mop and the bucket into the kitchen. After she turned on the dishwasher, she pulled out a pair of rubber gloves from her supply carrier. Suddenly the back door crashed open then slammed so hard that she felt the vibration all the way in the kitchen.

Charlotte jerked around just in time to see a heavyset man stalk into the room. Momentary panic gripped her at the look of pure rage on his face as he made a beeline for her.

Chapter 4

The man was almost nose-to-nose with Charlotte before he stopped. "Where is he?" he shouted.

Charlotte eased back a step. "Wh-who?" she choked out, her insides quivering with terror.

"Robert!" he sneered. "I want to see Robert, and I want to see him right now!"

Charlotte swallowed hard. Where on earth were the bodyguards? And why hadn't they stopped this maniac? Suddenly her own temper erupted. How dare this man burst in like a raging lion, shouting at her, making demands, and scaring her spitless?

Though still a bit shaken and keeping a wary eye on him, Charlotte took a deep breath, stretched to her full five-foot-three inches, and in a stern, no-nonsense voice that she rarely used unless provoked, said, "Whom should I say wants to see him? If he's available," she added. But just as she backed away with the intentions of heading straight for the library, the rude man shoved past her.

"Never mind," he snarled. "I'll find him myself."

"Hey! Stop!" Charlotte hurried after him as he marched out of the kitchen and headed for the library. Where in the devil were those bodyguards and why hadn't they stopped him to begin with?

Other than tackling the man, something she had no intentions of doing, there wasn't a whole lot that Charlotte could do as she trailed behind him. In no time he reached the library, and before she could stop him he shoved open the door and stomped into the room.

Charlotte quickly entered behind him. There were four people in the room: Robert, the two men she'd met earlier, and Sophia. All turned to stare first at the man, then at Charlotte.

But the man ignored them, all except for Sophia. At the sight of the elderly lady, he hurried over to her, wrapped his arm around her shoulder, and kissed the top of her head. It was then that Charlotte noticed Sophia's red-rimmed eyes and her too-pale face. It was evident that she was upset about something, but what?

"What in the devil are you doing here?"

Robert's question was directed at the man, and the sound of his voice pulled Charlotte back to the problem at hand. Taking a deep breath, she faced Robert Rossi. "Mr. Rossi, I'm so sorry, but this *rude* man insisted on seeing you."

Robert Rossi's expression hardened as he glared at the man for several tension-filled moments. Then finally, with a resigned sigh, he said, "It's okay, Charlotte. This hotheaded man is my youngest brother, Joe. I apologize if he was rude to you."

Charlotte swallowed hard, and when Robert made a dismissing motion with his hand, Charlotte figured that was her cue to leave the room. But as she closed the door behind her, Joe let loose a string of expletives that burned Charlotte's ears.

"You thought you'd pull a fast one, didn't you?" Joe shouted. "Well I'm here to tell you that there's no way I'm letting you put Mama away in that hellhole you call a retirement home.

And neither will Mario or Tony when they find out. Mama is not crazy! If anyone around here is crazy, it's you!"

Charlotte paused outside the door. In spite of Joe's initial rudeness, she figured that surely a man who cared so much about his mother couldn't be all bad. Though she didn't approve of eavesdropping, she stood frozen in the hallway, mesmerized by the heated conversation between the brothers.

"Shut up, Joe, and I'll explain," Robert ground out, his tone cold and menacing.

Joe laughed, but the sound was insolent and bitter. "What's to explain?" he retorted. "What Mama needs is her family, not strangers. But you're too pigheaded and greedy to see that? First Papa and now Mama. She'd go crazy for sure in a place like that. And what about the Medinas?"

"I'm warning you, Joe."

"Warn all you want," Joe shouted. "But if you go through with the Medina job, there *will* be payback. With Mama in that place, she'll be a sitting duck with no one to protect her."

The Medina job? Payback? Charlotte felt as if someone had just punched her in the stomach. This was some serious stuff, not the kind of conversation meant for an outsider's ears.

With her knees knocking and as quietly as possible, Charlotte eased back away from the door. If they caught her listening . . .

"Shut up, Joe!" Robert roared. "Shut your stink'n mouth and get out or I'll have you thrown out."

"Throw me out!" Joe shouted back. "But you're not getting away with this. I've already lost a father because of you, and I'll be damned if I lose Mama too. I'll see you in hell first!"

The voices faded as Charlotte tiptoed away from the library. Certain that at any minute, someone would come out of the library and catch her, she didn't breathe easy until she reached the kitchen doorway.

"That's what you get for eavesdropping," she muttered, disgusted with herself for giving in to the temptation.

The words had no sooner left her lips than she heard the library door bang open and Joe's voice echo down the hall. "This ain't over, Robert!" he yelled. "Not by a long shot!"

He was finally leaving. Best to look busy. Charlotte hurried over to the sink. Seconds later Joe stomped through the kitchen and, without even a glance her way, stormed out the back door. For once, Charlotte was truly grateful that no one ever paid attention to the maid.

Charlotte jumped when the back door slammed shut. Someone should really teach that man some manners, she thought as his dire words kept swirling in her head. *But if you go through with the Medina job, there* will *be payback.*

With a shudder, Charlotte grabbed the mop she'd left propped against the sink cabinet, dunked it into the mop bucket then squeezed out the excess water. Best not to think about what she'd heard, she decided. And healthier. The sooner she finished her chores, the sooner she could leave. She slapped the mop onto the floor and began mopping as if her very life depended on how soon she could get the chore done.

She was almost halfway finished when she heard a commotion in the hallway and froze. What if Robert suspected that she'd overheard the confrontation? Though she kept telling herself that there was no way he could have known she was eavesdropping, she held her breath.

Footsteps went past the kitchen entrance, and Charlotte finally breathed. Maybe the guests were leaving.

"We'll see you tomorrow night," she heard one of the men tell Robert.

The footsteps continued on toward the front door. They *were* leaving, thank the good Lord.

"And don't worry about Joe," the man continued, his voice muffled but still audible. "He'll come around."

The man's voice faded, but his words still echoed in Charlotte's head. *He'll come around?* What did that mean? Charlotte grabbed the mop bucket and headed for the laundry room. Had he meant that Joe would agree to putting Sophia in a home . . . ? *But if you go through with the Medina job, there* will *be payback* . . . or had he meant that Joe would go along with whatever they had planned for the Medinas?

Charlotte took a deep breath. *This is none of your business. Just do your job and get out.* She hefted the mop bucket and dumped the dirty water into the laundry sink.

"Charlotte?"

Charlotte frowned at the sound of Sophia's voice and hurried back into the kitchen.

Still pale and looking even more fragile than she had in the library earlier, Sophia attempted a weak smile. "There you are," she said. "If anyone comes looking for me, I've gone up to my room and I'd rather not be disturbed."

Charlotte gave the elderly lady a sympathetic smile. "I'll be leaving soon. Before I leave though, can I get you anything to eat or drink?"

"Oh, bless your heart, but no, thank you." Sophia shook her head. "I just need to rest a while. See you tomorrow. You are coming back tomorrow, aren't you?"

Charlotte nodded. She had no choice. If she didn't come back, Robert might get suspicious.

"Good. See you then."

After Sophia disappeared, Charlotte began gathering her supplies. Within minutes she had everything rounded up. All she had left was to find Emily and let her know that she was leaving.

Suddenly a shout loud enough to wake the dead reverberated throughout the house and Charlotte jumped.

"Emily! Get in here!"

Charlotte frowned. Robert again. What now? She poked her head outside the kitchen doorway just in time to see Emily hurrying down the hall toward the library.

With intentions of catching Emily before she reached the library, so she could tell her that she was leaving, Charlotte called out, "Emily." But Emily didn't slow down or even indicate that she'd heard Charlotte.

"What's wrong?" Emily asked when she reached the library doorway.

"Another one's missing!" Robert snapped. "That's what's wrong."

Another what was missing? Charlotte wondered, but as she moved closer, she heard Robert let loose a string of curse words that made her cringe with distaste, and she thought better of interrupting.

Emily stepped into the library. "There were twenty eggs when I counted this morning," Robert shouted. "Now there are only seventeen. Three more are missing. That makes five in the past two weeks. I want to know who took them."

Charlotte frowned as she eased back down the hall toward the kitchen. Emily hadn't mentioned that someone was stealing the Fabergé eggs when she'd showed them to her earlier. Even so, that would explain why she had been so particular about the instructions she'd given.

"So where are they?" Robert yelled.

"I—I don't know." Emily's voice quavered with fear. "Maybe one of the bodyguards is stealing them."

Robert cursed, and at the sudden sound of a crash, Charlotte froze. "What on earth?" she whispered.

As if in answer to the question, sounds of deep wracking sobs erupted from inside the library. "No, please, Robert," Emily pleaded in between sobs. "I don't know who's stealing them." Her voice rose. "I'm sorry, I'm—"

The sudden silence unnerved Charlotte and her imagination went wild as flashes of Robert's weapon collection flitted through her mind. Surely he wouldn't . . . Charlotte shook her head as if the action would make the evil notion disappear. Torn between checking on Emily and minding her own business, she groaned in frustration. *What to do? What to do?*

Don't be such a coward. Just do it.

Taking a deep breath and gathering her courage around her like a suit of armor, Charlotte took determined steps toward the library. She had almost reached the entrance when Emily suddenly appeared in the doorway, her face ravaged, her hands clutching her stomach. When Emily saw Charlotte, her red-rimmed eyes widened in startled surprise.

"I—I was just about to leave," Charlotte told her softly.

Emily's eyes filled with tears and she nodded. "Be-before you go," she whispered, "c-could you please clean up the mess in the library? Th-there's some broken glass." Without another word, Emily brushed past her, but not before Charlotte saw her lean forward and wince as if in pain.

For several moments, all Charlotte could do was watch until Emily disappeared around the end of the hallway. Though she didn't want to believe it, every bone in her body ached with outrage; deep down she knew what had happened. Just as sure as the sun rose in the east and set in the west, Charlotte was certain that Robert Rossi, in a fit of rage over the stupid missing eggs, had punched his wife in the stomach. Charlotte figured that this time he'd hit her in the stomach so there wouldn't be visible bruises like the last time. After all, it wouldn't look good for their party guests to speculate as to how Emily received a bruise on her face.

Charlotte glared furiously at the library door. Her temper flared and her outrage boiled within. Any man who hit a woman was reprehensible and a low-down coward. Someone should take Robert Rossi out and give him a good old-fashioned horsewhipping.

Slowly though, Charlotte's fury subsided. When all was said and done, there wasn't one thing she could do about the situation. She hadn't actually witnessed the assault, so she couldn't call the police. Only Emily could file a complaint. For right now the best thing she could do was simply do as Emily had asked and clean up the mess.

Charlotte turned and trudged down the hall. She retrieved the broom, the dustpan, and a paper bag from the laundry room, but just before she stepped through the kitchen doorway into the hall, a noise caught her attention and she paused.

Whispers, she decided after listening a moment. Someone was whispering. The bodyguards? Or the children? It was certainly possible that the children had overheard their father's rampage. They would have to be deaf not to have.

And I'm going to kill him *just like he killed Papa, if he hurts Mama again.*

Snippets of the conversation she'd overheard between Amanda and Brandon earlier flitted through her head. Fully expecting to see the two children hovering near the staircase, Charlotte stepped out of the kitchen. With a frown, she craned her head first one way, then another, searching the foyer area and the stairwell, but no one was there.

Now she was hearing things. "Great," she muttered. Next thing, she'd be seeing ghosts. "Just peachy."

Once back at the library door, Charlotte took a deep breath, knocked on the door frame a couple of times, then stepped inside.

Robert was standing with his back to her, hands on his hips, staring at the glass-enclosed shelves that contained his egg collection.

Charlotte cleared her throat. "Emily asked me to clean up the broken glass."

Robert said nothing and didn't bother to even acknowledge her presence. Feeling a bit uneasy, Charlotte looked around. The mess wasn't hard to find. Broken glass and a bouquet of mangled silk flowers were scattered on the floor in front of the fireplace. It was an arrangement that she had noticed on the mantel earlier when she had cleaned the library. Robert must have somehow knocked them over during his fit of rage. . . . Before he'd punched Emily.

Charlotte's unease grew even as her temper flared again. She walked over, bent down, gingerly picked up the silk flowers, and shook them gently to rid them of any shards of glass. Then she placed them back on the mantel.

As she swept the glass into the dustpan, she was careful to keep a wary eye on Robert. More than once she had to bite her tongue to keep from telling him just exactly what she thought. But each time she got the urge, her gaze strayed to the wall where his collections of weapons hung. There were handguns, rifles, and one particular nasty-looking gun large enough to kill an elephant. Then there were the knives, every size imaginable, the blades gleaming with menace. Charlotte shuddered.

By the time Charlotte had finished sweeping up the glass, Robert had yet to move a muscle, and he continued to stare at the eggs as if frozen or hypnotized.

With a one-shouldered shrug, Charlotte dumped the broken glass into the paper sack, then, armed with the sack, dustpan, and broom, she backed out of the room.

On Friday morning it was with great trepidation that Charlotte forced herself return to the Rossi household. True to Emily's word, the bodyguards recognized her and allowed her to enter the house without searching her or her cleaning supplies.

Since Emily wasn't at the door to greet her this time, Charlotte went straight to the kitchen and began cleaning.

Half an hour later she had just finished loading the dishwasher when Emily walked into the kitchen.

"Good morning, Charlotte."

"Good morning." Charlotte turned, but her smile of greeting melted. Emily was dressed and every hair on her head was in place, just like yesterday. But there was something different about her, something that Charlotte couldn't quite put her finger on. For one thing, not even her makeup could cover the pallor of her face. But it was more than that. Emily's eyes had a look of sadness tinged with a bit of fear, and there was a subdued air about her that made Charlotte want to reach out to comfort her and reassure her that whatever was wrong could be fixed.

"Are you feeling okay?" Charlotte asked.

Emily flashed her a tiny fake smile. "Just a bit tired. I didn't sleep too well last night." She shrugged. "Just stress. Guess I'm uptight about this party. And speaking of the party, I want to decorate a bit and was hoping that you wouldn't mind helping me. Not a lot," she hastened to add. "Just a few things here and there."

"I'll be happy to help," Charlotte reassured her. "But didn't you want me to clean the carriage house today?"

Emily shrugged and waved away Charlotte's concern. "You

can always clean it tomorrow. Getting ready for the party is more important. I think we should start right after lunch. Will that give you enough time for your other chores?"

"No problem," Charlotte told her.

Immediately after lunch, Emily instructed the bodyguard named Mark to bring down some boxes from the attic. There were three large boxes in all, which Mark placed on the floor in the kitchen, per Emily's directions.

When Emily bent down to open the first box, a small moan escaped her lips. Wincing, she placed her hand on her stomach.

She's sore from being punched. Charlotte felt her temper rising. *Mind your own business.*

At the moment, the last thing Charlotte felt like was minding her own business, but when, after a moment, Emily resumed digging in the box, Charlotte tried to control her temper.

"I think the tinsel is in this one," Emily said as she dug around in the box. "I thought we could drape it around in the parlor."

It turned out that the purple, gold, and green Mardi Gras tinsel was in the last box they opened, and as they draped the shiny strands over the tops of the windows and around the door opening, Emily's soft moans of pain came more often.

When all the tinsel was used up, Emily opened the second box that contained several large cardboard Mardi Gras masks. She handed Charlotte a stack of the masks. "I think we'll hang these around the door casing on the parlor side and on the hall side." She dug around in the box then pulled out several small packages. "We'll use these to hang the masks." She handed a package to Charlotte. "It's mounting adhesive. It will hold them, but it will also come off without leaving a mark."

While Charlotte worked on the hall side, Emily hung the masks on the parlor side. They were almost finished when the phone rang.

From the face that Emily made, it was clear that the interruption aggravated her. With a sigh, she walked over to a small table by the sofa and picked up the receiver. "Hello?"

For several moments Emily simply listened, then, if possible, her face turned even paler than before. "What? You've got to be kidding!" Her voice shook with disbelief. "But—but what am I supposed to do?" she cried. Seconds later she hung up the receiver.

Since Emily looked as if she were going to pass out at any minute, Charlotte rushed over to her. "What's wrong?"

Tears filled Emily's eyes and spilled over onto her cheeks. A low moan escaped her lips. "Th-that was Thomas with Big Easy Catering—the company catering the party. He's still bringing the food, but"—she swiped at the tears on her cheeks and stared at the floor—"all of the servers he was providing are sick with the flu," she said, her voice quivering. "He said that he'd try to find someone to help, but he doubted that anyone would be available." She raised her head and stared at Charlotte. "There won't be anyone to serve the food." She glanced at the fat phone directory next to the telephone. "I—I could try to hire more servers, but with all of the Mardi Gras festivities going on . . ." She slowly shook her head. "Impossible. What am I going to do?"

Emily staggered over to the sofa and collapsed. Covering her eyes with her hands, she began to cry. "Robert will be furious," she moaned. "And he'll blame me if this party doesn't go well."

Charlotte rushed over to Emily and knelt down in front of

her. "Surely he won't blame you for something like this—I mean, after all, this type of thing is beyond your control."

Emily nodded. "Oh, he'll blame me all right. You just don't know."

Charlotte reached up and gently pulled Emily's hands away from her face. "Then why do you do it, Emily? Why do you stay with him? This is only my second day to work for you, and it's obvious, even to me, that he abuses you. You don't have to put up with that."

Emily stared at Charlotte with dead eyes. "Yes—yes, I do," she whispered. Then louder she said, "You know who and what my husband is, and you're a smart enough woman to *know* why I have to stay."

Charlotte had no response to give. She did know who and what Robert Rossi was, and from the little she'd seen already, she also knew what he was capable of.

With a last knowing look at Charlotte and a sad little smile, Emily's brow furrowed in concentration. "Maybe, just maybe I could get a couple of Robert's men to help," she whispered. After a moment she shook her head and fresh tears filled her eyes. "That won't work," she finally admitted. "None of them know the first thing about being a waiter."

Charlotte's heart ached for the younger woman, and though she hated admitting it, she was afraid that Emily was right about there being no way out of her abusive situation, just as there was no solution for her dilemma about the servers. The whole thing was impossible. There was just simply no solution. Unless . . .

Chapter 5

"I can help," Charlotte blurted out before she let herself really think it through.

When Emily gave her a blank look, Charlotte quickly explained. "I can show the men what to do and supervise them during the party as well as help serve. I've done it before for clients."

Emily's face suddenly brightened with hope. "You would do that? You really think the guys could handle it?"

Charlotte nodded. "I don't see why not. If I stay until midafternoon, that should be enough time to give them a crash course on serving. No one can replace professionals, but as long as they don't dump the trays in anyone's lap, they should do okay. But I will need a couple of hours to freshen up at home before coming back for the party."

"Oh, Charlotte, that's a wonderful idea! Thank you, thank you." Spontaneously Emily reached out and hugged Charlotte. "You've just saved my life. How can I ever repay you?"

Charlotte awkwardly patted the younger woman's back. She wouldn't go so far as to say that she was "saving" Emily's life, but helping out might keep Robert from venting his anger on the poor woman.

After a moment Charlotte gently extracted herself from

Emily's embrace. "I don't expect you to repay me, but I do expect you to seriously consider what we discussed earlier."

Emily abruptly sobered, and from the look on her face, Charlotte knew that Emily realized exactly what she was saying to her. Then Emily bowed her head and nodded.

"Okay, then," Charlotte exclaimed. "We'd better get to work. Now where are those men you promised me?" Charlotte snickered. "That didn't exactly come out right, did it?"

For the first time since Charlotte had arrived, Emily laughed. "No, I guess not, but since I know what you meant, I won't tell if you don't." She stood. "Guess I'd better see about drafting you some help."

While Emily left to make arrangements for the men to be available, Charlotte put the boxes away in the laundry room then headed for the dining room. With narrowed eyes, she glanced around the room and began making mental notes as to how it should be arranged to accommodate the food and drinks for the party.

With an eye on the festive Mardi Gras centerpiece sitting in the middle of the table, and wondering if it might be a bit large, it suddenly occurred to Charlotte that Emily hadn't mentioned anything about a bartender. As she made yet another mental note of things to ask Emily, Charlotte hoped that she'd contracted the bartender separately; otherwise they needed to address the situation immediately.

"Charlotte?"

"I'm in the dining room," Charlotte called out to Emily. "Be right there."

When Charlotte entered the kitchen, she immediately recognized the two men with Emily. They were the same ones who had frisked her when she'd arrived the day before.

"I believe you've already met Mark and Gino," Emily said,

pointing first to the younger man, then to the one with the voice that sounded like a meat grinder. "I've apprised both of them of the situation and instructed them to do exactly what you tell them to do. Now I'll get out of your way so you can start."

"Ah, Emily, just one more thing before you leave. What about a bartender? Was that part of the catering deal?"

Emily shook her head. "No, thank goodness. Robert took care of that."

After Emily left the room, Charlotte turned her attention to the two men. "Thanks, guys, for agreeing to help out. Now, the first rule is to be polite and keep smiling." When Gino rolled his eyes, Charlotte ignored him.

During the next hour Mark was respectful and attentive, even eager to help out, but Gino was another matter. By the end of the hour, his disgruntled attitude was getting on Charlotte's last nerve, and she found it harder and harder to ignore his insolence. Though Gino never came right out and said so, he made it clear on more than one occasion that he didn't appreciate being reduced to a glorified waiter.

After one particular incident, Charlotte's patience snapped. She was on the verge of giving him a tongue-lashing, when Emily entered the room, a garment bag draped over one arm.

"Everything going okay in here?" Emily asked.

Emily's eyes glittered with eagerness and her voice was so full of hope that Charlotte didn't have the heart to burst her bubble with complaints about Gino. Praying that she wouldn't be proven a liar, Charlotte told her, "The guys will do just fine. In fact, I think we're finished."

Emily beamed. "Oh, good." She turned her attention to Gino and Mark. "Before y'all go, I've rented tuxedos for you. But you'll need to get over to Marty's Gladrags on Magazine right away to get fitted, because he's closing up shop early." She faced Charlotte. "And this is for you." Her eyes twinkling, she handed the garment bag to Charlotte. "It's your costume for tonight."

Charlotte took the bag and frowned. "Costume? I guess I didn't realize that I would need one."

"I just hope it fits," Emily told her as a suspicious-looking smile tugged at her lips. "I got a size eight."

"Size eight should do just fine," Charlotte answered.

All the way home, for reasons Charlotte couldn't figure out, the whole deal about the costume bothered her. It wasn't so much the fact that Emily wanted her to wear one. Charlotte had worn costumes for special occasions before. But there was something . . .

Several minutes later when Charlotte unzipped the bag in her living room and saw the costume inside, she groaned. "Surely she doesn't expect me to wear this," she grumbled as she inspected the outfit. The tacky costume was a caricature of a French maid's uniform, complete with a sinfully short black skirt and black fishnet stockings.

Still grumbling to herself, Charlotte headed straight for her clothes closet. There was no way she intended wearing that short black skirt. *Why, that skimpy thing probably won't even cover my behind*, she silently fumed as she searched her closet. After going through the closet piece by piece a second time, she concluded that the black skirt that she had planned to use as a substitute had to be in the bag of soiled clothes that she'd dropped off at the cleaners on Wednesday . . . and had never picked up.

An hour later Charlotte stared at her reflection in the full-length mirror that was attached to the back of her bedroom door. Contrary to what she had first thought, the costume skirt actually hit her about midthigh. Though it covered more than she'd thought it would cover, it was still a heck of a lot shorter than she was comfortable wearing. "Not exactly grandmotherly," she muttered. With a sigh and an oh-well shrug, she gathered her purse and headed for the door.

"See you later, Sweety," she told the little parakeet. But just as she reached for the doorknob, a loud knock sounded and she jumped out of surprise.

"Who is it?" she called out.

"Charlotte, it's just me."

"Just a second, Louis." Charlotte sighed. Louis Thibodeaux, her next-door neighbor and tenant, was a retired New Orleans police detective, and had, in fact been her niece Judith's partner for a while. After his retirement, he'd hired on with Lagniappe Security, a company that provided bodyguards. He was also the last person she wanted to see her in the outrageous costume.

Most of the time he aggravated the stuffings out of her, but there were other times . . . Only months earlier she had thought, had dared to hope, that their relationship was developing into more than just friendship.

Even now, it still embarrassed her to think of the day that it all changed, the day that Louis had returned from one of his trips with Joyce, his ex-wife, in tow. Since that day, it seemed like Louis only sought her out if he needed a favor, never just to visit or have a friendly cup of coffee.

So what did he want this time?

With a quick, self-conscious tug on the back of the short skirt, Charlotte opened the door.

Louis was a stocky man with gray hair and a receding hairline. But Charlotte still considered him attractive in a rugged sort of way.

"Hey, Charlotte, I need a favor." Louis's mouth suddenly dropped open and his eyes widened in surprise. Taking a step backward, he gave her the once-over from her head to her toes and back again. Then he let loose with a shrill wolf whistle, flashed a leering grin, and waggled his eyebrows. "That's some outfit you've got on there."

Charlotte suddenly felt like her face was on fire. "It—it's a costume," she blurted out.

Louis chuckled. "And here I thought that maybe you'd decided to get new uniforms for Maid-for-a-Day."

Charlotte rolled her eyes. "Oh, yeah, right," she replied, sarcasm dripping.

Louis shrugged. "One can always hope."

Ignoring the flirtatious gibe and ever conscious of the time, she said, "Didn't you say something about needing a favor?"

"Ah—well, yeah, I do. I have to go out of town again."

"But didn't you just get back from a trip?"

"Yeah, two days ago. I'm beginning to think I should have stayed retired."

"And do what?" she quipped. "You know you'd be miserable."

Louis shrugged. "Yeah, I suppose I would." He sighed. "Anyway, I have a favor to ask."

Here it comes, she thought.

"Joyce hasn't been eating too well lately."

Joyce, Louis's ex-wife, had cirrhosis of the liver—too many years of a poor diet and drinking herself into oblivion after she'd abandoned Louis and their son, Stephen, who had been a troubled teenager at the time. After over a decade of not knowing where she'd disappeared to, Louis had finally located her. At the urging of Stephen, Louis had paid her a visit, mostly to inform her that she had a granddaughter. When Louis learned of Joyce's medical condition, the thought of her dying among strangers had been more than he could bear.

Louis grimaced. "There are times that I almost have to force-feed her, and I was wondering if you could cook a little extra and bring her a plate in the evening, just for a couple of days. And maybe stay a few minutes to make sure she eats it?" he added hopefully. "Stephen will check on her in the mornings, and I'll be glad to give you some money for extra groceries."

Charlotte narrowed her eyes. "I don't need you to *pay* me to be neighborly, Louis. I always cook too much for just me anyway, and I'll be glad to take Joyce a plate. One thing though, just out of curiosity and not that I mind helping out, but when you have to go out of town, why don't you check with meals-on-wheels, or better yet, why doesn't Joyce just go stay with Stephen?"

Louis shoved his fingers through his hair then shook his head in frustration. "Meals-on-wheels is out. It would just be a waste because she wouldn't eat it, whereas if she knew that *you* had cooked it, she would be more inclined to eat it. As for staying with Stephen, she won't do it. We've tried to get her to, but she's refused. She says it wouldn't be right for her to interfere in his life now, not after she abandoned him when he needed her. Besides, she doesn't want Amy to see her so sick. Says it will scare her."

Charlotte nodded slowly. "Hmm, I forgot about that. If I remember right, Amy is about four or five now, isn't she?"

"She's five now," Louis said.

"Then Joyce is right. Little kids that age have vivid imaginations and are very impressionable."

"Yeah, I suppose so," Louis agreed. "Amy does have a big imagination, that's for sure."

"So, how long will you be gone this time?"

"Shouldn't be more than two or three days at the most." Louis suddenly glanced at his watch. "And speaking of going, I've got to get a move on if I want to get to the airport on time, but there's just one more thing, Charlotte. If—"

When he hesitated, his Adam's apple bobbed as he swallowed, and Charlotte knew what was coming.

Louis took a deep unsteady breath. "If she should get worse, just call 911 and call Stephen. He knows how to reach me. You have his number, don't you?"

Charlotte nodded, knowing that what Louis really meant was that if Joyce should die while he was gone.

"Thanks a lot, Charlotte. I won't forget this. I owe you bigtime." He narrowed his eyes. "Just out of curiosity." He motioned toward her costume. "Why are you wearing that getup? Going to a party?"

"I have a temporary job I'm working tonight. The Rossis—that's who hired me—are having a Mardi Gras party, and this is what I was given to wear."

Louis suddenly frowned. "The Rossis?"

Again Charlotte nodded. "Yes, the Rossis, as in Robert and Emily Rossi."

"Please tell me you're joking."

When Charlotte shook her head, Louis glared at her. "You do know who Robert Rossi is?"

"Yes, I know who he is, but I didn't know when I accepted the job," she said defensively.

"How could you not know?"

"Emily was the one who hired me, and I didn't make the connection until later."

Louis stared at her as if she had grown horns. "Well, once you knew, then why on God's green earth didn't you quit? Why would you go to work for someone like that?" Louis's voice rose. "I swear, you've pulled some stunts before, but this one takes the cake."

"It's just a temporary job," Charlotte retorted. "Not that it's any of your business."

"I don't care if it is only temporary. You have no business working for those people. Why, Hank would—"

"That's enough!" Charlotte cut him off. "And just leave my son out of this."

"No, it's not enough—not by a long shot." Louis glowered at her. "Of all the harebrained—I swear, I'm beginning to believe that you need a keeper. Well, you can just forget it." He sliced the air with the heel of his hand. "Even if I have to lock you in a closet, you're not going!"

Something inside Charlotte snapped. Slapping her hands on her hips and narrowing her eyes, she leaned forward until she was almost nose to nose with Louis. "You just try it and see what happens," she yelled. "Besides, given your present situation with your ex-wife, I don't believe you're in any position to tell *me* what I can or cannot do. Now get out of my way before I start screaming bloody murder!" Charlotte placed one hand squarely on Louis's chest and shoved.

Caught by surprise, Louis stumbled backward. Once he regained his balance, he glared at her, shook his head, and muttering to himself he stomped across the porch, jerked open the door to his half of the double, and slammed it behind him.

For several moments Charlotte stared at the other door with unseeing eyes as she willed her heart to stop pounding. Then, taking a deep breath, she adjusted the strap of her purse over her shoulder, stepped out onto the porch, pulled her own door closed, and locked it.

On parade nights, Charlotte knew to avoid the main streets. But even the traffic on the side streets was heavy with parade goers trying to find parking spots within walking distance of the parade route. Besides the bumper-to-bumper traffic, there was also a steady stream of pedestrians attempting to make their way to St. Charles Avenue.

As Charlotte inched along, carefully watching out for pedestrians, the angry words she'd flung at Louis haunted her, and her chest felt heavy with regret.

You should be ashamed of yourself, Charlotte LaRue . . . losing your temper like that . . . saying all of those hateful things.

"What I do is none of his business," she muttered defensively in an attempt to excuse her actions. Charlotte groaned as she threw on her brakes to avoid hitting a pedestrian who ran out in front of her.

As she eased off the brake and accelerated, she finally admitted that her excuse didn't hold water. Deep down she knew that Louis had a valid reason for saying what he'd said and that he'd only had her best interest and well-being at heart.

Charlotte winced as she recalled the way she'd taunted Louis about Joyce. In her heart of hearts, she truly admired him for what he was doing for Joyce, and was deeply ashamed, ashamed for being jealous of a dying woman, and ashamed for stooping to such a petty level. The next time she saw him she owed him an apology, she silently vowed. But right now she needed to pray for forgiveness for being so selfish and mean-spirited.

When Charlotte finally parked in front of the Rossis' house, a van, sporting a logo for Big Easy Catering Company pulled in behind her.

Two bodyguards that Charlotte hadn't met were on duty, but Mark and Gino, both decked out in tuxedos, were standing on the porch. When Mark spotted Charlotte, he signaled to the guard at the gate to let her pass.

"Looking good, Charlotte," he teased as she crossed the porch.

Since Mark was young enough to be her son, she didn't take his teasing seriously, nor was she insulted by it. "Same back at you," she quipped with a smile. "And I think the deliveryman could use some help. Y'all can bring it all into the kitchen."

As Charlotte walked through the entrance hall, out of habit she glanced into the parlor as she passed by the doorway. Though it was still basically straight, she noticed that some of the furniture had been moved away from the piano. Either they had hired a small band or the empty space was where the bar would be set up, she decided.

By the time the men unloaded the last of the food from the caterer's van, every available surface in the kitchen was covered with white boxes. Charlotte signed the receipt for the food, and as soon as the deliveryman left, she turned to Mark and Gino. "Okay, guys, it's time to get to work. We've only got about an hour before the guests begin to arrive. Let's open all these boxes first and see what's inside."

Once all the boxes were open Charlotte motioned toward the ones containing small triangular-shaped sandwiches. "Take two of those boxes into the dining room," she told Mark.

"Yes, ma'am." Mark gingerly stacked one box on top of another one, then disappeared with them into the dining room.

"Ah, hello? Excuse me."

Charlotte turned toward the raspy feminine voice. The attractive, dark-haired woman wearing glasses and standing in the kitchen doorway looked to be in her mid-to-late-forties and was dressed in a white blouse and black skirt, a standard serving uniform. Puzzled, Charlotte asked, "Can I help you?"

"If you're Charlotte, you can. I'm Anna—Anna Smith. I'm here to help serve."

Charlotte frowned. "But I thought that everyone at Big Easy was out sick with the flu."

Anna smiled and nodded. "Everyone but me."

Charlotte nodded. "Good. Welcome aboard. Glad to have the extra help."

Gino stepped forward. "Does this mean that Mark and me don't have to be waiters tonight?" he asked Charlotte.

Reminding herself that patience was a virtue, Charlotte faced the aggravating man and said, "Sorry, Gino. This just means that you might not have to work quite so hard." To Anna, she said, "Come on in. This is Gino."

Gino nodded, and at that moment Mark reentered the kitchen.

"And that's Mark," Charlotte said. "Mark, this is Anna. She's from Big Easy Catering and is going to help out with the serving tonight."

At the sight of Anna, Mark frowned. "A-Anna?" he repeated, clearly puzzled.

"From Big Easy Catering," Charlotte repeated.

Anna stepped forward and held out her hand to Mark. "Anna Smith," she said. "Nice to meet you, Mark."

For a moment, Charlotte wasn't sure if Mark was going to

respond. Then, as if he'd suddenly emerged from a trance, Mark reached out and briefly shook her hand.

Though Charlotte was puzzled over Mark's odd reaction, for the moment there was no time to dwell on it. "Okay, people, time's a'wastin'. Let's get busy."

After assigning each of her three helpers a task, Charlotte went into the dining room. She was arranging the food on the table when Emily appeared in the doorway.

"Oh, Charlotte, everything looks lovely."

When Charlotte turned to face Emily and saw what she was wearing, she smiled. "Thanks, and you look lovely too, Ms. Catwoman. I don't know many women who could wear that costume and wear it so well. In fact"—she laughed—"I don't think I know any."

Stains of scarlet appeared on Emily's cheeks. "Amanda picked it out. It's a bit more snug than I'm comfortable with, but I didn't have the heart to say no."

"And is Robert dressing as Batman?"

Emily shook her head and snickered. "Not hardly. He's dressed as Rex, King of Carnival."

Charlotte nodded, but bit her bottom lip to keep from laughing out loud. *He just wishes he could be Rex,* she thought. *No way would someone like Robert Rossi ever be considered for the prestigious honor of being selected as Rex.*

"Ah, Charlotte, I noticed a woman helping out in there." She motioned toward the kitchen. "I thought all of the servers were sick with the flu."

"I thought so too." Charlotte shrugged. "Everyone but Anna, it seems."

"Oh, well, the more the merrier, I guess. And speaking of more, the bartender and the musicians should be here any minute now." Emily waved a hand toward a small, portable bar standing in the corner of the dining room. "The bartender will be setting up over there and the musicians will set up around the piano."

When the chimes of the doorbell rang out, Emily glanced at her watch, then raised her eyebrows. "Maybe that's them now. I certainly hope so."

When Emily turned to leave, Charlotte called out, "Emily, wait up a second." When Emily paused, Charlotte continued. "It's just that—well, when the guests begin arriving, do you want me to answer the door and show them in?"

Emily shook her head. "Heavens, no. You've got enough to do already. Besides, Robert has already made arrangements for one of the men to do that. Security, you know. But thanks for offering."

Music from the jazz combo blended with the drone of chatter from the guests and was punctuated occasionally with laughter as the parlor and dining room steadily filled with people. Charlotte figured that there were already around thirty people milling around, with more still arriving.

As Charlotte glanced around the parlor to make sure that everything was in order, her gaze landed on Robert. If she didn't know better, she would swear that Robert's Rex costume was the real deal. She finally decided that he'd probably had the costume custom-made.

Unfortunately Emily wasn't the only Catwoman. Another one arrived on the arm of Batman. But of the two women, Charlotte still thought that Emily looked the best in her costume. Then Adam and Eve, complete with a fake snake wrapped around Adam's neck, made their entrance, and not far behind were Peter Pan and Tinker Bell followed by Cinderella and Prince Charming. But it was Mr. and Ms.

SpongeBob's arrival and silly antics that really loosened up the crowd, that and the tall glasses of Hurricanes that the bartender kept making.

Much to Charlotte's aggravation, as the evening progressed and the crowd grew more rowdy, Gino became even more disgruntled and uncooperative. He was lazy for one thing and seemed to take forever to complete even the most minor task.

The more that Charlotte mingled among the guests, the more she began noticing the men, sans costumes, strategically stationed throughout the house. Thinking about Emily's earlier statement concerning security also brought to mind what Joe Rossi had said the day before about the Medina family and payback, and a shiver snaked down Charlotte's spine. She'd noticed that the other three Rossi brothers had yet to make an appearance. Joe's absence she could understand, but what about the other two? Was tonight the night? Was it possible that the party was just a ploy to cover up Mario and Tony leading a strike on the Medina family?

Best not to think about that, Charlotte decided as she stared at a small group of men huddled around Robert Rossi in the back corner of the parlor as Robert talked on his cell phone. Though all of the guests had come in costumes, Charlotte still recognized several prominent figures. There was a U.S. senator dressed as an old-fashioned English judge, complete with white wig and black robes, a city councilman dressed like Spiderman, and an Elvis look-alike whom she recognized as a leading businessman whose picture had often been featured on the Money Page of the *Picayune.* All three were among the group huddled with Robert.

When Robert ended the cell phone call, he said something to the small group of men, and they erupted in cheers. Then

Robert held up his glass. "To success and a long, profitable relationship," he toasted.

All of the men chimed in. "To success!" They clinked their glasses against his and downed their drinks. Afterward, there was a lot of backslapping and laughter.

Now what on earth would a senator, a councilman, and one of New Orleans's leading businessmen have in common with the Mafia? she wondered. Nothing good, she was sure, but what?

Curiosity was eating Charlotte alive, and for a moment she wished she could be a little fly on the wall near the group of men. Then, with a shake of her head, she reminded herself to rein in her overactive imagination and mind her own business.

As she turned and headed toward the doorway, a woman dressed as Cleopatra approached her. Charlotte had noticed the Egyptian queen standing near the piano earlier, mostly because the costume was so stunning, almost an exact duplicate of the one that Elizabeth Taylor had worn in the movie *Cleopatra.* But she'd also noticed her because, unlike most of the guests, Cleopatra seemed to be there unescorted and seemed uninterested in chitchatting with the other guests. Seeing the Egyptian queen up close, Charlotte realized that she was a lot younger than she had first thought.

"Could you please direct me to the ladies' room?" the woman asked.

Charlotte smiled. "Of course. Just turn to your left in the hallway. The bathroom is located beneath the staircase—first door on the right. And by the way, that's a lovely costume."

Cleopatra pulled her lips into a semblance of a smile, and murmuring "Thanks," she made her way through the crowd toward the hallway.

* * *

By the time midnight rolled around, all Charlotte could think about was soaking her aching feet in a nice hot tub of water. When she noticed that some of the guests had begun to leave, she signaled for Gino, Mark, and Anna to meet her in the kitchen.

"It looks like things are winding down," Charlotte told the little group. You've all done a great job tonight, but it's not over yet. We still have the cleanup to face." She turned to Gino and Mark. "You two go ahead and begin collecting any dirty dishes and glasses that are left in the parlor." She faced Anna. "You can—"

"I saw some people milling around near the library," Anna interrupted. "If you want, I'll check in there."

Charlotte nodded. "Good thinking, Anna. And while all of you are picking up, I'll straighten the dining room. Just bring the dirty dishes back here. Set the glasses on the counter near the sink. Scrape off any food that's left on the plates into the trash can, then stack the plates inside the sink. I'll load the dishwasher later."

Once her crew had dispersed, Charlotte walked into the dining room and began straightening up the table. Several of the cut-glass platters only had one or two items of food left on them. By combining the food onto two of the platters, she was able to free up the other four.

The caterer had furnished all of the serving dishes, and Charlotte figured that most of them, with the exception of the large platters, would fit inside the dishwasher. Figuring that she would go ahead and hand-wash the platters she'd emptied, Charlotte carried them into the kitchen.

When Charlotte entered the room, she was surprised to find a pajama-clad Amanda washing her hands in the sink. Earlier

Charlotte had heard Emily give the children strict instructions that they were to stay in their rooms. So what was Amanda doing downstairs?

Amanda abruptly shut off the faucet and pulled a wad of paper towels off the towel holder.

Charlotte frowned. And why was the girl using the kitchen sink, instead of her bathroom sink, to wash her hands?

"Amanda?"

When the girl whirled around, Charlotte gasped. The poor child's face was as white as the paper towels in her hands. "What on earth?" Charlotte murmured. "Are you ill?"

If possible, Amanda turned even more pale. Looking like she'd been caught with her hand in the cookie jar, she shook her head. "No, ma'am, I'm just fine," she said as she quickly stuffed the paper towels into the trash can. "I was just—"

"Amanda!" Emily suddenly appeared at the hall doorway and headed straight for her daughter. "What are you doing down here?"

"N-nothing, Mama. I—I was just thirsty, that's all. Just thirsty . . ." Her voice faded away.

"You know you shouldn't be downstairs," Emily scolded. "Besides which, you could have gotten a drink of water from the sink in your bathroom." Emily glanced over her shoulder then back to Amanda. "If you know what's good for you, you'd better get back upstairs fast before your father sees you."

Amanda bowed her head and stared at her feet for a moment. "He won't see me," she whispered.

A sound of frustration emerged from deep in Emily's throat. "Don't argue with me, young lady. Just go back upstairs. Now!"

Amanda shrugged. "Okay, Mama."

Once Amanda had left the room, Emily sighed. "Please tell

me that things get better. I don't think I'm cut out to raise teenagers."

Charlotte laughed. "If it makes you feel any better, no one is."

Emily rolled her eyes upward. "Thanks for nothing, Charlotte." Then she sighed. "The reason I came in here in the first place was to let you know that one of the guests spilled her drink all over the back of my sofa, and of course she just happened to be drinking a Bloody Mary."

"Ah, yes, the joys of tomato juice. Don't worry, I'll get it cleaned up right away."

A few minutes later, armed with waterless hand cleaner, two towels, one damp and one dry, Charlotte headed for the parlor. Once she'd cleaned up the mess on the sofa she returned to the kitchen, washed the food trays, then began loading the dishwasher.

"I think this is the last of them in the dining room," Gino grumbled as he entered the kitchen and unloaded another tray of dishes.

After a moment, it suddenly occurred to Charlotte that she hadn't seen Mark or Anna for a while. Gino was the only server bringing her the dirty dishes. "Ah, Gino, where are Mark and Anna?"

Gino shrugged. "How should I know?"

Charlotte leveled a narrow-eyed look at him. "Take a guess."

Gino heaved a heavy sigh. "Okay, okay. Mark's probably on the porch smoking."

"What about Anna?"

"I don't know," he complained. "Maybe she's in the bathroom or something."

"Humph! Maybe I'll find out." Charlotte rinsed off her hands and dried them, then headed for the parlor.

Neither Mark nor Anna was in the parlor, so she decided to check the dining room. After a moment, she finally spotted Mark. His back was to her and he had cornered Cleopatra.

"It figures he'd be fooling around instead of working," Charlotte grumbled to herself. But actually she was surprised. Out of the three servers, he'd been the most helpful and enthusiastic of the bunch for most of the evening. Even so, the evening wasn't over yet, and he was supposed to be working, not flirting with the guests.

But as Charlotte made her way toward Mark, she got a side view of him that made her pause. If the strained expression on his face and his tense body language was any gauge to measure by, then maybe she was mistaken. Maybe he wasn't flirting, after all. In fact, he looked as if he was pretty upset about something. But upset about what?

Charlotte sighed, then continued walking toward Mark. She was probably reading more into the situation than there really was. More than likely Mark was upset because Cleopatra wasn't interested in flirting with the hired help.

When Charlotte tapped Mark on the shoulder, he whirled around to face her. "Oh, Charlotte."

Giving Cleopatra a brief, apologetic smile, Charlotte said, "Mark, we could use your help."

"No problem," Mark said. Then, with one last glance at Cleopatra, he followed Charlotte out into the hallway.

"Go ahead and check again for any dirty dishes in the parlor," Charlotte told him.

"Sure thing," Mark responded, and headed for the entrance to the parlor.

"Now for Anna," Charlotte murmured, deciding that she should probably check the half bath under the staircase first.

The door to the half bath was ajar, and when Charlotte peeked inside the small room, she found it empty.

Still staring into the empty room, she remembered that Anna had said something about checking in the library for dirty dishes. "Of course," Charlotte whispered. "She's probably still in the library."

When Charlotte turned she saw Cleopatra headed her way. "Is anyone in the bathroom?" the Egyptian queen asked her.

Charlotte shook her head. "It's empty."

"Oh, good. I'm about to pop. Too much wine." With a quick smile, Cleopatra hurried past Charlotte into the bathroom.

With a slight smile of her own, Charlotte walked away. She still needed to find Anna.

Charlotte had just turned the corner to the hallway leading to the library when a woman's bloodcurdling scream rent the air.

Emily.

Chapter 6

Charlotte froze. "What on earth?" she whispered as a cold knot of fear took root in her stomach.

"Help! Help! Somebody help me!"

The sound of Emily's terrifying screams for help catapulted Charlotte into action. Her heart pounding, she sprinted down the hallway in the direction of the cries.

"Help me!" Emily cried out again. "Help!"

"Emily?" Charlotte yelled. "Where are you?"

"The library! Help!"

Charlotte skidded to a halt at the library door. Behind her she could hear voices and the clatter of approaching footsteps. But all she could do was stare in horror and disbelief.

Emily was kneeling on the floor beside a body—Robert's body. Her hands were pressed against the small of his back, and she was sobbing. Tears streamed down her cheeks and blood oozed from beneath her hands. On the floor, just to Emily's left, was a wicked Rambo-looking knife, also covered with blood.

"I—I can't stop the bleeding," Emily cried. "Call 911! Please get help!"

At that moment a man dressed as the Grim Reaper, followed by two more men, shoved past Charlotte.

"Emily, what happened?" the Grim Reaper asked.

Charlotte immediately recognized the Grim Reaper's voice as belonging to Leo Acosta, Robert's attorney. Though she'd only seen them once, she also recognized the two men with him. Both were bodyguards that she'd noticed earlier. A fat lot of help they had been, she thought. So much for security.

Leo dropped down beside Robert's body and placed the tips of his fingers along the side of Robert's neck. After a moment he grimaced and shook his head. "I'm so sorry, Emily." He reached over, grasped Emily's wrists, and pulled her hands away from Robert. "He's gone."

Emily began to shake with gut-wrenching sobs as Leo helped her to her feet. He turned to the two bodyguards. "Keep everyone out of here!" he ordered as he reached beneath his robe, pulled out a cell phone, and tapped in numbers. After a moment he said, "There's been a murder . . ."

Murder . . . murder . . . The word reverberated through Charlotte's head as the murmurs of the crowd behind her drowned out the rest of Leo's conversation.

The two bodyguards stepped over to the doorway and blocked the entrance. "Move back," one of them demanded.

"We need everyone to return to the parlor," the other one said.

As far as Charlotte could tell, nobody moved.

"What's going on in there?" a shrill voice from the crowd cried out.

Charlotte turned in time to see the crowd part for Sophia. "Move—get out of my way," the old lady demanded.

One of the bodyguards attempted to stop her. "Miss Sophia, don't—" But Sophia dodged him and pushed her way to the library entrance. Then she froze.

"Oh, my dear Lord," she cried. "Not Robert too! Noooo!" she screamed. Then, without warning, Sophia grabbed her chest, gasped, and with a groan of pain, she fell to the floor.

"Sophia!" Emily cried. She started toward the old lady, but Leo stepped in front of her.

"Stay here, Emily. You'll get blood on her."

Emily froze then stared down at her hands.

The bodyguard who was closest to Sophia immediately knelt down beside her and checked for a pulse. A second later, Leo was standing over both of them, and two more bodyguards had pushed their way through the crowd.

"Well?" Leo snapped at the guard hovering over Sophia.

The bodyguard glanced up. "She's alive," he said. "I think she just passed out."

"And who gave you a medical degree?" Leo retorted. "Someone get her heart medicine!" he yelled. "Upstairs, third door on the left, bedside table." To the two bodyguards who had just arrived, he said, "Take her into the parlor. One of you stay with her, and you"—he pointed to the other bodyguard who had just arrived—"come back and help move everyone else in there too. And don't let anyone leave before the police get here," he added.

As the two bodyguards lifted Sophia, Leo shook his head. "All of these people here," he grumbled, "and not a doctor in the whole bunch."

Once the men left with Sophia, Leo returned to Emily. Placing his arm around her waist, he said, "She's okay. I think she just fainted. How are you holding up?"

Emily murmured something, and after a moment Leo frowned, hesitated, then nodded. He turned his gaze toward the doorway, and when he spotted Charlotte, he motioned for her to come forward. "Charlotte, come in here, please."

Her legs still shaking and wondering what in the world he wanted with her, Charlotte entered the library.

"I need you to take Emily upstairs," Leo told her. "Help her get cleaned up. She needs to change clothes before the police arrive."

Charlotte had read enough mystery books and had seen enough *CSI* shows on TV to know that, considering the circumstances, such a thing could be viewed as tampering with the evidence. She didn't want to believe that Emily had murdered Robert and, in fact, didn't believe that Emily could murder anyone, but it sure looked that way. And the last thing she wanted was to get in trouble with the police.

"Isn't that tampering with evidence or something?" she asked.

"Just do it, Charlotte. I'll take full responsibility."

Yeah, right. Sure you will, Charlotte thought, still hesitating. *Right up until they haul Emily and me off to jail.*

"Please, Charlotte," Emily whispered. "Please help me. Th-the blood—I can't stand having all of this blood on me."

Though Charlotte still didn't like it, she couldn't ignore Emily's plea for help. Swallowing further objections she nodded and, placing one hand at the small of Emily's back, she took a firm hold of Emily's arm with her other hand. As gently as she could, Charlotte urged her forward. "Let's get you upstairs."

Out in the hallway murmurs of speculation ebbed and flowed through the crowd like waves on a seashore, but the moment Charlotte and Emily stepped through the library doorway, the whispers abruptly ceased. After all the noise and commotion, the sudden silence was so eerie that Charlotte felt as if she'd entered another dimension.

"I—I know how it looks," Emily said, her voice fragile and shaky as she leaned heavily against Charlotte. "But I tried to *save* him."

At first Charlotte wasn't sure if Emily was trying to convince her or the people surrounding them. She finally decided that Emily was simply still in shock and more than likely talking to herself.

"It's okay," Charlotte soothed softly. "Let's just get you upstairs."

"There was too much blood," Emily continued, her voice thick with tears. "So much blood . . . I couldn't stop it."

"Of course you couldn't," Charlotte murmured sympathetically, feeling as if every eye in the hallway were staring holes through them.

In spite of Charlotte's attempt to console Emily, and in spite of what she wanted to believe, a silent battle raged in her head as she guided her down the hallway through the crowd then up the staircase.

They all think she did it, and who can blame them? Given the evidence, only a fool would think otherwise.

But looks can be deceiving, she silently argued. *Not everything is always as it seems.*

But sometimes things are exactly as they seem.

When they finally reached the master bedroom, Charlotte led Emily to the bathroom. "Let's get your hands washed first," she said as she turned on the faucet and handed Emily a bar of soap.

"So much blood," Emily whispered, scrubbing her hands and arms.

Once Emily had washed and dried her hands, Charlotte helped her get undressed. "Here," Charlotte said as she handed

Emily a robe that was hanging on a hook on the back of the bathroom door, "put this on until we find you something else to wear."

After she'd help Emily with the robe, Charlotte stared down at the floor at the bloodstained costume. Should she fold it or stuff it into the dirty clothes hamper? Or should she just throw it in the garbage?

No, definitely not throw it in the garbage, she decided. In spite of Leo Acosta's assurances, she was probably already in trouble for helping Emily wash up, but the police would take a really dim view of her trashing the costume.

Only if they know, a little voice whispered in her head. *Of course they'll know,* she silently argued. *There were at least thirty witnesses who saw her in the bloody thing.*

With a grimace of distaste, she decided that the best thing to do would be to simply leave the costume on the floor for now.

"Let's find you something else to wear," Charlotte told Emily.

Emily motioned toward the bodice of the apron that Charlotte was wearing. "I got blood on your apron."

Charlotte frowned and looked down at her frilly white apron. Sure enough there was a smear of blood right at the bustline. Charlotte reached behind her and untied the sash. Once she'd slipped off the apron, she carefully folded it and left it on top of the cabinet by the sink.

"I didn't do it, you know," Emily said as they walked back into the bedroom. "I didn't kill him."

Charlotte wasn't quite sure yet if she believed Emily and wasn't comfortable responding one way or another, so she said nothing.

"You do believe me, don't you?"

Though faint, Charlotte could hear the sound of sirens outside. She swallowed hard and busied herself rifling through Emily's closet.

When Emily realized that Charlotte wasn't going to answer her, she slowly shook her head and fresh tears filled her eyes. "Of course you don't believe me," she whispered. "No one's going to believe me." Then Emily reached out and grabbed Charlotte's wrist. "Please, there's not much time. At least let me explain."

Charlotte went still. Outside, the sirens grew louder. Finally, with a sigh, Charlotte nodded.

A look of relief washed over Emily's face. "Some—some of the guests had started to leave," she said. "So—so I went looking for Robert so that he could tell them good-bye." Her face twisted as if she were in pain. "When I got to the library, he—he was already on the floor with the knife in his back. It's the truth. As God is my witness, it's the truth."

Emily shook her head and her eyes glazed over with the memory of what she'd seen. "Blood was gushing out, and I knew if I didn't do something right then and there, he was going to bleed to death." She paused, blinked several times, and the glazed look disappeared. "It was a really stupid thing to do, but I thought I could . . ." She gave a one-shouldered shrug. "I pulled out the knife so that I could apply pressure to the wound to stop the bleeding. By then it was already too late."

Outside, the sound of sirens grew louder then abruptly died.

"They're here," Emily whispered as she stared toward the front window at the flashing lights piercing the darkness.

Though everything Emily had told Charlotte made perfect sense, deep down she knew that proving Emily's innocence was going to be almost impossible. And though Charlotte wasn't sure she believed it herself, she said, "Everything will work out."

Then, because she didn't know what else to say, she turned back to the closet and selected a pair of navy slacks and a pink blouse. She held them out for Emily to see. "Are these okay?"

Emily gave a one-shouldered shrug again. "Does it really matter?"

Charlotte sighed. "Yes, it matters, and for the record, I believe you," she finally admitted. And at that moment she meant it. "You only did what you'd been trained to do—what any good nurse would do. And what any good wife would do," Charlotte added. The look of relief on Emily's face tugged at Charlotte's heart.

"Maybe it's not so hopeless after all," Emily whispered as she slipped off the robe and pulled on the blouse. "If you believe me, maybe others will too," she said as she buttoned the blouse.

Charlotte hated to be the bearer of doom and gloom, but she felt that Emily should be prepared for the worst. "I believe you because I know you and don't truly think that you're capable of murder, but I think you have to be prepared for the worst. Others, including the police, might not be so inclined to take you at your word. Especially when they find out that Robert abused you," she added with a grimace. "And they will find out, one way or another." And that was putting it mildly.

"I know they will." Emily stepped into the slacks, buttoned and zipped them. Then, as if she didn't want to think about it or discuss it any longer, she completely changed the subject. "I hope Sophia is okay."

* * *

Downstairs, policemen were everywhere, and the party guests huddled in small groups scattered throughout the entrance hall, the dining room, and the parlor. Charlotte could feel the guests' eyes staring holes through Emily and her as they descended the last few steps.

"I've got to check on Sophia," Emily told her, ignoring the stares and whispers coming from the groups.

When Emily and Charlotte entered the parlor, two EMTs, a man and a woman, were lifting Sophia onto a stretcher. From the little that Charlotte could see, it appeared that Sophia was still unconscious.

Emily approached the woman EMT. "Is Sophia going to be okay?" she asked.

"Are you family?"

Emily nodded. "I'm her daughter-in-law."

"There's a possibility that she's had a light heart attack, so we're taking her to St. Charles General."

Moments later, as they watched Sophia being wheeled out of the parlor, Emily murmured, "I should go to the hospital with her."

"I don't think the police are going to allow you or anyone else to leave just yet." *But especially you,* Charlotte added silently. "What about one of her other sons or their wives?" she suggested. "You could have your lawyer call them."

Charlotte suddenly frowned. Come to think of it, why hadn't the brothers shown up yet? And where were Mark and Gino? With all that had happened—Robert's murder, Sophia's collapse—she would have thought that the brothers would have been notified right away. "Speaking of Robert's brothers, where are they? And where are Mark and Gino?" she asked Emily.

"I'm not sure, but I hope they're with the children. Before

we went upstairs, I told Leo to get the children out of here, away from the house."

"The children!" Charlotte whispered. She couldn't believe she hadn't once thought about Amanda and Brandon. "Guess I'm more tired than I thought. I forgot all about the children."

"Yes, well, I hate to admit it, but there's always the possibility that Robert's killer was sent to murder all of us. That's just one of the reasons we live with six bodyguards. Leo probably gave Mark and Gino orders to take the kids to one of their uncles' homes for protection."

But if you go through with the Medina job, there will *be payback.*

Unbidden, Joe Rossi's words swirled through Charlotte's head. It stood to reason that if Emily didn't kill her husband, Robert's death could be a part of the retaliations that Joe had warned his brother about, thus the need to squirrel the children out of harm's way.

A small groan from Emily jerked Charlotte from her thoughts, and when she glanced over at the younger woman, she was shocked to see how pale Emily had turned.

"What's wrong? Are you okay?" Charlotte reached out to steady her.

"I—I don't know," Emily whispered. "Just all of a sudden I feel weak in the knees."

"Maybe we'd better sit down before you pass out too." Charlotte motioned toward the sofa. "Why don't we sit over there?"

Once they had settled on the sofa and several moments passed, Charlotte noticed that Emily had a bit more color in her cheeks. For herself, she felt like moaning with relief just to be off her feet. But Charlotte's relief was short-lived when two men dressed in sports coats entered the room. The men glanced around as if looking for someone, then they walked back out into the foyer.

One look at the men, and Charlotte would have bet her last nickel that they were detectives. She had met a few of the detectives and several of the uniformed officers from the sixth precinct, but she couldn't recall ever having met those particular two men before.

In the back of her mind, she'd hoped that her niece Judith and Judith's partner, Brian Lee, would have caught the case. Then again, after second thoughts and given the circumstances, maybe it was better that they hadn't, she decided.

"I suspect those two men who just walked out are the detectives who will be investigating the case," Charlotte told Emily.

Once again Emily paled, and Charlotte wished that she had kept her mouth shut about the detectives. The one thing that Emily didn't need at the moment was added stress. The woman was nobody's fool. She knew that she had to be the prime suspect, and anyone with a half a brain would be worried out of their mind. If only there was a positive way of distracting Emily, something that would make her feel less helpless.

Then an idea occurred to Charlotte—the perfect solution to take Emily's mind off what was to come. "You know, Emily, you might want to go over the invitation list and check off the guests who left earlier. I'm almost certain that the detectives will want that list, and if you've already checked off the ones who left, it might save some time."

Emily stared at the doorway thoughtfully. "That's probably a good idea. Only one problem—the list is in the library."

Charlotte grimaced. "Yeah, well, that could be a problem, all right. Let me see what I can do."

Charlotte pushed off the sofa and, with the intentions of finding the detectives she'd seen, she walked out into the entrance hall. A uniformed officer she didn't recognize was posted at the front door, but where had the detectives gone? Maybe the dining room, she decided.

As Charlotte headed for the dining room, out of the corner of her eye she spotted Anna Smith standing alone near the foot of the staircase. With Mark and Gino missing and herself being MIA because of Emily, poor Anna was probably at a loss as to what to do. Charlotte sighed. She supposed she should probably say something to the server. And she would. But not right now. First things first.

The detectives weren't in the dining room, nor were they in the kitchen, which left the library. "Should have looked there in the first place," she grumbled.

Just as Charlotte turned the corner to the hallway leading to the library, a uniformed policeman stepped in front of her and blocked her path.

At the sight of Billy Wilson's familiar face, Charlotte felt some of the tension and fear she'd been experiencing fade. Billy and her niece's ongoing relationship had long been a bone of contention between Charlotte and her sister. Because Judith was a detective, Madeline thought that Judith could do a lot better than dating just a patrolman, but Charlotte figured that as long as Judith was happy with the relationship, Madeline should keep her snobby opinions to herself. And, to give Madeline credit, she'd been almost civil to Billy on Sunday.

"Ms. LaRue, what are you doing here?"

"Oh, Billy! Am I glad to see you."

Billy frowned and eyed Charlotte speculatively. "Are you one of the party guests?"

Billy's question reminded Charlotte that she was still dressed in the silly maid costume. Tugging self-consciously at the short skirt of her costume, she said, "No, not a guest."

Billy's frown deepened. "I don't recall Judith telling me that you work for Robert Rossi. And that's something she definitely would have mentioned."

"Oh, I don't work for him—at least not on a permanent basis," she quickly explained. "This was just a temporary job, just to help out with the party." More temporary than either of them had planned on. Certainly a lot more temporary than Robert Rossi had planned on.

Charlotte grimaced. "Ah, speaking of the party," she said, "Emily and I—Emily is Robert Rossi's wife—anyway, we were talking a few minutes ago. We both figured it might be of help if the detectives had a copy of the guest list. Emily could go over the list and let the detectives know which guests left before"—Charlotte swallowed hard—"before Mr. Rossi's body was discovered."

Billy nodded. "Sounds like a good idea to me."

"Only one problem," Charlotte said. "The list is in the library, probably either on top of the desk or in one of the drawers. Do you think you could get that list for us?"

"I can't make any promises," Billy told her. "But I'll see what I can do."

Charlotte reached out and squeezed Billy's forearm. "Thanks, Billy."

"Why don't you wait here a minute?"

Charlotte nodded. "Okay."

"Not a step farther, though," Billy warned. "I have strict orders to keep everyone away from the library until the crime lab and the investigator from the coroner's office get here."

"I'll stay here," Charlotte reassured him.

With a nod, Billy turned, walked down the hall, and disappeared around the library doorway. As Charlotte stared at the entrance to the library, flashes of light kept going off. Had to be the detectives taking pictures of the crime scene, she figured, and she shuddered as a mental image of Robert Rossi came to mind.

A few minutes later, Billy emerged from the library, and in his hand was what appeared to be the list.

"Thanks, Billy," she said as he handed over the list.

"Take care, Ms. LaRue."

With a quick smile for Billy, Charlotte hurried back to the parlor to where she'd left Emily.

"Got it," she told Emily as she handed her the list.

Emily's gaze rested on the paper for a moment, and then she glanced nervously around the room. "I guess to be accurate, I need to, as they say, eyeball everyone."

Charlotte figured that the last thing Emily wanted was to face each of her guests, and who could blame her? Still, it was something that had to be done. "Why don't I come with you?" Charlotte suggested.

The grateful look of relief on Emily's face was so pathetic that it made Charlotte want to cry. "Besides," Charlotte added, "two heads are better than one."

Over the next twenty minutes, Emily, with Charlotte's help, began checking off names. Once they had checked off all of the guests who were still present in the parlor, they moved into the entrance hall, then into the dining room and did the same.

"I think that about does it," Emily murmured, eyeing the list.

Charlotte leaned over and read the names that hadn't been checked. "Which one of those is Cleopatra?" she asked.

"Cleopatra?"

Charlotte nodded. "There was a young woman here who was dressed like Cleopatra, and since I didn't see her while we checked off names . . ."

Emily frowned. "You know, I do remember seeing a woman dressed like Cleopatra, and I also remember wondering who she was." Emily lowered her gaze and glanced over the list of the guests who had already left. "Hmm, now that's strange. I remember what each of these were wearing and none of them was dressed like Cleopatra." She lifted her gaze. "So who was she?"

Charlotte slowly shook her head. "I haven't the foggiest, though at one point, I did see her talking to Mark. But if she's not here and she's not on the list of guests who have already left, then where did she go?"

Emily narrowed her eyes. "But more to the point, how did she get past the bodyguards in the first place without being on the list?"

Chapter 7

"Okay, everyone, listen up!"

At the unexpected sound of the loud booming voice, Charlotte forgot all about Cleopatra for the moment. With a frown of annoyance, she turned to see what was happening. One of the men whom she had suspected was a detective stood near the staircase with a megaphone in his hand.

"We need to question everyone about what happened here tonight," he continued. "And the sooner everyone cooperates, the sooner you can go home. What we'd like right now though is for everyone to go into the parlor."

Step into my parlor said the spider to the fly . . .

Charlotte shivered as the words popped into her head. *And now it begins,* she thought. Taking a firm hold of Emily's upper arm, she said, "Come on, let's go. The sooner we move into the parlor, the better chance we'll have at getting a place to sit."

Once everyone had crowded into the double parlor, the same detective gave further instructions. "We will be interviewing each of you individually. We appreciate your cooperation and ask that you be patient."

The detective left for a moment and immediately the buzz of voices filled the room. When, suddenly, the room grew quiet, Charlotte glanced toward the door opening to see what was happening, just in time to see a body bag on a stretcher being wheeled past.

"They're taking Robert now," Emily whispered tearfully.

Once the stretcher had passed, the room began to buzz again. In an attempt to offer comfort, Charlotte gathered Emily's hands in hers and held them. But no words of comfort came to mind.

Then the room abruptly grew quiet again.

What now? Charlotte thought as she glanced toward the doorway again. One of the detectives, accompanied by Leo Acosta, had entered the room and was headed straight for Emily.

When the two men reached the sofa, Leo held out his hand to Emily. "The police want to ask you some questions now, Emily, but I don't want you to worry. I'll be there the whole time."

Emily's gaze shifted back and forth between the attorney and the detective. After a moment, she finally nodded and allowed the attorney to help her to her feet.

The moment that Emily and the lawyer disappeared from the room, the silent room erupted in a hum of voices.

During the time Emily was being questioned, no one else was singled out for an interview. *Not a good omen,* Charlotte thought, *considering the circumstances.* Things looked bad for Emily. It was a sure bet that she was their number one suspect, and the poor thing was probably being put through the wringer by *both* of the detectives.

In Charlotte's heart of hearts, she couldn't believe Emily was the one who had stabbed Robert. For one thing, Emily was intelligent enough to know that killing Robert with a house full of guests as witnesses then calling for help would be a really stupid thing to do. But if Emily didn't do it, who did?

Charlotte grimaced and rolled her eyes upward toward the ceiling. *Well, duh,* she thought. Considering the number of enemies Robert had, it probably made more sense to ask who *didn't* kill him.

Charlotte slowly shook her head and reminded herself that though the list of possibilities was probably endless, not everyone had the opportunity. The thing to do was to figure out who had motive *and* opportunity?

Charlotte frowned in thought. Almost everyone in the house had opportunity, but the first person who came to mind that had motive was Joe Rossi, Robert's own brother. Joe had made it crystal clear that he blamed Robert for their father's death and that he blamed Robert for the way he'd been treating their mother. Only problem with Joe being a suspect was that he hadn't attended the party at all. Joe didn't have the opportunity . . . or did he?

After all, except for the bodyguards, everyone at the party was in costume and most wore masks. It was possible that Joe could have dressed in a costume and slipped in and out without anyone being the wiser. And who would have stopped him? Not the bodyguards. They would have recognized him as part of the family . . . part of the family . . . the family.

And I'm going to kill him *just like he killed Papa, if he hurts Mama again.*

Charlotte winced at the memory of Amanda's angry threat. Though she hated to even think about it, she couldn't ignore what she'd overheard Amanda telling Brandon.

Charlotte froze as a wave of apprehension swept through her. Amanda in the kitchen . . . Amanda, pale, and in her pajamas . . . Amanda washing her hands at the sink right before Robert's body was discovered. Why had she been washing her hands downstairs in the kitchen when she had a perfectly good bathroom of her own upstairs? *Because she had blood on her hands?*

Charlotte squeezed her eyes shut and cringed. *Ridiculous!* For one thing, she seriously doubted that a girl Amanda's age would have the courage to do such a thing. And for another thing, Charlotte was sure it would take a lot more strength than someone Amanda's size possessed to plunge a knife into a man Robert's size and strength.

Not if she sneaked up on him.

No! Charlotte refused to believe it. But if Amanda didn't do it and if neither Emily nor Joe did it, then who did kill Robert?

Charlotte suddenly stiffened. The eggs! Of course. Why hadn't she thought of them in the first place? Robert had been furious about the missing Fabergé eggs and had claimed that someone was stealing them . . . someone already in the house. What if, during the course of the party, he'd walked into the library and caught the thief red-handed, and the thief had killed him?

Then again, maybe not, she thought. If that were the case, then the thief would have more than likely stabbed Robert in the chest instead of the back.

Mind your own business. Let the police do their job.

Yeah, yeah, she countered the nagging voice in her head. *And sit back and watch them railroad Emily for something she didn't do?*

At that moment, the drone of chatter died, and when Charlotte glanced around to see why, Emily and Leo Acosta walked through the door.

"Oh, you poor thing," Charlotte whispered to no one in particular. Emily was alarmingly pale and evidently so shaken up from her interrogation that Leo Acosta felt the need to assist her back to her seat.

"You did good in there, Emily," Charlotte heard the lawyer tell Emily as they approached the sofa, his voice sounding abnormally loud in the quiet room. "Everything's going to be okay. Just stay calm and focus."

Once Emily was seated, she covered her face with both hands and leaned forward, resting her elbows on her knees.

Leo patted Emily on the shoulder, and turned to Charlotte. "They were pretty rough on her, so stay with her."

As if suddenly aware that everyone in the room was staring and listening, he grimaced and lowered his voice. "I have to make some phone calls, and I'd rather she wasn't left by herself right now, and I'd rather she didn't talk to anyone."

Charlotte wasn't sure how she felt about the lawyer giving her orders, but since she couldn't leave anyway, she really had no choice.

"Can I depend on you to stay with her?"

Charlotte sighed. "Yes, I'll stay with her."

With a nod of satisfaction and one last glance at Emily, the attorney turned and headed toward the doorway. The minute that he disappeared through the door, the rumble of voices again filled the room.

Satisfied that, within reason, for the moment everyone in the room was too busy gossiping and speculating to pay attention to her and Emily, Charlotte leaned toward Emily. "Are you okay?"

Emily turned her head to the side. "No," she whispered. "I'm not okay. I'm worried about my children and Sophia. And I'm tired. Very tired."

Charlotte was curious as to what the detectives had asked

Emily, but one look at the fear and desperation in Emily's eyes, and Charlotte reined in her curiosity. She figured that the poor woman had been interrogated enough for one night, and the last thing Charlotte wanted was to add to Emily's stress.

Charlotte patted Emily's back. "Just know that if you need to talk, I'm here."

Emily simply stared at Charlotte for a moment, finally nodded, and then turned away and covered her face with her hands again.

Now what? Charlotte wondered, suddenly feeling tired to the bone. If only she could simply leave, go home, and forget everything that had happened.

Charlotte glanced around the room. Given the number of people yet to be interviewed, going home anytime soon was just wishful thinking. There was no telling how long it could take for the detectives to question each guest.

Resigning herself to the fact that there was nothing she could do but wait, Charlotte crossed her arms, bowed her head, and fixed her eyes on the fishnet stockings that covered her knees.

Stupid stockings. Though it had been at least a couple of decades ago, she could still remember when they were in fashion. She hadn't liked them then and liked them even less now. In fact, she'd always thought that they looked like something only a hooker would wear with hot pants. Too bad she couldn't figure out some way to take them off.

Louis seemed to like them.

Charlotte winced. Louis was going to have a cow when he found out that she was yet again involved in a murder investigation. A sinking feeling settled in her stomach. And so were Judith and Hank. Charlotte's stomach knotted. She hated admitting it, but Louis had been right. Once she'd found out who had hired her, she should have run the other way. And if she'd listened to him, she wouldn't be in the fix she was in now.

"Ah, excuse me, ma'am."

Charlotte gave a start, and her gaze flew up to the man standing in front of her. One of the detectives. Now where on earth had he come from? She must be more tired than she'd thought, letting him sneak up on her like that. More tired and dreading having to face Judith, Hank, and Louis.

"Would you please follow me?" he said. "We'd like to talk to you in the kitchen."

Can I depend on you to stay with her?

Leo Acosta's orders came to mind, and Charlotte hesitated.

"Now, please," the detective demanded.

"I'm coming, I'm coming," Charlotte told the detective. As she pushed up off of the sofa, she patted Emily's shoulder. "I'll be back. Just don't talk to anyone." Emily's only response was a slight shrug.

But would she be back? Charlotte wondered as she followed the detective through the crowded room. Once they finished questioning her, they might tell her to go home. And if they told her to go home, then who would stay with Emily?

Outside in the hallway, Charlotte spotted Leo Acosta coming down the hallway. "Sorry," she told him, motioning toward the detective as they passed each other. "But I told Emily not to talk to anyone."

Leo nodded. "I'm headed that way now."

The first thing Charlotte noticed when she entered the kitchen was the mess. Catering boxes and dirty wineglasses were still stacked on the counter; dirty dishes filled the sink.

Her gaze roved over the kitchen. The detective had said "we." So where was the other one?

"Have a seat over there." He motioned toward the breakfast table.

"How soon before I can get in here to finish cleaning up?" Charlotte asked him as she seated herself at the table.

The detective frowned. "Clean up?"

Charlotte nodded.

His frown deepened as his eyes honed in on the costume she wore. "Then you really are a maid, and that's not just a costume you're wearing?"

Stung by his assumption that someone her age would actually choose to wear the ridiculous getup, Charlotte glared at him. "I am a maid, but this *is* just a costume. I was asked to wear it for tonight's party."

The detective stared at her a moment more as if trying to decide if she was telling him the truth. Then, with a nod, he pulled a small notebook from his pocket and seated himself across the table from her. "Name please."

"Charlotte LaRue."

The detective started to scribble her name but paused. With eyes narrowed, he tilted his head to one side and stared at her for several moments. "I've heard that name before. Have you ever been arrested?"

Charlotte stiffened with indignation. "No!" she snapped. "Of course not."

"We will check, you know."

"Check all you want. *I have never been arrested*," she said, emphasizing each word.

"What about parking violations?" he shot back.

"Oh, for pity's sake! You've probably heard my name before

because my niece is Judith Monroe—Police Detective Judith Monroe."

The moment she said Judith's name, a look of dawning comprehension came over the detective's face, and Charlotte suddenly wished she could stuff the words back inside her mouth.

"Aha!" The detective nodded knowingly. "Now I know why your name sounds so familiar. You're *that* maid."

Charlotte felt like a worm squirming on a fishhook. Was he referring to the other murder cases that she'd been involved in or simply referring to her being Judith's aunt? Though she wanted to ask what he meant, she figured it was probably best to let sleeping dogs lie, so to speak. "So—what's your name?" she asked, hoping to divert his attention.

"I'm Detective Gavin Brown, and I'll be asking the questions around here."

Well, excuse me, she fumed silently.

As Gavin Brown scribbled something in his notebook, a patrolman entered the kitchen. "Sorry to interrupt, Detective Brown, but just thought you'd want to know that the press has arrived. They're crawling all over the place."

The curse words that came out of Gavin Brown's mouth made Charlotte wince, and though she was on the verge of telling him that gentlemen didn't use such language around ladies, she thought better of it.

"Just do the best you can," the detective told the patrolman. "Someone will be out later to give them a statement, but whatever you do, don't let them inside."

The patrolman nodded. "Yes, sir."

As soon as the patrolman left the room, the detective turned his attention back to Charlotte. "So, Ms. LaRue, how long have you worked for the Rossi family?"

"Two days, counting today." At the detective's puzzled expression, she explained. "I'm not the regular maid. I was hired just to help out with the party."

"So where's the regular maid?"

"I was told that she had a family emergency and wouldn't be back until next week."

"I don't suppose you happen to know her name?"

"Just her first name," Charlotte answered.

"And?"

"Her name is Jennifer."

"O-kay." Nodding, the detective jotted down the information in his notebook. When he finished he raised his gaze and stared at her with narrowed, unblinking eyes.

Charlotte figured that for some reason he thought he could intimidate her. Why he even felt the need to intimidate her was beyond her. But what he didn't know, couldn't know, was that better men than he had tried and failed. She figured the best thing to do would be to use the old "catch more flies with honey than vinegar" trick. Dredging up the most innocent smile she had, and using the sweetest tone she could muster, she said, "Is there anything else you need to know, Detective Brown?"

The look on his face was priceless, and Charlotte had to bite her bottom lip to keep from laughing out loud.

He cleared his throat and shifted uncomfortably in his chair. "I'd like for you to tell me in your own words what happened here tonight."

Just the facts, Charlotte. Nothing more and nothing less. Taking a deep breath, Charlotte began at the point when she'd heard Emily scream, and though she briefly considered telling him about the attorney instructing her to help Emily change clothes, she decided against it. "Right after I got to the library, Leo Acosta showed up and called the police."

"Did you see anyone in the hall when you first heard her scream?"

Charlotte shook her head. "No one."

"Was there anyone else in the library besides Ms. Rossi and Mr. Rossi?"

Again Charlotte shook her head. "No, no one. But Emily didn't kill him," she added.

"And just how do you know that? Did you *see* who killed him?"

"No, of course not."

"Then how do you know that Ms. Rossi didn't do it?"

"I just know," she retorted.

"Yeah, well, maybe you'd better leave the detective work to the professionals."

Charlotte felt her temper flare at the sarcasm dripping from his voice when he'd emphasized the word *professionals,* but telling herself just to cool it, she counted to ten.

"Now, is there anything else you'd like to add?"

"There is one thing," she said, squashing the urge to tell him to go butt his head against a stump. His attitude was beginning to get on her last nerve. *Not nice, Charlotte. Antagonizing the police won't help Emily.*

Charlotte cleared her throat. "You may have noticed that in the library, Robert—ah, Mr. Rossi, I mean—has a large collection of Fabergé eggs. What you may not know is that someone has been stealing the eggs."

"And how do you know that?"

Charlotte shrugged. "Yesterday I overheard Robert tell Emily that three more eggs were missing."

The detective narrowed his eyes and stared at Charlotte for several moments. "So, how long has this series of thefts been going on?"

"I really don't know. Like I said, I just started working for the Rossis yesterday."

Gavin Brown jotted something in his notebook, then, after a moment he fixed his gaze on Charlotte. "Okay, Ms. LaRue, is there anything else you want to tell me?"

As Charlotte stared at the detective, a cold knot formed in her stomach. He'd just asked the same question a few minutes earlier, which could mean that he was fishing for more information or a particular piece of information. She lowered her eyes and stared at the tabletop. *Tell him about Emily changing clothes. He's going to find out anyway . . . unless he already knows.* It was possible that either Emily or the lawyer had already told him about her helping Emily change clothes. Then again, they might not have.

Charlotte drew in a deep breath and looked the detective straight in the eyes. "No," she finally answered. "There's nothing else that I can think of right now." Technically she wasn't lying. After all, he'd asked if there was anything else that she *wanted* to tell him.

"You're sure about that?" he retorted.

The minute he asked the question, Charlotte knew she'd made a mistake. But to backtrack now would look like she was trying to cover up something.

Well, aren't you?

Charlotte ignored the pesky voice in her head. "I'm sure," she answered. "Now, can I go home?"

The detective shook his head. "Sorry, no. Not yet."

"When can I go home?"

"When I say so," he shot back. "Until then, please return to the parlor."

Charlotte fumed all the way back to the parlor, but even while she fumed her head swirled with questions. Did Gavin

Brown already know that she had helped Emily change clothes? Did he already know about the blood on her apron? Was she a suspect too? Should she call Judith, or even better, maybe she should call her nephew Daniel? After all, Daniel was a lawyer.

As Charlotte entered the parlor, the knot in her stomach tightened. The time to have called Daniel was *before* she'd been questioned, and she should have told the detective about Leo Acosta asking her to help Emily change clothes. It was stupid of her not to tell him. Unless some little elf had done away with Emily's bloody clothes and the stained apron, the police were going to find the things.

During the following hours, Charlotte watched as one by one, the guests were called in to be questioned by the detectives, then were allowed to leave. As the number of guests dwindled and the room gradually emptied, her unease grew.

Finding it harder and harder to stay awake, Charlotte walked over to the front window. As she stood there watching daybreak chase away the last remnants of night, she heard the front door open and close. A moment later she saw the remaining two guests, a couple dressed as a devil and an angel, walk toward the front gate.

Two of the bodyguards and several patrolmen were still milling around on the front porch, and the two detectives and the crime scene team were still in the house, but other than her, Emily and Leo Acosta, and the reporters hanging around outside, everyone else had left.

"Ms. LaRue?"

Charlotte turned to see Gavin Brown enter the parlor. He motioned for her to come over to the sofa where Emily was curled up asleep. Leo Acosta was bent over Emily, gently shaking her shoulder to wake her up.

"Wh-what's happening?" Emily asked. As she pushed herself into a sitting position, Gavin Brown stepped forward.

"Ms. Rossi, you're under arrest for the murder of Robert Rossi. You have the right to remain silent . . ."

Chapter 8

Though Charlotte had expected Emily to be the primary suspect, she hadn't expected her to be arrested on the spot, and it was a blow to listen as the detective read Emily her rights. She'd been certain that they would take Emily to the police station and question her further there before arresting her.

Fighting her own fears, Charlotte braced herself as anticipation and dread spread through her veins. When they finished with Emily, would they then arrest her as well?

Emily was still half-asleep, and from the look on her face, Charlotte could tell that the poor woman had yet to comprehend what was happening. When Emily did finally realize that the worst had happened, that she was being arrested, she covered her face with her hands, and shaking her head from side to side, she sobbed. "Nooo . . . nooo . . ."

"Do you understand your rights?" the detective demanded, raising his voice to be heard over her weeping.

Leo Acosta sat down by Emily and wrapped his arm around her. "Emily, it's okay. I promise it's going to be okay." He glanced up at the detective. "Could you give us a second?"

At first Charlotte didn't think that the detective was going to back down, but after a moment, he nodded. To her dismay though, he turned his attention to her. *Uh-oh, here it comes,* she thought.

"We know what you did, Ms. LaRue. We found the clothes upstairs and we found your apron. In case you don't know, accessory to murder is a crime. The *only* reason you aren't being arrested too is because of your niece Judith. We've talked to Detective Monroe, and she has assured us that you will make yourself available when needed and that she will keep an eye on you."

Charlotte's heart sank. When had they talked to Judith? She had hoped that she could keep Judith out of it. If Judith knew, then it was a sure bet that Judith had called Hank. *Great, just wonderful,* she silently groaned.

She turned and glared at Leo Acosta. A snake in the grass. That's what he was. A low-down snake in the grass. She'd known not to trust him, known in her heart of hearts that helping Emily was wrong, and she'd also known that if push came to shove, Leo Acosta would be the first one to throw her to the wolves. The fact that he was pointedly ignoring her only proved it.

"One more thing, Ms. LaRue," the detective said. "Don't leave the city. If I learn that you've left for any reason, I'll put out an arrest warrant on you so fast it'll make your head swim."

All Charlotte could do was stare at the detective and pray that she could hold on to her temper and not say something that would make things worse.

"You can go home now," Gavin Brown told her. "But you best remember what I said. And another thing—don't be talking to the news media about any of this."

As if she would, thought Charlotte. The last thing Maid-for-a-Day needed was to be linked with the murder of a mobster. Now wouldn't that be just peachy for business?

Charlotte bit her tongue and counted to ten. Then, with one last glare at the detective, she glanced down at Emily. She wanted to say something to Emily, to offer her some kind of comfort. But Emily was still crying and Charlotte doubted that she would hear anything she said anyway. With a sympathetic look at Emily and a hateful glare directed at Leo Acosta and the detective, Charlotte turned and hurried out of the room before they could change their minds about her leaving.

The moment Charlotte stepped out onto the porch, someone shouted, "It's the maid!"

Suddenly video camera lights and camera flashes momentarily blinded her. Charlotte threw her hands over her eyes. Reporters. She'd completely forgotten about the reporters.

By the time she could see again, her knees were knocking, and two reporters had shoved microphones in her face and were shouting out questions.

Remembering the detective's warning about not talking to the media, all that she knew to do as she plowed through the throng of reporters was shake her head and keep repeating, "No comment."

When she reached her van, at least three other vans that represented different television stations were parked along the curb.

By the time she'd climbed inside and locked the doors, her heart was pounding like a jackhammer and her hands were trembling so badly that it took three tries before she was able to insert the keys into the ignition. Would her picture end up in the newspaper, or worse, on television? Dear Lord in heaven, she hoped not. Then the next thought horrified her even more. The stupid maid's costume. Charlotte groaned. Not only was everyone in the whole city—in the whole country—going to identify her as the mob's maid, but they would also see her in the ridiculous costume.

To her further distress and aggravation, she was still so shaken that she ran a stop sign and barely escaped being clobbered by a truck. With her ears ringing from horns blaring, all she could think about was getting home.

Only when she turned down Milan Street did her heart finally slow to a tired thud. Though it wouldn't have surprised her in the least to find Judith or Hank waiting on her doorstep, she sent up a prayer of thanksgiving when she pulled into her empty driveway.

Inside her house, as she changed into her pajamas, she began to fantasize that when she awakened, she would find that the whole thing had been just a bad dream.

But as she crawled into bed, sleep didn't come right away. Each time she felt herself drifting off, she would suddenly remember some detail that she'd overlooked when Gavin Brown had questioned her. In between fits of sleep, over and over she relived the night and the party from the beginning up until the point when she'd discovered Emily hovering over Robert's body in the library. And then the real nightmares began, nightmares of her standing on the Rossis' porch, dressed in nothing but the stupid fishnet stockings.

The first time Charlotte heard the phone ring, she was sorely tempted to ignore it and let the message machine take the call. But once again, her old fears rose up to haunt her. What if it was an important business call, or what if it was an emergency call?

Surely just this one time wouldn't matter though, and besides, she couldn't seem to force her eyes open anyway.

When the ringing finally stopped, Charlotte sighed with relief and felt herself drifting back to sleep. She wasn't sure how much time had passed, but it seemed that only seconds later the phone began ringing again.

Ignoring it the first time had bothered her, but ignoring it a second time was more than she could stand. Forcing her eyes open and making a mental note to call the phone company and have a phone installed in the bedroom, something she should have done ages ago, she climbed out of bed and stumbled to the living room. Still half-asleep, she picked up the receiver.

"Maid-for-a-Day, Charlotte speaking," she muttered.

"What in the devil is going on down there?"

Charlotte frowned. "Bitsy?" Maybe she was having yet another nightmare. After all, Bitsy was supposed to be in California.

"Of course it's me," Bitsy retorted in her squeaky voice. "Imagine my shock when I was watching Fox News channel this morning and heard that Robert Rossi had been murdered. That's national news, all the way out here in California. I swear. I've only been gone for a couple of days and everything falls apart. So what on earth happened?"

Not a nightmare. Too bad, Charlotte thought, and too bad she hadn't bothered to check the caller I.D. *before* she'd answered the phone. But as Charlotte opened her mouth to explain everything, in true Bitsy fashion, the old lady didn't give her a chance and kept talking.

"Is Emily okay? The children? Oh, dear Lord, please tell me that the children are okay. Why, I can't imagine—"

"Bitsy," Charlotte said firmly. "If you'll just slow down a

minute and let me get a word in edgewise, I'll tell you what happened."

"Well, of course you will. Why do you think I called in the first place? I—"

"Bitsy," Charlotte ruthlessly interrupted, "Robert was murdered last night during their Mardi Gras party. The children are just fine as far as I know, but Emily has been arrested for Robert's murder."

A full ten seconds of silence hummed over the phone line, and Charlotte began to worry that Bitsy had fainted or something.

"That's ridiculous," Bitsy suddenly blurted out, her voice brimming with indignation. "That's the most asinine thing I've ever heard, and I'd like to know just which ignoramus is responsible for doing such a thing. Why, I've known that woman for years and she wouldn't hurt a fly."

Charlotte blinked. She had seen Bitsy upset before, but she didn't remember Bitsy ever being so furious.

"You have to help her, Charlotte. You have to find out who did this. You've done it before and you can do it again. In the meantime I plan to make some calls. Believe me, by the time I get through, some heads are going to roll."

Charlotte blinked again and for a moment she was speechless. While it was true that she had been instrumental in solving a couple of other murders, with the exception of one particular incident, playing sleuth wasn't something she set out to do. Besides, she'd already helped Emily and had gotten herself into a heap of trouble for doing so. As for Bitsy making phone calls, Charlotte didn't doubt that the old lady had once known some influential people in high places, but it had been years since her husband was mayor and, like Bitsy's husband, many of their old cronies had also passed away.

"Ah—Bitsy, I'll help as much as I can." No use telling Bitsy *how* she'd already helped. She certainly didn't want that blabbed all over the country.

"You promise?"

Charlotte swallowed hard. At times Bitsy could be a bit childish about things, and Charlotte knew that anything less than a promise would be unacceptable in Bitsy's eyes. "Yes, ma'am, I promise."

"Good! I knew I could count on you to do the right thing. And if there's any way I can help, you call me, night or day. I want Emily cleared of this mess, once and for all and as soon as possible."

When Charlotte heard the distinct click in her ear, she suddenly realized that Bitsy had hung up on her. With a sigh, she hung up the receiver as well.

Charlotte narrowed her eyes. Bitsy had said that the news of Robert's murder had been telecast on national news. Charlotte swallowed hard. She should have asked if Bitsy had seen any films of the people or the house, more specifically, any shots of the maid. Since Bitsy didn't mention seeing her, and Charlotte felt sure that she would have said so if she had, that must mean that none of the pictures taken of her had been used.

Feeling some measure of relief, Charlotte looked up at the ceiling. "Thank you, thank you," she whispered. Maybe the old saying was true after all. Maybe the good Lord did look after fools and children. "And right now, this old fool could use a hot cup of coffee." But just as Charlotte turned toward the kitchen, she heard a sharp rap on her front door.

"Now what?" she groaned. Executing an about-face, she glared at the front door. "I swear, Sweety," she grumbled as she walked over to the front window, "a body can't get a moment of peace around here."

The little parakeet preened and whistled until he realized that Charlotte had no intention of letting him out of the cage. Then he bristled and squawked in protest.

"Sorry, boy," Charlotte told him as she peeked out the window to see who was at the door. When Charlotte caught a glimpse of her niece, a feeling of dread washed through her.

"Aunt Charley?" Judith called out, her voice muffled as she knocked on the door again.

"Hold on a minute," Charlotte responded as she threw the dead bolt. The moment she opened the door, the blast of cold, damp air from outside sent goose bumps chasing up her arms.

"Did you get any sleep?" Judith asked as she stepped past Charlotte and entered the living room.

"Well, good morning to you too." Charlotte closed the door. "But to answer your question—" She glanced over at the cuckoo clock on the wall behind the sofa. "I got maybe four hours or so."

Seemingly unfazed by her aunt's sarcasm, Judith said, "Are you doing okay?"

Charlotte gave her niece a quick smile. "I'm okay, hon. I was just about to make myself a pot of coffee. But first, I think I need to pay a visit to the little girl's room."

"Coffee sounds good," Judith said. "I could use a cup myself." Judith grinned and motioned toward the general direction of the bathroom. "But by all means, take care of business first."

A few minutes later Charlotte joined Judith in the kitchen.

To give Judith credit, she waited until the coffee was brewed before she began grilling her. While the coffee brewed, they talked about the prospect of yet another baby in the family. Though Hank and Carol's baby was still months away from being born, Judith was already planning a baby shower.

Once the coffee was ready, Charlotte poured them both a cup.

"You do know why I'm here, don't you, Auntie?" Judith accepted the cup of coffee that Charlotte handed her.

Charlotte took a quick sip of her own cup of coffee and tried, unsuccessfully, to keep from smiling as she seated herself across the kitchen table. "Why, of course, hon. You missed me and came to have coffee with me."

"Get serious, Auntie, 'cause this is some serious business."

"This?" Charlotte asked in the most innocent voice she could fake.

Judith twisted in her chair and drummed her fingers against the tabletop. Then she uncrossed her legs and crossed them again.

The nervous fidgets. Charlotte had learned that any time Judith began fidgeting was a sure sign that she was nervous.

"Aunt Char-ley!" Judith finally said, her tone growing impatient. "You know good and well what I'm talking about. For Pete's sake, what on earth possessed you to work for the mob?"

Aha, finally. Now we get down to it. Charlotte placed her cup on the table, crossed her arms on the tabletop, and leveled a glare at her niece. "In the first place, I didn't know they were the mob when I agreed to do the job. And in the second place, I only agreed to do the job because it was a temporary thing—just a couple of days to get ready for the party."

Judith narrowed her eyes. "You didn't know they were the mob! Aw, come on, Aunt Charley. Everybody in the entire city knows who and what Robert Rossi is."

Charlotte rolled her eyes. *Shades of Louis Thibodeaux.* "Well, I didn't," Charlotte retorted. "At least not until Bitsy Duhe told me. All I knew was that a woman named Emily Rossi needed help cleaning because her regular maid had family problems."

Judith waved a hand. "Okay, okay. That's all beside the point now anyway. But once you knew, you should have high-tailed it in the opposite direction."

"Yeah, yeah. Shoulda, woulda, coulda."

Judith sighed. "Please don't be like that. I'm trying to help you."

Guilt reared its ugly head. *Shame on you. Besides being your own flesh and blood and trying to protect you, Judith is just trying to do her job.* Wincing, Charlotte finally nodded. "I know, hon, and I'm sorry. It's been a long night and I'm tired."

"I'm sure you are, but the faster we get through this, the sooner you can put it behind you and get some rest. Now, what's this I hear about you tainting the evidence? I would have figured that you, of all people, should know better."

Charlotte lowered her gaze to stare at her coffee cup. "Yes, you're right. I did know better," she admitted, albeit reluctantly. "But it was one of those situations where you would have had to been there to understand. There was no way Emily could have waited until the police arrived before she cleaned up." Charlotte lifted her gaze to Judith's face. "Emily had blood all over her hands and clothes from trying to *save* her husband." She paused a second. "You do know that she was once a nurse, don't you?"

When Judith nodded, indicating that she did, Charlotte continued. "Anyway, the poor woman was in shock and close to hysteria. Besides, that lawyer of hers—Leo Acosta—he's the one who told me to help her get cleaned up. He said that it would be okay. Not that I believed him," Charlotte quickly added. "But"—she shrugged—"what's done is done. And of course when push came to shove—" Charlotte's tone dripped with sarcasm, "Mr. Acosta didn't bother to tell the detective that *he* was the one who insisted that I help Emily clean up. At least not that I know of," she added.

"Hmm, interesting," Judith murmured, nodding thoughtfully. "So, what you're saying is that when the detective questioned you, Mr. Acosta didn't bother to let him know that he was the one who had told you to help Ms. Rossi clean up?"

"Hmph! When I was questioned, Acosta wasn't anywhere around."

Again Judith nodded. "Okay, why don't we talk about you being questioned?" Judith reached down and pulled a small notebook and a pen out of her purse. She opened the notebook to a blank page, and with pen poised in hand, she leveled a no-nonsense look at Charlotte. "I want you to tell me exactly what you told Gavin Brown."

Charlotte took another sip of her now-tepid coffee, and, as best as she could remember, she told Judith about her interview with the detective.

When she'd finished, Judith tapped her pen against the notebook. "Okay, now I want you to tell me what you left out."

Charlotte purposely widened her eyes and tried to look as innocent as possible. "What I left out?"

Judith nodded knowingly. "No use playing dumb with me, Auntie," she warned. "You forget, I've known you all of my life. And don't hand me any of that bullsh—"

"Judith!"

Judith rolled her eyes. "Okay, okay. Don't hand me any of

that *stuff* about your confidentiality, no gossip policy either, not if you want to stay out of jail."

"Well, if you put it that way . . ."

"Yeah, I thought that might get your attention."

"Watch it, young lady. You may be a big bad police detective, but I'm still the same aunt that changed your diapers. So just can the sarcasm and show a little respect."

Judith smirked. " 'Well, if you put it that way,'" she said, throwing Charlotte's own words back at her.

In spite of herself, Charlotte couldn't help grinning. "Smarty pants."

"Had a good teacher," Judith quipped. Then Judith sobered. "Okay, Auntie, let's have it."

"Actually, I do have a few thoughts about other possible suspects."

"I figured you would, and I suppose this means that you're convinced that Emily Rossi didn't do it?"

Charlotte shrugged. "I just can't feature her killing him and certainly not stabbing him with a knife. For one thing, she's smarter than that. Only someone crazy or really desperate would risk murdering the man with a house full of guests. For another thing—call it a gut feeling or whatever—she's simply not the type."

Charlotte hesitated as it occurred to her that Emily could have been desperate enough at the moment. And she could be crazy, crazy like a fox. Crimes of passion happened all of the time. *You should probably tell Judith about how mean and abusive Robert was to Emily.* But Charlotte ignored the pesky voice in her head. To say anything about Emily being abused would only make the poor woman look even guiltier.

"There was an incident the day before," Charlotte said

quickly before she could change her mind. "It was with Robert Rossi's brother Joe."

As Charlotte told Judith about the incident, including what Joe had said about the Medina family and possible payback, Judith jotted down notes.

"I figure that it's possible that Joe Rossi could have sneaked in undetected if he wore a costume and mask."

Judith nodded. "My thoughts exactly."

"And there was that business about the Fabergé eggs, but I've already told you about that."

Judith nodded. "Yes, ma'am. Gavin wrote that up in his report. Anything else? Or maybe I should ask, anyone else?"

Amanda . . . looking pale and frightened . . . washing her hands in the kitchen sink . . . Charlotte swallowed hard, and praying that she wasn't making a mistake, she shook her head. "No, no one else."

"You're sure?" Judith's eyes narrowed suspiciously.

When Charlotte nodded again, Judith gave an oh-well shrug and flipped the notebook closed. "If you think of something else—anything else—you will let me know, won't you?"

"Of course," Charlotte murmured.

"And, Auntie, one more thing. Stay out of it. Let the police handle this. Don't interfere. And don't look at me like that."

"Like what?" Charlotte asked, widening her eyes in an attempt to appear clueless.

"Don't give me that. You know exactly what I'm talking about." Judith reached over and covered Charlotte's hand with her own. "I'm serious, Auntie." She squeezed Charlotte's hand for emphasis. "Did it ever occur to you that the reason Leo Acosta insisted that you help Emily was so that he could manipulate things to make it look like *you* were the one who murdered Robert?"

"Me! Why that's ludicrous. What possible motive could I have to murder the man?" But even as she protested, a sinking feeling settled in the pit of her stomach. It had never once occurred to her that the attorney could have been setting her up to cover the tracks of the real killer. But why her?

Because you were handy.

Charlotte's stomach turned sour. How could she have been so naive, so stupid?

"You don't have to have a motive. He could manufacture one. He could either be trying to cover up for Emily or someone else, or— Gavin doesn't agree with me," Judith explained, "but personally, I think Mr. Acosta should be a suspect as well. He could have been trying to blow smoke to cover his own tracks. In fact, just between you, me, and the fence post, I think Gavin jumped the gun arresting Ms. Rossi so soon. But not my call and not my case." Judith squeezed Charlotte's hand. "I don't want you worrying about this, Auntie. I'm just cautioning you to watch your back."

A few minutes later, as Charlotte stood at the front window and watched Judith drive away, her niece's words about the attorney setting her up haunted her. Surely Judith was wrong, she thought, turning away from the window.

"She's got to be wrong," she whispered to Sweety Boy. "And I've got to get a shower and put on some decent clothes," she said louder, in an attempt to dismiss the disturbing thoughts. "Before anyone else decides to pay a visit," she added. "Before Hank shows up."

Though Judith hadn't mentioned it, Charlotte was sure that her niece had probably called Hank to warn him about what was going on. And knowing Hank, he wouldn't hesitate to seize the opportunity to once again nag her about retiring.

After the night she'd been through, the last thing she wanted was to argue with her son. But if he did show up, she didn't want to be caught still in her pajamas.

Charlotte turned away from the window, and headed across the room. Just as she reached the doorway the phone rang.

With every nerve in her body screaming in protest, Charlotte halted in her tracks. Curling her hands into tight fists, she whirled around and stomped over to the desk. Narrowing her eyes, she glared at the phone as it rang a second time. When she didn't recognize the number displayed on the caller I.D., she was sorely tempted to ignore the call. The phone rang a third time, and Charlotte took several deep breaths. *Pick it up, ignore it, pick it up, ignore it* . . . On the fourth ring, she snatched up the receiver. "Maid-for-a-Day," she said between gritted teeth. "Charlotte speaking."

"Charlotte, Leo Acosta here."

Chapter 9

Charlotte swallowed hard and her heart began hammering beneath her breasts. What if Judith was right? What if Leo Acosta had intentionally set her up when he'd told her to help Emily? If he had, then he was either trying to cover for someone or trying to cover for himself.

"I'm calling because I need your help," the attorney said. "Emily has been denied bail."

I'm just cautioning you to watch your back. Judith's last words swirled in Charlotte's head, and it was on the tip of her tongue to tell the lawyer that he could go take a flying leap, that she'd already helped more than she should have. Then the rest of what he'd said finally registered. *Emily has been denied bail.* "But why?" she exclaimed.

"Because of who she is, the D.A. convinced the judge that she's a flight risk. Anyway, like I said, I need your help. Sophia is insisting that she and the children want to go home, and once the crime scene people are finished, the house will need a good cleaning."

"Then Sophia is okay? She didn't have a heart attack?"

"No, not a heart attack. More like an anxiety, panic-attack-type thing, according to her doctor. But for the time being, everyone feels it's best that Sophia and the children be allowed to return to the house, at least until it can be determined what's to be done with them."

"Of course. The children," Charlotte murmured. "What on earth is going to happen to them now?"

"Like I said, that's still to be determined. There was some talk about sending the children to a boarding school, and there was talk about Sophia either moving in with Joe or into a retirement home. But Sophia put her foot down. She told them in no uncertain terms that neither she nor the children are going anywhere, and she insists that she and the children are going to stay at Robert's house until Emily is freed from jail." He paused. "The reason I'm telling you all of this is because I'm hoping that you will agree to help out. Just until things are settled."

"What about Jennifer, the regular maid? And can't something be done for Emily right now?"

"Jennifer won't be back. For one thing, Sophia doesn't want her back. But that's neither here nor there since Jennifer already has another job. As for Emily, nothing can be done right now, but I have all the confidence that if it goes to trial she will be acquitted. But that's going to take some time. If you agree to help out, you'd be paid well."

Just say no. Charlotte opened her mouth to say no, then a picture of Bitsy flashed in her head and the sound of her squeaky voice rang in Charlotte's ears. *You promise?*

Charlotte's protest died in her throat, and she sighed. "It's not a matter of money," she explained. "It's more a matter of being shorthanded on help at the moment. But let me check my schedule and see what I can work out. Can I get back to you later this afternoon?"

"Of course. Let me give you my cell number."

Charlotte grabbed a pen and jotted down the attorney's number.

"I do need to know as soon as possible," he reiterated. "If you can't help, then I have to make other arrangements. I just thought that since the family already knows you and feels comfortable around you, it would be better for everyone concerned to have someone familiar with the house and the family at a time like this."

"Like I said, I'll get back to you this afternoon. Talk to you then."

The second that Charlotte hung up the receiver she immediately regretted that she hadn't simply said no right up front in spite of her promise to Bitsy. While she was sure that the need for help was genuine, she didn't trust Leo Acosta or his so-called concern for the family.

Fool me once, shame on you. Fool me twice, shame on me.

"Yeah, yeah," Charlotte grumbled. "And forewarned is forearmed, yada, yada, yada." With an irritable sigh and determined to finally take a shower and dress, she once again headed for the bathroom.

Charlotte had just finished dressing when a wave of dizziness suddenly swept over her and she went weak in the knees. Even as she grabbed hold of the bedpost with both hands to steady herself and sank down onto the bed, she recognized the symptoms for what they were.

It had been almost two years since she'd been diagnosed as a diabetic, and during that time she'd been diligent about doing the things she was supposed to do. She checked her blood sugar on a regular basis, exercised, ate her meals on time, watched her diet, and twice a day took the white oval pill that had been prescribed for her.

As she sat there taking deep breaths and praying that the weak feeling would pass, with each breath she silently condemned her own carelessness for allowing her blood sugar level to drop. And if her memory served her, she was also out of the glucose tablets that she carried in her purse.

She knew she'd neglected taking her pill this morning, but for the life of her she couldn't remember if she'd taken it last night. For that matter, she couldn't remember the last time that she'd eaten anything other than a bite or two of the catered food during the party.

"Wonderful," she complained, still feeling like she'd been wrung out to dry. Now all she had to do was figure out how to get to the kitchen without passing out. A glass of orange juice and her medicine would help until she could get some food down.

Charlotte turned her head and stared at the bedroom wall that separated her half of the double from Louis's half. The walls were thin enough that if she yelled really loud, Louis would hear her and come running.

The thought froze in her brain. "Oh, no," she whispered. With everything that had happened, she'd completely forgotten about Louis being gone. And Joyce . . . she'd also forgotten about helping out with Joyce.

Taking a deep breath, Charlotte braced herself. She could do this. She *had* to do it. *One step at a time*, she kept silently repeating as she eased off the bed. Slowly, and ever so carefully, she made her way out of the bedroom, through the living room, and finally, into the kitchen.

Holding on to the kitchen countertop to steady herself, she retrieved her bottle of pills, a glass out of the cabinet, and the juice from the refrigerator. Once she'd poured the juice, she popped the pill into her mouth, then drank every drop in the glass. She eased over to the kitchen table and sat down. Placing her elbows on the table and supporting her head with her hands, she waited and prayed that the episode would pass soon. Finally, slowly but surely, the weakness and dizziness subsided, and she began to feel a bit better.

After an early lunch of soup and crackers, Charlotte took a package of chicken parts from the freezer and set it in the sink to thaw. Then she checked to make sure that she had all of the other ingredients she needed to make chicken gumbo.

"No andouille." She sighed as she closed the refrigerator meat drawer. She'd made the gumbo before without the special sausage, but it never tasted as good as when she used it.

Charlotte pulled open the vegetable drawer and sighed again. No celery or green onions. Maybe she should consider cooking something else instead, but what?

Disappointed, Charlotte closed the refrigerator door. She loved gumbo, and today was the perfect kind of day for it. Nothing tasted better on a cold, blustery day than a hot, spicy bowl of the deep rich stew. Ordinarily, she didn't cook gumbo unless she was having a crowd over, since there was no way to make just a little bit for one person. But taking Joyce a meal was just the excuse she had needed.

Charlotte glanced at the kitchen clock. She still needed to go over her schedule for the upcoming week, but if she left right away she'd have just enough time to run to the grocery store, pick up the missing ingredients, and get back home. Once she got the gumbo cooking, she just might still have a minute to glance over her schedule before the time for her first interview.

A few minutes later, Charlotte was almost to the front door when the phone rang. Squinting at the caller I.D., she sighed when she saw the name on the display. The last thing she wanted at the moment was to talk to Hank, but if she didn't talk to him on the phone, she risked him showing up on her doorstep. Better to talk to him on the phone than in person.

Charlotte picked up the receiver. "Hi, hon."

"Mom, are you okay? Judith told me what happened and I just wanted to check on you."

"Other than being tired, I'm fine, son."

"Be sure and watch your blood sugar. You know that stress isn't—"

"My blood sugar is fine," she interrupted. *At least now it is.* No use in telling him otherwise, she decided.

"Have you called Daniel yet?"

Charlotte frowned. Did Hank know something she didn't know? "Calling him crossed my mind, but at this point, I don't think I need an attorney."

"You should call him anyway, Mother."

"Honey, if I think I need an attorney, Daniel will be the first person I call, but right now I don't think that's necessary. So, how's Carol feeling?"

"Carol is feeling fine, and don't change the subject. You do realize if you would stop being so stubborn and go ahead and retire, you wouldn't get into these fixes?"

Suddenly Charlotte felt even wearier than before. "Honey, I know you mean well, but could we please not have this discussion today? I only got about four hours of sleep, I've got dozens of things I need to get done this afternoon, and I really don't feel up to arguing with you."

For several seconds silence hummed over the phone line, then Charlotte heard Hank release a huge sigh.

"Okay, Mom. You win this time, but we *will* discuss this again. And I think you should call Daniel anyway, just as a precaution."

Charlotte bowed her head and closed her eyes. Time to end

this conversation. "I'll think about it," she conceded as she opened her eyes and lifted her head. "Got to go now. I love you, son, and be sure and give Carol my love too." Then, without waiting for Hank to reply, she hung up the receiver.

With her hand still on the receiver, she glanced over at the birdcage. "Well, things could be worse, Sweety. He could have just shown up at the front door."

The little parakeet ruffled his feathers and burst into a series of chirps and whistles as he pranced back and forth along his perch.

Still thinking about Hank, Charlotte grimaced. "You know, Sweety, sometimes, having a doctor for a son can be a real pain. No pun intended," she added with a smirk.

For a moment the little bird simply stared at her, then, as if realizing that she had no intentions of letting him out of the cage, he sidled over to his cuttle bone and began pecking away.

Charlotte rolled her eyes. "What's the matter? Cat got your tongue? Get it? Cat got your tongue?" When Sweety continued pecking at the cuttle bone, Charlotte shook her head. "Humph, just because I won't let you out right now is no reason to pout. I promise I'll let you out later."

The little bird kept pecking, and with an oh-well shrug, Charlotte grabbed her purse and headed for the door again.

When Charlotte returned from the grocery store there was an unfamiliar car parked alongside the curb in front of her house and a heavyset woman knocking on her front door. Charlotte groaned with frustration. The woman had to be Marla Whitney, her first interview, and she was early—a good thirty minutes early, exactly the amount of time it would have taken her to put the gumbo on to cook.

When Charlotte parked her van in the driveway, the woman turned and walked to the edge of the porch.

"Are you Marla?" Charlotte called out as she stepped down from the van.

The heavyset woman nodded curtly. "Yes, I am, and I have a two o'clock interview with Ms. Charlotte LaRue for a job."

Charlotte walked to the back of the van and opened the door. "I'm Charlotte," she told the woman as she took out the two sacks of groceries that she'd bought. *And you're early,* she added silently, still aggravated that the woman had arrived sooner than she was supposed to. But out loud she said, "I hope you haven't been waiting long." Charlotte gave the door a nudge with her hip to close it.

"Well, I was hoping to get this interview over with as soon as possible. I have another interview scheduled for three o'clock."

It wasn't so much *what* the woman said as the imperious tone she'd used, and a red flag went up in Charlotte's head. If Marla talked to a prospective employer like that, how would she treat a client?

"As soon as I put these away, we'll get started," Charlotte told her as she trudged up the steps to the porch.

Charlotte had to juggle the sacks in order to unlock the front door, and another red flag went up. Anyone with half a brain could plainly see that she could use a helping hand. Instead of offering to help though, Marla simply stood and watched her struggle to open the door.

Once inside the living room, again Charlotte had to juggle the groceries to close the door. "You can wait in here," she told the woman. "Just have a seat on the sofa, and I won't be but a few minutes."

Too bad the woman had an attitude problem and poor manners, thought Charlotte as she quickly put away the groceries.

Out of all the résumés she'd received, Marla's had seemed the most promising.

Charlotte considered herself a fair judge of character, and she would give the woman a chance to redeem herself, but her gut feeling was that Marla Whitney wasn't the type of person she needed to deal with clients who could sometimes be a bit eccentric as well as demanding.

When Charlotte returned to the living room, Marla was nowhere in sight. Had she left? Charlotte didn't think so. She hadn't heard the front door open or close, and Marla's purse was still sitting on the floor near the sofa. So where was she?

With a frown, Charlotte walked to the entrance to the short hall. "Marla? Hello, are you still here?"

"Yeah, I'm here." The muffled reply came from the direction of the bathroom. "I'll be out in a minute. I have to pee."

Charlotte's frown deepened and warning spasms of alarm erupted within her at the thought of a complete stranger wandering through her home, especially when she'd told the woman to wait in the living room. The least the crude woman could have done was *ask* to use the bathroom.

Charlotte marched to her desk, pulled Marla's file from the stack and sat down. By the time that Marla finally returned to the living room, Charlotte had made her decision. There was no way she could trust this woman with her clients. Even so, now came the sticky part. How to tell her.

"You've got a nice little house here," Marla said as she seated herself on the sofa.

"Thank you," Charlotte said curtly.

"So, how soon do I start work?"

Charlotte cleared her throat. "I have several other applicants to interview, so I'll have to get back to you."

"But you haven't interviewed me yet."

"I don't think that's going to be necessary," Charlotte replied.

Marla suddenly jumped to her feet. "What? You've got to be kidding!"

Charlotte stood. "No, I'm not kidding. I'll either call you or send you a letter with my decision by the end of next week."

Marla stepped toward the desk. "Well, I can't wait that long. I need to know now, today."

Ignoring her, Charlotte walked around Marla to the front door and opened it. "If you need to know today," she said, "then the answer is no. You're not qualified for what I'm looking for," she added bluntly, and motioned for the woman to leave.

"Well!" Marla glared at Charlotte. "I never!"

At the look of pure malevolence on Marla's face, a whisper of fear seized Charlotte. Then Marla headed straight toward her, a stalking, purposeful intent to each step she took.

Chapter 10

Charlotte figured that Marla outweighed her by a good fifty pounds, if not more.

The bigger they are, the harder they fall.

Yeah, right, she thought. All the woman had to do was sit on her. Charlotte tensed. If it came down to a physical confrontation, she'd have to defend herself as best she could. She'd have no choice. But for the moment, all she could do was stand her ground, wait, and pray that the woman was all bluff.

Marla continued giving Charlotte the evil eye right up until the second she flounced past her out the door. The moment she crossed the threshold, Charlotte slammed the door behind her and threw the dead bolt. Only then did she draw an easy breath. On shaky legs she stepped over to the window and watched until Marla got into her car and left.

With a deep sigh of relief, Charlotte headed for the kitchen. What she needed was a good, strong cup of coffee, and she needed to get the gumbo cooking before the next scheduled interview. And she needed time to go over her schedule for the following week. If she hurried, she just might be able to get the gumbo to the cooking stage with a bit of time to spare.

In the kitchen, Charlotte prepared the coffeepot and turned on the switch. Then she set about preparing the ingredients for the gumbo. Once she'd cleaned and chopped the onions, celery, bell peppers, and garlic, and she'd sliced the andouille, she set the ingredients aside. As she stirred equal amounts of flour and oil in a heavy skillet over a low fire for the roux, she thought about the incident with Marla. Conducting the interviews in her home was a mistake, she decided . . . and dangerous. But if not at her house, then where?

Charlotte stared at the roux that was beginning to turn a nice caramel color while she thought about other possibilities. The only place she could come up with was a coffeehouse. At least at a coffeehouse there would be a lot of people around; it was less dangerous and not as risky in case she got another nut case.

Just thinking about what could have happened with Marla, Charlotte shivered. Between Robert's murder and Marla, she was sorely tempted to cancel the second interview. She glanced at the kitchen clock and frowned. Too late. Dale Harris was probably already on her way.

With a sigh of resignation, Charlotte returned her gaze to the roux. The muddy mixture had turned a nice dark brown, so she determined it was ready. Dumping the chopped vegetables into the roux and continuously stirring the mix, she cooked it until the vegetables were coated with the dark roux and had softened. Then she scraped the mixture into a larger pot, added water, the chicken pieces, the andouille, salt, and pepper. Once the gumbo came to boil, she turned the burner down to low and set the timer for one hour.

Ever conscious of the passing time and armed with a cup of coffee, Charlotte headed for the living room. Seating herself behind her desk, she selected the next file on the stack of prospects. Dale Harris was Charlotte's second choice and due for an interview at three o'clock. According to Dale's résumé, she'd worked for the same janitorial service for the past five years.

Charlotte glanced at the reason she had left her former job. "Good reason," she murmured. The company that she'd worked for had gone out of business.

Charlotte set aside Dale Harris's folder. Now, finally, the schedule for the upcoming week. Just as she opened the schedule book, a knock sounded at the front door. Charlotte looked up at the cuckoo clock and frowned. She couldn't believe that it was already three o'clock. Where in the devil had the time gone? she wondered as she stood and headed for the door.

Still a bit uneasy from Marla Whitney's interview, Charlotte peeked through the front window first. "Oh, great," she grumbled when she saw the clean-cut young man standing on the porch. He was medium height and medium build with short, dark brown hair.

Charlotte eyed his navy suit. "Just what I need," she muttered. "Another salesman." Lately there had been a rash of door-to-door salesmen trying to sell her everything from vacuum cleaners to magazines.

Since the young man didn't have a briefcase or any other visible items with him, Charlotte's next thought was that he was either lost or up to no good.

At the door, Charlotte eyed the security chain. As a precaution, she slipped the slide bolt into the door plate of the chain lock, then opened the door.

"May I help you?"

"Yes, ma'am, I hope so. I'm looking for Ms. Charlotte LaRue."

Charlotte's frown deepened. "Whatever you're selling, I don't want any."

He quickly shook his head. "Oh, no, ma'am. I'm not selling anything. My name is Dale Harris and I'm here for an interview."

For several moments, all Charlotte could do was stare at him while she wrapped her mind around the fact that Dale Harris was a man, not a woman. She'd never had a male employee before, and, in fact, had never heard of a man being a maid. The idea of hiring a man as one of her maids had never even occurred to her . . . until now.

"Are you Ms. LaRue?"

"Ah . . . yes—yes I am. Could I see some identification?"

Dale Harris reached inside his pants pocket, pulled out a billfold then flipped it open and held it up for Charlotte to see.

Charlotte glanced at it, then nodded. "Thanks. Just a minute, please." She closed the door, slipped the slide bolt out of the door plate, then opened the door again. "Sorry about that. Come in, come in." She motioned for him to come inside. "It's just that lately I've been bombarded with door-to-door salesmen and one can never be too careful nowadays."

Dale Harris grinned knowingly and stepped inside. "Oh, I totally understand."

Charlotte pointed to the sofa. "Have a seat."

Dale Harris eased down onto the sofa.

"Can I get you something to drink? Coffee? Tea?"

He shook his head. "Oh, no, ma'am, I'm just fine."

Charlotte nodded, and as she seated herself behind her desk, she made a mental note that so far, he seemed to have really nice manners.

"O-kay." She took a deep breath and decided to plunge right in. "You do realize that I don't run a janitorial service. Maid-for-a-Day is exactly what it implies. We clean houses."

"Oh, yes, ma'am, I understand. Why? Is there a problem because I'm a man and not a woman?"

Charlotte took her time answering him. Said any other way, his question could have been construed as being a bit on the defensive or combative side, but the way he'd asked made her feel like he genuinely wanted to know. "No," she finally answered. "I don't see it as a problem, though I will admit it is a bit unusual. Maybe if you'd tell me why you want to be a maid . . . ?"

Dale grinned. "I did a little research on your company, and when I learned that your maids work exclusively in the Garden District, well . . . honestly, I think it would be a real hoot to clean those big old homes. I'm interested in historical architecture, you see, and I want to go for a degree. But I still need to support myself while doing it. I'm hoping that my hours would be such that I would still have time to go back to school part-time."

Charlotte narrowed her eyes. "You don't happen to know a young woman named Cheré Warner, do you?" It would be just like Cheré to try and find her own replacement.

Dale slowly shook his head. "Not that I recall. Should I know her?"

Charlotte flashed him a smile. "No, no, that's okay. It's not important."

Charlotte liked Dale Harris and liked the reason he'd given her. His explanation seemed honest and heartfelt, and she was sorely tempted to hire him on the spot. But she quickly squashed her impulsive reaction, and instead said, "Now it's my turn to be honest. I have another applicant to consider and several more résumés to look at, so it might be a week or so before I'm able to make a final decision. In the meantime . . ."

She picked up a paper that contained the standard services that Maid-for-a-Day provided each client, as well as her policies and procedures. She stood and handed it to him. "You can read through this."

Hoping that he would interpret the action as a signal that the interview was over, she remained standing and smiled.

A momentary look of disappointment crossed his face, but then he stood. Thrusting out his hand, he said, "Thank you for seeing me, and I look forward to hearing from you."

Charlotte shook his hand. "Thank *you* for being so prompt, and I'll be in touch with you within the next week or so."

Such a nice young man, she thought as she closed the door behind him.

While Charlotte waited for her four o'clock interview to show, she cooked a pot of rice to go with the gumbo. Just as the rice got done, the timer went off, indicating that the gumbo was ready.

Charlotte glanced at the clock and frowned. Four-fifteen. So where was her next appointment? Back at her desk, Charlotte took out her schedule for the upcoming week.

Too bad she hadn't thought to ask Acosta how long he wanted her to work for the Rossi household. It would help to know whether he expected her to work every day, just a couple of days, a week, several weeks . . .

Just as a precaution, she should probably think about clearing her schedule for the entire week to begin with. But if she did that, then he might assume that she could work full-time, and working full-time, every day, for any of her clients was impossible.

Frustration welled within and Charlotte suddenly threw back her head and stared up at the ceiling. "For Pete's sake, get a grip." She could second-guess what the lawyer had in mind till doomsday and still not get it right. She should have asked.

"But you didn't," she muttered. And since she didn't ask and didn't relish talking to the lawyer again until she had to, the only thing left was to decide what days she *could* work instead of worrying about what days he *wanted* her to work.

Taking a deep breath, once again she looked at the schedule. Since Sally Lawson was back from vacation, she'd need someone to clean Sally's house on Monday.

Charlotte made a note to call her part-time employee Janet Davis and ended the note with a large question mark. The last few times she'd called Janet, her part-time employee had been tied up and had turned down the opportunity to work.

Charlotte's gaze moved to Tuesday. With Bitsy out of town, at least Tuesday wouldn't be a problem. She didn't have to clean Bitsy's house. All she had to do was drop by and just check on it.

Her gaze moved over to Wednesday. Wednesday would be a problem. She'd need someone to clean for Sandra Wellington on Wednesday.

She wrote Wednesday beneath Janet's name and underlined it. Though she didn't hold out much hope that Janet would be able to work at all, she'd ask her about Wednesday as well.

Charlotte tapped her pen against the book as she stared at the Thursday and Friday spaces. Cheré still had one week left to work, which meant that at least for this week, she'd still have Thursday and Friday off, but the following week would be another matter. Unless she found replacements, she'd have to fill in for Cheré.

Sending up a prayer that Janet would be available, Charlotte picked up the receiver and tapped out Janet's phone number.

"Hi, Janet, this is Charlotte," she said when Janet answered. "How are you?"

"Oh, Charlotte, hi. I'm fine, and you?"

"Doing okay."

"That's great. Listen, I've been meaning to call you, but things have been so hectic lately. I wanted to let you know that you shouldn't count on me to work for the next month or so. I'm sorry. I hope this doesn't put you in a bind, but we've bought a new house. We're doing some of the renovations ourselves—painting and stuff, then with the packing and moving, well . . ." Her voice trailed away.

"I didn't even know you were thinking about buying a new house."

"We weren't," Janet said. "This was one of those deals too good to be true."

"I can certainly understand that," Charlotte replied. Falling for a deal too good to be true . . . an offer too good to refuse . . . same thing and the very reason she'd gotten herself into this mess to begin with. "Shades of the *Godfather*," she whispered, rolling her eyes toward the ceiling.

"Excuse me?"

"Oh, nothing," Charlotte said. "Just thinking out loud. Tell you what. Why don't you just give me a call once you're settled again and want some part-time work? And by the way, congratulations on your new house."

"Thanks, Charlotte. Not many employers would be as understanding as you are."

After saying her good-byes, Charlotte hung up the receiver and stared at the schedule book. *Now what?* she wondered. Her gaze strayed to the stack of prospective employee files on the corner of the desk, then she glanced up at the cuckoo.

Obviously, the four o'clock interview was a no-show, and again she had to ask herself, now what?

Now you get busy and hire some more help.

She truly needed to interview a few more applicants, but doing so was going to take time, and time was one thing she didn't have. Charlotte reached over and tapped the file labeled Dale Harris. Before she could change her mind, she slid the file in front of her, opened it, found Dale's phone number, and placed the call.

Dale answered on the third ring.

"Dale, this is Charlotte LaRue. I hope I didn't call at a bad time."

"Not at all, Charlotte, especially if you're calling for the reason I think you're calling."

Charlotte smiled and suddenly felt as if the weight of the world had been lifted from her shoulders. "I know it's really short notice," she told him, "but something's come up and if you're serious about working for Maid-for-a-Day, then I'm ready to give you your first assignments. I don't suppose you've had a chance to go over the paper I gave you about the services that Maid-for-a-Day provides and the policies and procedures?"

"Yes, ma'am. As soon as I got home I read that paper."

Charlotte's smile widened. "Good. Just the answer I wanted to hear. You also need to know that this is a trial period. Standard uniforms for my maids are navy pants and shirt. The cotton scrubs like nurses wear are fine. My other maids wear a white apron as well, but I don't think that's necessary for you."

Dale laughed. "Whew, that's a relief."

"Now that that's out of the way, grab a pen and paper,"

Charlotte told him. For the next few minutes, Charlotte gave Dale the names and addresses of the clients that he would be working for, and the days and times. Then she went over certain idiosyncrasies of each of the clients.

When Charlotte had finished talking with Dale, she depressed the switch hook, and with a sigh of dread, she tapped out Leo Acosta's phone number.

"Leo Acosta here," he answered.

"This is Charlotte LaRue."

"I hope you're calling to give me good news."

"I've gone over my schedule and I was able to clear next week."

"That's great!" he responded. "Would tomorrow be too soon for you to start? The police have assured me that they'll be done with the house by noon."

After a moment of hesitation, Charlotte said, "I guess that's okay, since this is not exactly normal circumstances. But just for future reference, I don't work on Sundays."

"Good enough. Now—about tomorrow. Sophia and the children are planning on returning to the house after lunch. Why don't you plan on cleaning the carriage house first? I'll meet you there and let you in, say about nine?"

"Nine it is. See you then." Charlotte hung up the phone and sighed. Now, for making sure Joyce ate some dinner. She tapped out Louis's phone number. After four rings, the call was answered.

"Hello?"

To Charlotte's ears, Joyce's voice sounded weak and raspy and a bit sleepy. "Joyce, this is Charlotte, next door. I hope I didn't wake you."

"No, no. It's this medication I'm on. It makes me kind of out of it, if you know what I mean."

Charlotte knew exactly what Joyce meant. Louis had told her that the pain medication Joyce took was enough to sedate an elephant.

"Listen," Charlotte told her, "I was hoping I might persuade you to share some of this chicken and andouille gumbo I cooked. Please say yes, because there is no way I can eat all of this by myself."

"It's been a long time since I had gumbo."

"Good, I'll be right over with a big bowl." Before Joyce had time to refuse the offer, Charlotte hung up the phone.

"I'm not really hungry right now," Joyce protested a few minutes later when Charlotte set the tray of food on the table in front of the sofa.

"You many not be hungry," Charlotte told her, "but you really need to eat anyway."

"You sound just like Louis." Joyce narrowed her eyes suspiciously. "And speaking of Louis, he put you up to this, didn't he?"

Charlotte smiled. "So what if he did? He's just trying to take care of you the best he can. And I'm not leaving until you eat something, so if you want to get rid of me . . ."

Joyce gave Charlotte a wan smile. "Louis said that you were stubborn. No offense meant," she quickly added.

Charlotte couldn't help wondering just what else Louis had said about her, but decided against asking. After all, the whole point for her being there in the first place was to get Joyce to eat.

"No offense taken," Charlotte replied with a grin. "Tell you what, though. If nothing else, at least try a few bites and drink your milk." She handed Joyce a soup mug and a spoon. "And if you eat, then I promise I'll leave you in peace."

Joyce sighed. "Just remember, you promised," she said as she spooned up some of the gumbo and rice.

By the time that Charlotte climbed into the bed that night, she was exhausted. While Joyce ate, Charlotte had straightened up Louis's half of the double. When Charlotte had returned to her side of the double, she'd placed a call to her sister to let her know that she wouldn't be at church the next morning and she would be unable to eat Sunday lunch with the family.

Such a shame about Joyce, Charlotte thought, as she switched off the bedside lamp and snuggled down beneath the covers. She genuinely liked Joyce, and under other circumstances they might have become good friends. Not that she approved of a mother abandoning her husband and child, especially a child as troubled as Stephen had been as a teenager. But Joyce had paid for her mistakes and paid heavily. She'd had a hard, lonely life full of guilt and remorse, and now she was dying. Charlotte figured that if Louis and Stephen could forgive Joyce, then she of all people had no right to judge her.

On Sunday morning, Charlotte awoke early feeling a bit stiff and out of sorts. What she needed, she decided as she climbed out of bed, was some exercise.

At least three times a week she tried to make time to walk. In her line of work, being physically fit was imperative. Besides, ever since her sixtieth birthday, when she'd been diagnosed as a diabetic, Hank constantly nagged her about getting exercise.

Once she'd dressed in her warmest jogging suit and put a pot of coffee on to brew, she headed for the front door.

Outside, the thermometer on the porch showed that it was

only fifty degrees, but the dampness made it feel much colder. In spite of the long-sleeved fleece-lined pullover, Charlotte shivered as she locked her door.

Across the street, her neighbor's Doberman pinscher set up a howl, but Charlotte ignored him. When she reached the sidewalk in front of her house, she turned around and stared at the old Victorian double.

Charlotte lived in the same house that she'd grown up in. She, along with her sister, had inherited it after their parents' untimely deaths. Though Milan Street was only a few blocks from the Garden District, her particular neighborhood was referred to as Uptown. Unlike the huge mansions that she and her crew cleaned, the majority of the houses on her street were like hers, older, smaller homes owned by regular working folks.

Even so, Charlotte loved her neighborhood and her old home. Unlike her sister, who had long ago sold her half of the double to Charlotte, Charlotte had never felt the urge or the need to live anywhere else. Besides being the home she'd grown up in and the home in which she'd raised her son, it was the perfect location for her thriving, sometimes-hectic cleaning service.

Charlotte tilted her head to one side and narrowed her eyes. It was hard to believe that only a week ago she'd been eagerly anticipating the money she would make working for the Rossis, money she could use to finally spruce up her house. And now . . .

With a shake of her head, Charlotte turned away and set off walking down Milan toward St. Charles Avenue. Now Robert Rossi was dead, and his wife, Emily, was in jail, accused of murdering him.

Careful to keep a wary eye on the gaping cracks in the sidewalk, Charlotte shivered. And to top it off, she was under suspicion as well.

Charlotte picked up her pace. Maybe she should call Daniel after all. And maybe she should call Leo Acosta and cancel.

You promise?

Trying to ignore the memory of Bitsy's plea, Charlotte picked up her pace again until she was doing a slow jog. By the time she reached St. Charles Avenue, she'd warmed up considerably and was breathing hard.

Stopping for a moment to catch her breath, she stared at the Avenue. Traffic was lighter than usual, even for a Sunday morning. There were only a few vehicles out and about, but people were already setting up ladders and lawn chairs in anticipation of the Okeanos and Thoth parades that would roll down St. Charles just before noon.

"Mardi Gras," she grumbled as a bell clanged from a streetcar as it rumbled its way down the tracks in the middle of the Avenue. Above the tracks the branches of hundred-year-old oaks formed a green canopy over the Avenue. And caught on the branches and in the lacy gray moss hanging from the evergreens were several colored strands of beads.

With a shake of her head, Charlotte did an about-face and headed back down Milan. It wouldn't be long now before the crowds would be back, lined up at least ten deep along St. Charles.

Charlotte loved Mardi Gras and the tourism was good for the city, but the crush of the crowds, the extra traffic, and the blocked-off streets due to the numerous parades could be aggravating at times, not to mention the littered streets full of beer cans and other garbage.

At the thought of the garbage Charlotte rolled her eyes. New Orleans was the only city that she had ever heard of that measured the success of an event by the amount of garbage left in the streets.

By the time that Charlotte caught sight of her house, she was more than ready for a hot shower and a cup of coffee before leaving for work. She was also sure that she'd never be able to even think about Mardi Gras again without remembering the sight of Robert Rossi, dressed as Rex, lying dead on the library floor with Emily hovering above him.

Charlotte shivered at the thought of having to return to the Rossi house.

Chapter 11

When Charlotte drove up to the Rossi house, an NOPD crime scene van, a patrol car, and a sleek black Jaguar were parked along the curb in front. As she climbed out of her van, she spotted a patrolman stationed at the front gate.

After nodding a greeting to the patrolman, she unloaded her supply carrier and vacuum cleaner from the rear of the van and approached the gate.

"I'm Charlotte LaRue with Maid-for-a-Day," she told the policeman. "I believe Mr. Acosta is expecting me."

The patrolman nodded and opened the gate. "He's waiting for you at the carriage house. Like I told him, you can clean the carriage house but the main house is off-limits for now. I'll let you know when the crime lab techs are finished. Shouldn't be too much longer."

With a nod and a "Thanks," Charlotte stepped through the gate. A movement at the front door of the main house caught her eye. Another patrolman stood guard on the porch. Since she didn't see hide nor hair of the Rossis' bodyguards, she figured they were all probably with Sophia and the children. Even so, it still seemed strange that there were none of them around.

As Charlotte walked toward the carriage house she could

feel the eyes of both policemen watching every step she made.

Though the day was cool it wasn't cold. The sun was shining and there was barely a breeze stirring the air, but a sudden shiver ran through Charlotte. Knowing that her every move was being observed was just one more reminder that, along with Emily, she was also considered a suspect.

Now don't go getting paranoid, Charlotte. Things could be worse. They could have arrested you.

Paranoid or not, it wouldn't hurt to stay on her toes, and, as Judith had cautioned, it wouldn't hurt to watch her back, especially around Leo Acosta.

Just as the patrolman had said, the attorney was waiting at the carriage house. When Charlotte approached, his back was facing her and he was talking on his cell phone. He was so engrossed in his conversation that Charlotte was sure that he didn't realize she was there, so she cleared her throat to get his attention.

The attorney stiffened then spun around to face her, his expression tight with strain. When he saw Charlotte, the startled, wary look disappeared. "Gotta go," he said into the cell phone and immediately ended the call.

"I hope you haven't been waiting long," Charlotte said, setting the vacuum cleaner down on the stoop. Not that she really cared, since she was fairly certain that she was right on time, but she figured it was the polite thing to say.

He shook his head. "Not long at all." He slipped the tiny phone into the pocket of his jacket, then glanced at his watch.

A flash of gold glinted in the sunlight, and Charlotte had no doubt that the Rolex on his wrist was the real thing, just as she suspected that the suit he wore was an Armani and the shoes on his feet were Gucci.

"You're right on time." His mouth curved into a fake smile, and then he motioned toward the front door. "It's open." He reached inside his pants pocket and fished out a set of keys. "I have to go now, but"—he handed the keys to Charlotte—"these are the keys for both places, so if you finish up and the police have left, go ahead and start on the main house. I should be back sometime after lunch with Sophia and the children."

Charlotte returned his fake smile with one of her own and dropped the keys into the pocket of her apron. "Guess I'd better get busy then."

When she picked up the vacuum, he made a show of opening the door for her. "Thanks," she said, stepping past him.

"See you later," he called out, and by the time that she set down the vacuum and the supply carrier, he was already halfway to the front gate.

Charlotte closed the door. Out of habit and because she didn't want anyone sneaking up on her, she shoved the dead bolt into place.

As always, when Charlotte cleaned an unfamiliar house, she performed a walk-through to analyze what needed to be done. The carriage house was bigger on the inside than it appeared on the outside. In fact, Charlotte figured that even if she counted both sides of her double it was still larger than her house.

The first room was a huge living area that was furnished with two full-size sofas and several lounge chairs. One entire wall was taken up by an entertainment system, complete with one of the biggest wide-screen televisions she'd ever seen. From the looks of the room it was evident that Robert Rossi had wanted his bodyguards to have all the comforts of home.

Charlotte rolled her eyes. "Nice work if you can get it," she muttered.

The next room was as large as the living area but divided into a kitchen on one side and dining room on the other side. A set of double doors at one end of the dining area opened to reveal a closet that contained a washer and dryer. Though all of the kitchen appliances were state-of-the-art and appeared to be fairly new, Charlotte wrinkled her nose with distaste as she glanced around the smelly, messy room.

"Men!" She shook her head with disgust. Dirty dishes filled the sink and overflowed onto the countertops. A peek inside the dishwasher revealed that it was completely empty. The least they could have done was put the dirty dishes in the dishwasher.

She closed the dishwasher door and turned to the stove. The stove was going to take some major scrubbing, she decided as she eyed what appeared to be dried spaghetti sauce and some other splattered food that she didn't recognize.

As Charlotte walked through the kitchen, she felt a sucking sensation with each step that she took on the tiled floor. "Yuck!" She peered down at the floor and frowned. Someone had spilled something sticky and hadn't bothered cleaning it up properly. There was no telling what had been spilled and no telling how long ago it had been spilled. It was a wonder that roaches weren't crawling everywhere.

No sooner had the thought entered her mind than a huge cockroach appeared from beneath the cabinet and scurried across the floor toward the laundry closet. Charlotte immediately gave chase, but the sneaky little bugger was too fast for her and disappeared beneath the washing machine before she got within stomping distance. Executing an about-face, she marched over to where she'd left her supply carrier, took out the can of bug spray she always kept handy, then headed back for the laundry closet.

"You can run, but you can't hide," she muttered as she saturated the baseboard and the floor around the front and sides of the washer and dryer.

With a shudder and disgusted shake of her head, she returned the can of bug spray to the supply carrier, then continued her inspection.

Off the back of the dining area was a long hallway that reminded her of a hotel hallway. On either side were three identical doors, six doors all total. Each door opened into separate but identical tiny bedrooms, and each bedroom had its own small bathroom.

After her initial inspection, Charlotte decided to tackle the kitchen first, the living room next, and the bedrooms and bathrooms last.

It was getting close to noon by the time she entered the last of the bedrooms. In comparison to the other five, it was by far the neatest, and it was the only one in which the bed had been made. Not only had the bed been made, but the adjoining bathroom was almost spotless. Even so, the bedroom needed dusting and vacuuming, and she scrubbed the shower, the sink, and the toilet in the bathroom for good measure.

Also, in comparison to the other bedrooms, this last one had a few more personal items strewed about, one of which was a small, framed picture sitting on the dresser top.

Out of curiosity, Charlotte picked up the five-by-seven picture and stared at it. The photo was of a skinny teenage girl with white-blond hair, a boy with dark hair who looked to be about twenty, and a woman. Possibly a family portrait, she decided.

From the moment Charlotte really looked at the picture though, she couldn't seem to take her eyes off the woman. The woman's hair was blond, though not quite as blond as the girl's, but it was her face that held Charlotte's attention. One whole side of the woman's face was badly scarred; yet, in spite of the scar, there was also something that seemed really familiar about her. Charlotte was sure she'd seen the woman somewhere before, but she was equally sure that she would have remembered someone with such a terrible scar.

Had the woman been in an accident of some kind, or been badly burned? Still wondering what could have caused such a hideous scar and why she seemed so familiar, Charlotte's gaze moved on to the girl, then to the boy.

As she stared at the boy, the shock of recognition suddenly hit Charlotte full force. "Of course," she murmured, a smile pulling at her lips. Though much younger than he was now, Charlotte was certain that boy in the photo had to be Mark. Out of the six bodyguards, Mark had been the friendliest and the most helpful. If the boy in the photo was Mark though, did that mean the girl was his sister and the woman his mother?

By the time Charlotte had finished cleaning the carriage house, the growling of her stomach reminded her that it was lunchtime.

She eyed the table in the carriage house dining area. She could eat her lunch there. But no sooner had the thought entered her mind than a mental picture of the roach scurrying across the floor followed it.

Charlotte grimaced with disgust. Though she'd sprayed, there was no guarantee that she'd killed the nasty creature. It would be just her luck that the dirty thing would decide to come out of hiding about the time she began eating.

Her gaze strayed to the front window and to the main house beyond. Surely the lab techs had finished by now. If they had finished and it wasn't too chilly, she could eat her lunch on the front porch, out in the fresh air and sunshine. But if they hadn't finished . . .

"Some choice," she grumbled as she gathered her supply carrier and vacuum cleaner. She could either eat with the roaches or eat with the police watching her.

Outside, there was still a slight chill in the air, but Charlotte figured that if she sat in a sunny spot on the porch, she'd be warm enough. Though it took a minute, by way of elimination, Charlotte finally located the correct key on the key ring that Leo Acosta had given her to lock up the carriage house. Once she'd locked the door, she picked up her vacuum cleaner and supply carrier and headed toward the front of the property. Though the crime scene van and the police car were still parked out front, two of the lab techs were loading equipment into the van.

Charlotte spotted the patrolman she'd seen earlier standing guard at the front door, and she approached the steps leading up to the porch. "May I leave this stuff here?" she asked. When he nodded, she motioned toward a small grouping of wicker chairs at the end of the porch. "And if it's okay, I'd like to eat my lunch over there."

Again the patrolman nodded. "That's fine. By the time you finish, you can probably get inside the house. The guys are packing it up now."

Charlotte climbed the steps, set the vacuum and supply carrier down near the end of the porch, and then headed for her van. Once she'd retrieved her insulated lunch bag, she settled in one of the wicker chairs at the end of the porch. As Charlotte soaked in the winter sunshine and munched on a turkey sandwich, she stared up into the huge oak tree in front of the house.

You promise?

Charlotte winced as Bitsy Duhe's words popped into her head. So far, other than a lot of mental speculation, she'd done little toward keeping her promise to Bitsy. But where to start? After all, she was a maid, not a detective.

Charlotte eyed the policeman still standing guard at the front door. The man hadn't seemed especially friendly, but then again he wasn't exactly unfriendly either. Maybe she could pump him for information . . . assuming of course that he knew anything. But how to even begin was the big question.

Charlotte chewed thoughtfully, but none of the opening lines she came up with seemed appropriate. In fact, they all sounded like what they were—a fishing expedition for information. By the time she finished her sandwich, she decided that odds were, even if the patrolman did know something of value, there was no way he would be willing to share what he knew with the maid.

As she bit into the last of the apple slices she'd packed in her lunch, the two crime techs she'd seen going back and forth between the house and the van emerged from the entrance door. They stopped and talked a minute with the patrolman, and then they headed for their van. As they climbed inside the van and slammed the doors, the patrolman walked over to where Charlotte was sitting.

"We're all finished here," he told her. "You can go in now."

Charlotte smiled. "Thanks."

No sooner had the word left her lips then, out of nowhere, an unexpected surge of dread and apprehension swept through her. *Another library . . . another dead client . . . murdered . . .*

Charlotte doubled her fingers into a fist. Once before, she'd cleaned up a crime scene after a murder. Unlike Robert Rossi, with his sordid background, Jackson Dubisson had been a prominent, well-respected attorney . . . at least on the surface, until all of his dirty little secrets were found out. But like Robert, Jackson had ended up dead before his time. In her mind's eye she could still see the desk, the speckles of dried blood . . .

Charlotte swallowed hard and tried to draw a deep breath. At least this time no one could accuse her of contaminating the crime scene, though doing so then hadn't exactly been her fault. But now that she knew what to expect, she wasn't sure that she was willing to go through the whole ordeal again.

"Are you okay, ma'am?" the patrolman asked Charlotte, his eyes narrowing with concern. "You look a little green around the gills."

Chapter 12

Praying that she wouldn't choke on the apple, Charlotte swallowed the last bite, then forced a weak smile. "I'm okay," she murmured.

"You sure?"

Charlotte nodded. "I'm sure."

The officer shrugged. "If you say so." With one last worried look at her, he shrugged, gave her a two-fingered salute, and then he turned and walked away.

Still feeling a bit strange and still dreading the task ahead, Charlotte stuffed the empty Ziploc sandwich bags, the napkin, and thermos back inside her lunch bag. She zipped it up, and on shaky legs, returned the lunch bag to her van.

Once she was back on the porch she gathered her vacuum and supply carrier and entered the house. After making sure that she locked the front door behind her, she turned to assess what needed to be done.

Inside, the house was exactly how she remembered it. Though she and her makeshift crew had picked up most of the dirty dishes and glasses, there were still a few scattered around in the parlor.

In the dining room she eyed the platters of leftover, dried food on the dining table and sighed. *Waste not, want not.* The words of her grandmother rang in her head. Such a shame, she thought. All that food completely ruined, wasted.

With an oh-well shrug, Charlotte headed for the kitchen. Catering boxes and dirty wineglasses were still stacked on the countertops of the cabinets, and dirty dishes filled the sink.

Charlotte glanced at the doorway that led to the hall and the library, then stared at the mess in the kitchen again. Though she was sorely tempted to begin cleaning the kitchen first, doing so would mean ignoring her long-standing policy of giving priority to the worst mess. From experience, she knew that cleaning the library would be far worse than cleaning the party clutter. Not so much because of the physical mess, but more the mental distress from knowing that a man had been murdered in that room.

Charlotte sighed. Procrastinating wouldn't make the mess in the library or what she'd seen in there go away. "Just do it and get it over with," she muttered.

A few minutes later, armed with her supply carrier and dragging her feet, Charlotte headed for the library. Upon entering the room, she wrinkled her nose against the sour odor that hung in the air. She had smelled the same odor once before and recognized it for what it was. The stench of death and the violence that had provoked it always left a distinct smell.

An uninvited mental image slid into her head—Robert Rossi dead on the floor and Emily, hovering over him, her hands all bloody . . .

Charlotte shivered, and as if drawn by some unseen force she couldn't control, she dropped her gaze to the floor in front of the desk and stared at the spot where Robert had died. After a moment though, she narrowed her eyes. Something was wrong. Something was missing. The rug, she finally decided. The plush Aubusson rug that had covered the hardwood floor in front of the desk was missing.

After Charlotte thought about it for a moment, she finally decided that either the crime lab techs had taken it for evidence or Leo Acosta had already sent it out to be professionally cleaned. Whichever the case, she'd truly dreaded the task of trying to scrub the blood out of it and was thankful that was one less unpleasant ordeal that she'd have to contend with.

Feeling a bit better about the whole thing, she glanced around the rest of the room. As she'd expected, almost every surface was coated with a fine ashy residue left over from the police dusting for fingerprints.

Charlotte always worked from the top down, so she decided to begin with the glass-enclosed curio cabinet that held the Fabergé eggs, since it was the tallest piece of furniture in the room. After dusting and waxing the outside and cleaning the glass, she opened the doors of the cabinet. As she carefully dusted each of the eggs and the shelf that held them, she automatically counted them. When she had finished the last one, she frowned.

"That can't be right," she murmured. If she remembered correctly, the day before Robert was murdered there were seventeen of the original twenty-five left in the case.

Charlotte quickly counted them again, and her frown deepened. By her calculations, two more were missing. But how? And when?

For long moments Charlotte continued staring at the eggs as she went over the events in her mind. If there were seventeen eggs the day before the murder, but only fifteen now, that meant that somewhere between the time Robert had pitched his hissy fit and the time he was murdered, two more eggs had been stolen. But *when* were they stolen? Before the party or during the party?

With a sigh and a shake of her head, Charlotte closed the glass doors. A nagging feeling deep in her gut insisted that the theft of the eggs was important, but important enough to murder someone? Though she found it hard to fathom, she knew that people had been murdered for a lot less.

Still staring at the eggs, another thought suddenly occurred to her. She supposed it was possible that the police might have found fingerprints on two of the eggs and taken them for evidence.

Charlotte slowly shook her head, dismissing the idea. If that were the case though, surely they would have taken all of the eggs for comparison. But what if the eggs *had* been stolen during the party and Robert had caught the thief red-handed . . . if there was even the remotest possibility that the thief, and not Emily, had murdered Robert . . .

Charlotte sighed. Though certainly possible, unfortunately, without an eyewitness or a confession, there was no way of proving such a thing. But even without solid proof, surely a piece of information like that would cast some doubt about Emily having murdered Robert. Proof or no proof, she should tell someone what she found. But whom should she tell? The police or Leo Acosta? Or both?

Charlotte frowned. Since the police already had their eye on her, she would really prefer not to have anything to do with them, but she didn't trust the lawyer as far as she could throw him either. Maybe she should tell both the lawyer and the police or simply just tell Judith instead and let Judith handle the information.

* * *

Half an hour later, Charlotte had finished dusting the library and was ready to vacuum when she heard a noise that sounded suspiciously like the front door opening and closing.

Had she locked the door? She was positive that she had, which meant that only someone with a key could get inside . . . or someone like a thief, bent on robbery. The egg thief . . . returning for more eggs. . . .

Stop being so paranoid! Charlotte pursed her lips and tried to rein in her overactive imagination as she headed down the hallway to check out the noise. Just as she rounded the corner, she almost ran smack into Mark.

Charlotte let out a startled squeal and slapped her hand against her chest. Beneath her chest, she could feel her heart pounding like a jackhammer. "Dear Lord in heaven, Mark! You just scared ten years off my life."

"Sorry about that, Charlotte. I guess I should have called out or something."

" 'Or something,' " Charlotte grumbled.

"I really am sorry." Mark motioned toward the front of the house. "I just came in to warn you that Sophia, the kids, their nanny, and the guys are here."

"Their nanny? I guess I didn't realize they had a nanny."

"They don't, ordinarily," Mark replied. "But then these aren't ordinary times. Considering the circumstances, Acosta and the Rossi brothers felt that Sophia could use some help with the children."

To say the least, Charlotte thought as a commotion at the front door reached her ears. But how in the devil had they found someone qualified so fast?

Mark grinned and winked at Charlotte. "And speak of the little devils, here they come." No sooner were the words out of his mouth than both Amanda and Brandon appeared, each carrying an overnight bag. Behind them was a dark-haired young woman whom Charlotte assumed had to be the new nanny. And following behind her, carrying a large suitcase that she figured belonged to the nanny, was Gino.

But Charlotte had eyes only for Amanda and Brandon. Both of the children waved a polite greeting before heading up the staircase, but the lost expressions on their faces reminded Charlotte of pictures she'd seen on the news of orphaned children in war-torn countries, and her heart overflowed with sympathy. Though she'd been older than the Rossi children were, she too had lost her parents and knew all about the anguish and the heartache that Amanda and Brandon had to be experiencing.

"Jean, wait up a moment," Mark called out to the woman following the children up the stairs. "I want to introduce you to Charlotte."

The young woman paused, then turned and came back down the stairs.

"Charlotte, this is Jean. Jean, this is Charlotte LaRue, the new maid."

"The new *temporary* maid," Charlotte corrected.

Jean offered her hand and her lips curled into a smile that didn't quite reach her eyes. "Nice to meet you, Charlotte. I'm the new temporary nanny."

As Charlotte briefly shook Jean's hand, an unexpected feeling of déjà vu came over her and she narrowed her eyes. "Have we met before?"

Jean immediately pulled her hand away, and for the briefest moment her eyes darkened with some emotion that Charlotte couldn't identify. Then the moment passed, and Jean laughed and shook her head. "Not that I know of. Now, if you'll excuse me, I need to see about the children."

Without another word, she turned away, and as Charlotte watched the nanny climb the stairs, she racked her brain trying to figure out why the young woman seemed so familiar.

"Oh, Charlotte, there you are."

Charlotte turned to see a beaming Sophia bustling through the front door. Though Charlotte wasn't quite sure what she'd expected after Sophia's reaction to her son Robert's murder and her fainting spell the night he was murdered, what she would have never expected was to see Sophia looking so spry and alert . . . and happy?

"You know, I was so afraid that you wouldn't agree to keep working for us, especially after that unfortunate incident Friday night."

Unfortunate incident? Charlotte was too stunned to do anything but nod.

Sophia just gave her a sly, knowing smile. "I knew that if I insisted," she continued, "Leo would find a way to persuade you. I'm so glad you're here. Have you cleaned the kitchen yet?"

Still stunned by Sophia's odd behavior, Charlotte shook her head. "That's the next room on my list," she said, her voice a bit croaky-sounding to her own ears.

"Well, be sure and let me know when you're finished in there. I don't think my poor little darlings have had a decent meal since their blessed Mama left."

Blessed? Left? Sophia was acting as if Emily was off on vacation or something, and an uneasy feeling stirred in Charlotte's stomach. Either Sophia had slipped over the edge into senility or she was in complete and utter denial.

Charlotte slid her gaze to Mark to see what, if any, reaction he was having to the old lady's behavior, but nothing in his expression gave her a clue, one way or another.

"And I intend to remedy that tonight," Sophia continued. "It's been years since I fixed my famous lasagna, and tonight's the night." She leaned toward Charlotte and, in a sly voice barely above a whisper, she said, "Robert never would allow me to cook, you know. But now I can cook anything and any time that I want to cook."

Charlotte was utterly speechless, and when she did find her voice again, all she could think to say was, "I—I'll let you know when the kitchen is clean."

Still a bit dazed and confused over Sophia's attitude, Charlotte retrieved a tray in the kitchen, then gathered all of the dirty dishes from the parlor and dining room.

Cleaning the kitchen didn't take as long as Charlotte thought. Once she'd thrown away the leftover food and trashed all but one of the catering boxes, which she intended to use for the linens, it was only a matter of loading the dishwasher, wiping down the cabinets and stove, then sweeping and mopping.

While the kitchen floor dried, Charlotte busied herself in the dining room by gathering up the soiled linens that the caterer had provided for the dining room table. As she stared at the bunched-up tablecloth and matching cloth napkins, she frowned. With everything that had happened, there was no telling when the caterer would show up to pick up the stuff. Since there were several food and wine stains on the tablecloth and napkins, she debated whether she should go ahead and wash the linens herself or just leave them.

After only a moment's hesitation, she picked up the pile of

linens and, tiptoeing across the still-wet kitchen floor, she headed for the laundry room.

When Charlotte first entered the small room, she detected a faint, but distinctly unpleasant odor. With a puzzled frown, she glanced around the room but didn't see anything that could be causing the smell. Then she opened the lid of the washing machine.

"Oh, gross!" Wrinkling her nose against the foul, putrid odor, she swallowed several times to keep from gagging.

At least now she knew where the source of the smell was coming from. Ever so carefully and fully expecting to find that a mouse or a rat had somehow crawled in the machine and died, she peered down in the tub. Charlotte's frown deepened. As far as she could tell, all that was in the tub were just a couple of towels and some washcloths. But even if the stuff had soured and mildewed, that still didn't explain the awful smell.

What to do, what to do? Charlotte glared at the tub. She was sorely tempted to just dump in some detergent, turn on the machine, and wash the smelly things. But after a brief internal battle, she decided that there could still be something dead hiding beneath the towels, and then she'd really have a nasty mess. Best to check it out first.

Since there was no way she was going to touch something that smelled so nasty without protection and still fighting to keep from gagging, she reached inside her apron pocket and took out a pair of rubber gloves. She pulled on the gloves, then she reached inside the tub to gingerly retrieve the towels and washcloths and dropped them on top of the dryer.

Once the items were out, she peered down in the tub again, but she saw nothing but the tub itself, which meant that the smell had to be coming from the towels. Growing more curious by the moment, Charlotte spread out first one towel and then the other one on top of the dryer. Though both towels were royal blue, several dark dried stains were still evident.

Charlotte frowned. The only explanation for the stench had to be whatever had stained the towels. For several moments, she racked her brain trying to think what could cause such a stain and odor.

Blood!

"Of course," she whispered. The stains had to be the results of when she'd helped Emily clean up after Robert's body had been discovered, and old, dried-up blood would certainly stink.

Satisfied that the mystery was solved, Charlotte dropped the towels back into the washing machine, but as she reached for the laundry detergent, her hand froze in midair. "Oh, no," she groaned. There was no way the bloodstained towels could be from Emily's room. For one thing, they had left the towels and washcloths, along with Emily's costume and her apron upstairs in the master bathroom. The police would have taken those particular towels for evidence. For another thing, the towels and washcloths from the master bathroom were dark green, not blue.

Suddenly Charlotte's breath caught in her throat and she gripped the edge of the washing machine. Sophia's towels and washcloths were blue, royal blue. But why would Sophia's towels be stained with blood, unless . . .

Chapter 13

"Nooo," Charlotte protested in a voice barely above a whisper, horrified that she would even think such a thing about the sweet old lady. There was no way Sophia could have murdered Robert, no way a mother would murder her own son. Would she?

"No!" Charlotte protested louder, unwilling to believe such a thing. There had to be some other explanation.

Charlotte reached for the laundry detergent again, and again her hand froze in midair. *But what if Sophia is the killer? After all, mother or not, she had as much motive as anyone, and if you wash the towels, you'll be washing away the evidence.*

Again Charlotte gripped the sides of the washing machine. Though she wanted to ignore the pesky, unwelcome voice of reason, she couldn't ignore the fact that, according to Joe Rossi, Robert had made plans to put their mother in a retirement home. She also couldn't ignore the fact that Robert had been arrested and tried for the murder of his father. In spite of him being acquitted, even his own brother thought he was guilty, and if his own brother thought he was guilty, then, didn't it stand to reason that Sophia still might think so too? And suspecting that your son killed your husband had to be hard to live with.

Either of those reasons, along with watching Robert abuse Emily, could have been enough to drive the old lady to do something rash. Especially if she wasn't quite right in the head to begin with, Charlotte added, thinking about the way Sophia had been acting, almost as if she was glad that Robert was gone.

But what about her so-called heart attack?

"But it wasn't a heart attack after all," Charlotte murmured, narrowing her eyes in thought. Just a panic attack, according to her doctor. "Panic attack, my hind foot," Charlotte muttered. More like a clever way to avert suspicion from herself, a way to throw everyone off track.

With a huge sigh, once again Charlotte fished the towels and washcloths out of the washing machine. No matter how badly she wanted to believe that Sophia wasn't capable of such a heinous crime, she couldn't ignore the facts or the evidence. But why hadn't the police discovered the towels and washcloths? Surely they had searched the laundry room.

"Who knows?" she grumbled. Right now, what she needed was a paper sack. Though she couldn't remember why, in all of the mystery books she'd read and from watching *CSI*, she knew that putting the stuff in a paper sack was the best way to preserve this particular type of evidence.

Charlotte searched for and finally found a paper sack in the recycling bin. But even as she carefully placed the towels and washcloths in the sack to give to the police, she still wasn't totally convinced about Sophia. For one thing, she felt sure that it would take a lot more strength than someone Sophia's age would possess in order to plunge a knife into a man Robert's size and strength. And for another thing, just because the towels and washcloths came from Sophia's bathroom didn't necessarily mean that Sophia used them. With a house full of guests, anyone could have gone into Sophia's bathroom to clean up. Then, to hide the evidence, they could have put them in the washing machine. Whoever hid them could have figured that by hiding the towels and washcloths, they would be washed without anyone being the wiser.

"Kind of stupid not to turn on the machine then and there," she muttered.

But, if Sophia didn't kill Robert, then who did?

Unbidden, a picture of Amanda washing her hands at the kitchen sink came to mind. Back and forth. Back and forth. Charlotte winced and felt the beginnings of a headache coming on as she folded the top edge of the sack. If only she hadn't made that promise to Bitsy, she'd be tempted to dump the whole mess into the trash and forget it.

But you did promise her.

"Yeah, yeah," Charlotte grumbled as she tried to figure out what to do with the sack and its smelly contents until she got the chance to turn them over to Judith. The logical thing would be to stow it in her van, and though she hated the thought of stinking up her van, she couldn't think of anywhere else that would be safe to stow it.

Once the sack was locked up in the van, Charlotte returned to the house. Now all she had to do was get through the rest of the day.

That afternoon as Charlotte gathered her cleaning supplies and packed them into her supply carrier, the smell of bread baking in the oven and lasagna sauce bubbling on the stove filled the air. From the parlor came the sound of children's laughter.

"That nanny is absolutely wonderful with the children," Sophia commented to Charlotte as she stirred the lasagna sauce bubbling in a saucepan on the stove burner. "Why, right now she's in there playing charades with them." Sophia tapped the wooden spoon against the edge of the saucepan and placed the spoon on a saucer on the counter, then bustled over to check on the bread in the oven. "Not even Emily ever had time to play games with them," she continued. "Not with all the stuff Robert had her doing." Sophia peered in the oven at the bread. "Almost ready," she said. "Just needs to brown a bit more."

Placing her hands on her hips, she turned to face Charlotte. "I swear, I don't know where I failed with Robert. He was such a sweet little boy." She shook her head and stepped closer to Charlotte. "So how did he turn out to be such a mean, cruel man?" Suddenly she frowned and grabbed Charlotte's arm. "Did I tell you about the epiphany I had?"

"Er—ah, no, I don't believe you did," Charlotte answered, wondering how to tactfully extricate herself form the death grip that Sophia had on her arm. But if she remembered right, Emily had mentioned something about Sophia having some type of religious experience after Robert's father was murdered.

"It's the second one I've had," Sophia said, her voice soft with awe. To Charlotte's relief, Sophia released her grip on her arm. "I had the first one after my husband died, you know," Sophia continued. "Anyway, I had another one on Friday night, right before Robert was found in the library." The old lady's eyes glazed over, and in a soft, singsong voice that sent shivers up Charlotte's spine, she explained.

"Robert was my son, but he was a bad man who murdered people." Crossing her arms against her breasts, Sophia began to slowly sway from side to side. "Death was his punishment, you know, his punishment for killing his father and his wife.

Not Emily, of course, but Linda, his first wife," she hastened to add. "But people get paid back for the things they do." She nodded her head. "Yes, siree, they do, especially the bad things. And my Roberto and that sweet Linda came back to make sure Robert paid for what he did to them." Sophia suddenly smiled. "And to think I lived to see it."

To Charlotte's utter amazement, the old lady winked at her.

"And I helped too," Sophia told her.

All Charlotte could do was stare at the old lady and wonder what in the devil she meant. Was she actually confessing that she had killed Robert, or was she simply delusional? Had to be delusional, Charlotte decided. No one in their right mind would confess to murder, especially to a stranger . . . would they?

"Now, all I need to do is convince the police that Emily didn't do it," Sophia continued. "Can you imagine anyone believing Emily could do such a thing?" She shook her head and made a tut-tut sound. "Why, Emily wouldn't hurt a fly."

Sophia suddenly glanced down at Charlotte's supply carrier and frowned. "You're leaving?"

Stunned by Sophia's sudden change of subject and demeanor, Charlotte could do little but nod. *Yep, had to be delusional.*

"What time did Leo tell you to come in each day?"

Before Charlotte had a chance to answer, Sophia said, "The reason I'm asking is because there's a slight chance that the children and I might get to visit Emily in the morning. Tell you what? I don't see any point in you having to come in early. The children are out of school for Mardi Gras and usually sleep late, so why don't you plan on coming in around ten or so tomorrow?"

* * *

Sophia's crazy. Absolutely, totally crazy.

That was the only logical explanation, Charlotte decided, wrinkling her nose against the smell from the sack of towels and washcloths that filled her van as she loaded her cleaning supplies. No wonder Robert had been trying to get her into a retirement facility, she thought as she climbed into the van. After rolling down the window to let in some fresh air, she cranked the van, fastened her seat belt, and then pulled out into the street.

But was Sophia crazy enough to actually murder her own son?

And I helped too. A cold shiver ran through Charlotte as she recalled what Sophia had said. Half a block up the street the traffic light turned red, and after Charlotte slowed the van to a stop, she stared straight ahead with unseeing eyes and tried to recall everything else that Sophia had told her.

And my Roberto and that sweet Linda came back to make sure Robert paid for what he did to them.

Charlotte shivered again. What on earth would make Sophia think such a thing?

A horn blared behind her, and Charlotte jumped. Realizing that the traffic light had turned green, she eased off the brake and accelerated. There was no way that Charlotte fancied herself an expert in psychology. For the moment, the only answer she could fathom was that in Sophia's demented state, she had conjured up the ghosts of her dead husband and daughter-in-law in order to justify the fact that she had killed her son.

Charlotte frowned as she turned the van onto Milan and drove slowly down the bumpy, uneven street. Sophia had said something about "his punishment for killing his father and his wife." Did that mean that Sophia knew for a fact that Robert had murdered both his father and his first wife? Or was that too just another fantasy that Sophia had created in her deranged state?

After Charlotte had parked in her driveway and shut off the engine, she sat for several moments staring straight ahead. "This is another fine mess you've gotten yourself into," she complained. With a groan, she shoved open the door and climbed down out of the van. There had to be a way to get out of this mess, a way she could simply remove herself from the whole sordid affair. Maybe she could call Leo Acosta and say she was sick and couldn't work.

Charlotte retrieved the stinky sack from the back of the van, then hesitated as she stared at it. She couldn't leave it in her van indefinitely, and there was no way on God's green earth that she was taking the smelly thing into her house.

She glanced over at the door to the storage room connected to the carport, and for lack of a better place to keep it, she stuck it in the storage room on a shelf then closed and locked the storage room door.

Maybe she could claim to have the flu? Charlotte thought as she unlocked her kitchen door and went inside.

You promise?

"Yeah, yeah, Bitsy, I promised," Charlotte muttered as she opened a cabinet and took out a bottle of aspirin. Promising Bitsy had been yet another mistake, and just thinking about it all made her head feel as if someone was trying to squeeze her brain into mush. Maybe she was coming down with the flu after all.

Charlotte unscrewed the cap on the aspirin, shook out two of the tablets, popped them into her mouth, and chased them down with a glass of water.

From the living room Sweety Boy began squawking. . . . "Missed you, squawk, missed you, squawk."

Aw, that's so cute," she whispered, and it was also a reminder that she'd been so caught up in her work that it had been several days since she'd let the poor little thing out of his cage. No time like the present.

"Coming, Boy," she called out as she trudged into the living room toward his cage.

"You can come out now," she told Sweety Boy as she opened the birdcage door and stuck her forefinger inside. The little bird immediately hopped onto Charlotte's finger and she eased him out of the cage.

The moment he was clear of the opening, he took flight. "Just for a little while," she told him as she toed out of her shoes and settled on the sofa. For a moment she watched him flutter around the living room as he stretched his wings. Then she leaned her head back against the sofa and closed her eyes. "Just until the aspirin gets rid of this headache," she murmured.

Just before Louis kissed her, Charlotte awoke with a start.

Just before Louis kissed her!

Blinking several times, she yawned. Just a dream. Nothing but a dream. But why on earth would she be dreaming about Louis Thibodeaux?

A bit mortified at the thought, she shoved off the sofa, stood, then stretched. "Guess I was more tired than I thought," she murmured. Then suddenly she remembered. *Sweety Boy.* She'd let him out of the cage before she fell asleep.

Wondering where the little bird was hiding and wondering how long she had napped, Charlotte turned to check the time on the cuckoo clock. By her calculations she'd slept almost an hour. Now where had that bird got off to?

Charlotte glanced around the room. Ever since Sweety Boy

had accidentally joined her in the shower one day and the force of the shower spray had knocked him out cold, she'd tried to be more careful letting the little guy fly around free.

A fluttering sound drew her gaze back to the cuckoo clock. Charlotte narrowed her eyes as she stared at the clock. After a moment she saw Sweety Boy's head pop up from behind the decorative scrollwork that framed the front of the clock, and she smiled. "There you are, you little scamp," she told him. "I should have known you'd be hiding up there."

During the three years she'd had the bird, she'd learned that the clock was his favorite out-of-cage perch. Charlotte had long suspected that Sweety Boy thought that the mechanical bird in the clock was real. And she could swear that at times she could hear him trying to mimic the cuckoo.

"Poor little bird," she murmured as she reached up with her forefinger extended. Sweety hopped onto her finger. "So lonesome you'll settle for a mechanical bird for company," she cooed as she walked over to the cage, eased him back inside, and latched the door.

But in a sense wasn't that what she was doing? Settling? Was she so lonely that she was willing to settle for a man who was taking care of his dying ex-wife? After all, Joyce would eventually die, and then . . .

Charlotte froze, horrified at the directions of her thoughts. Now where on earth had that come from?

"I am not just sitting around waiting for Joyce Thibodeaux to die," she sputtered indignantly as she stomped into the kitchen.

With everything else that had happened in the past two days, why would she even think of such a thing, especially now?

Probably the stupid dream . . . and the devil, she decided as she jerked open the dishwasher and began putting away the clean dishes that were inside. "And I'm not lonely," she said aloud, wondering just who she was trying to convince. "Well, I'm not," she whispered with a bit less enthusiasm. After all, she had clients and her family to keep her company, and before too long, she'd have a little grandbaby as well.

And right now, instead of sitting on her pity pot and bemoaning her relationship with Louis Thibodeaux, she should be concentrating on keeping her promise to Bitsy. She should be trying to figure out who killed Robert Rossi. The sooner the better, as far as she was concerned. And, even more pressing at the moment, she needed to decide what she was going to fix Joyce for supper.

Liar, liar, pants on fire.

"Oh, for pity's sake," she grumbled in disgust as she slammed the dishwasher closed. So what if she was a bit lonely at times for male companionship? Big deal. Louis Thibodeaux wasn't the only fish in the sea. "So get over it," she whispered.

Taking a deep breath, Charlotte walked over to the refrigerator, and after a thorough search of her freezer, she decided that the fastest and easiest thing she could cook was chicken and dumplings.

By bedtime that night, Charlotte was more than ready. Though sorely tempted just to crawl into bed, she decided that tonight, of all nights, she needed to say her prayers.

Kneeling beside the bed, she bowed her head and closed her eyes, and with her earlier thoughts about Joyce and Louis in mind, she asked for forgiveness and strength to resist evil thoughts. Then she prayed for Joyce and her family and for Emily Rossi and Emily's family. Adding her thanks for all of her blessings, she finally climbed into bed.

Groaning with pure pleasure, Charlotte stretched out on the mattress beneath the covers then switched off the bedside lamp. But as she lay there, she couldn't stop thinking about Joyce.

After she'd cooked the chicken and dumplings, she'd sat with Joyce and encouraged her to eat. Though she'd been able to coax the rail-thin woman to eat most of the chicken and dumplings and green peas that she'd brought her, she could tell that Joyce had to force herself.

Once Joyce had finished, Charlotte had cleaned up Louis's kitchen and straightened the living room, while Joyce talked about Amy, her little granddaughter.

So sad, thought Charlotte as she stared up at the darkened ceiling. She could tell that Joyce truly wanted to spend more time with Amy, but was afraid the child might be frightened by the way she looked, and Charlotte could certainly understand why Joyce wouldn't want Amy to see her like she was.

Charlotte sighed, then, out of nowhere she recalled reading an article about how therapeutic it could be for older people or terminally ill patients to get their hair and nails groomed. Looking good and getting pampered a bit seemed to lift their spirits.

Joyce could certainly use a haircut and a manicure. And if she looked better, it might make her feel better, lift her spirits, and she might be willing to spend more time with Amy.

The more Charlotte thought about it, the more she became convinced that her thoughts were answered prayer, that what Joyce needed was a visit to the beauty shop. Charlotte was equally convinced that her own hairdresser, Valerie, would be willing to work Joyce into her schedule on short notice once she knew Joyce's circumstances. Money wouldn't be a problem. Charlotte smiled. She'd just have the bill sent to Louis.

Now, all she had to do was convince Joyce, first thing the next morning. If she timed things just right, she should be able to take Joyce to the beauty shop and get her back home before time to show up at the Rossis. And if she was a bit late showing up at the Rossis, then so be it.

With everything that had happened, Charlotte had completely forgotten about Monday being Lundi Gras. Because Lundi Gras, the Monday before carnival, had its own special celebrations, she feared that her hairdresser might have closed for the occasion.

When Charlotte called to check, she was relieved when Valerie answered the call. Convincing the hairdresser to work Joyce into her schedule wasn't a problem, but persuading Joyce turned out to be a bigger problem than Charlotte anticipated.

"I guarantee you'll feel so much better after a haircut and manicure," Charlotte told Joyce once she'd answered her call.

"I—I want to, Charlotte," she said, her voice still groggy from sleep. "And it's not that I don't appreciate what you're trying to do. It's just that I—I can't afford to—"

"You don't have to," Charlotte interrupted. "We'll have Valerie send the bill to Louis."

"Oh, no, I couldn't—not after all he's done already."

"Yes, you can," Charlotte insisted. "In fact, knowing Louis, I'm sure he'd be the first to tell you to do it."

"I—I don't know. I—"

Charlotte could tell that Joyce was weakening and decided it was time to play her trump card. "Look, Joyce, I know you'd like to spend more time with Amy, wouldn't you?"

"Yes, I would," she whispered.

"And I also know that if it was me and I had a grandchild, I'd want her to remember me looking the very best I could."

When Charlotte heard the soft sob through the phone line, she suddenly felt lower than a snake's belly and meaner than a junkyard dog. All she'd done was remind the poor woman that she was dying. "Oh, Joyce, I'm so so sorry. I shouldn't have said that."

Joyce sniffled. "No, it's okay. We—we both know that I'm dying, and believe it or not, it feels good for someone to finally acknowledge it out loud. Louis and Stephen tiptoe around the subject and won't discuss it at all. I know that they mean well, and it's not that I'm ungrateful for all they've done for me. I am."

"I know you are, Joyce, but won't you please reconsider letting me take you to the beauty shop?" There was brief silence, then Charlotte could swear she heard a faint giggle.

"Louis was right," Joyce said, and there was an amused lilt in her voice that hadn't been there before. "You are one stubborn lady."

Charlotte still couldn't get over the transformation of Joyce as she helped her navigate the steps leading to the front porch after their visit to the beauty shop.

Valerie had washed and trimmed Joyce's hair into a style that actually flattered the poor woman's thin face, and the manicurist had transformed Joyce's broken yellowed fingernails into smooth ovals then painted them a dark, flattering pink. But the small excursion had worn Joyce out.

When Joyce stumbled on the last step leading to the porch, Charlotte took a firmer grip on Joyce's waist. "Easy does it," Charlotte cautioned her.

"I'm okay," Joyce said, her voice breathy, barely above a whisper. "I just need to rest a while and get some strength back."

"A bite of food wouldn't hurt either," Charlotte told her as they approached Louis's front door. "It's a good thing we went through the drive-through at McDonald's. I expect you to eat every bite of those pancakes and sausage I bought."

Charlotte had already parked in front of the Rossi house and was almost to the front door when she remembered that she never had called Judith about the bloodstained towels and washcloths.

Eyeing the bodyguard at the gate and the one posted at the front door, Charlotte decided that calling Judith would have to wait. She certainly didn't want either of the men to overhear what she had to tell Judith.

When Charlotte entered the house, the first thing she noticed was the scent of fried bacon, and though muffled, she heard a commotion coming from the kitchen.

When she entered the kitchen, Amanda and Brandon, along with Jean the new nanny, were seated at the breakfast table, and Sophia was taking a pan of freshly baked biscuits out of the oven. In the center of the table was a platter of scrambled eggs, a bowl of steaming grits, a platter of bacon, and a pitcher of orange juice, enough food to feed an army, Charlotte decided.

The children were busy giggling and chattering. Jean was reading the morning newspaper. Though Jean was dressed casually in slacks and a sweatshirt, each of the children, as well as Sophia, were dressed in what Charlotte's mother had always referred to as Sunday-go-to-meeting clothes.

Abruptly the chattering stopped and all eyes stared at Charlotte.

"Oh, Charlotte, hi," Sophia said cheerily as she slid the hot biscuits onto a platter. "We'll be out of your way in no time, but I wanted the children to have a nice hot breakfast first."

"We're going to see Mama," Brandon announced with a grin.

"Just as soon as Mr. Acosta gets here," Amanda chimed in, a huge smile on her face.

"The children are so excited," Sophia told Charlotte as she buttered several of the biscuits.

And not the least bit remorseful about their father. "I can see that," Charlotte said instead, giving each of the children a smile of her own. "Is there something I can do to help you, Sophia? Breakfast looks wonderful."

Sophia shook her head. "No, I don't think so. But thanks anyway." She carried the platter of biscuits to the table. "I think this should do it." Setting the platter down on the table, she seated herself. After glancing over the table though, she frowned. "Oh, my goodness. I forgot the jelly." She looked up at Charlotte. "On second thought, if you wouldn't mind, could you please get the strawberry preserves out of the refrigerator?"

"I'll be glad to," Charlotte said.

Once Charlotte had placed the jar of preserves on the table, Sophia motioned toward an empty chair. "You're welcome to join us, Charlotte."

Though Charlotte was tempted and her own breakfast of oatmeal paled in comparison to the feast on the table, she was still full. "It looks delicious, but no, thanks, I've already eaten."

Sophia nodded and turned to Brandon. "Say the blessings, dear. And don't forget to thank the good Lord for Mr. Acosta being able to arrange it so that we can see your mother."

A few minutes later, Charlotte was upstairs dusting Sophia's bedroom when she heard the thump-thump of running footsteps in the hallway.

"Charlotte?"

"In here, Brandon."

Within seconds Brandon stuck his head through the doorway. "Mama Sophia says to tell you that we're leaving now and we'll be back after lunch."

Before Charlotte had a chance to even thank Brandon for the message, he disappeared, and she could hear his footsteps thudding back down the hallway.

Only moments later she heard the distinct sound of the front door slamming shut. "Boys!" She shook her head. Peeping out of the front window, she saw Brandon running toward a black Lincoln Town Car parked in the driveway. One of the bodyguards was assisting Sophia as she climbed inside, and Leo Acosta was holding the back door open for Amanda and Brandon.

With a shrug, Charlotte turned away from the window and went into the bathroom to clean. She'd finished wiping out the bathtub and was ready to clean the mirror, but when she reached in her supply carrier for the Windex, she sighed. The bottle barely had enough left in it to clean Sophia's bathroom mirror and she still had four more bedrooms and baths to clean.

With another sigh she trudged out of the bathroom back into the bedroom. If she remembered right, she should have an extra bottle in the van.

That's what you get for not checking your supply carrier. "Yeah, yeah," she grumbled as she hurried down the hallway.

Charlotte had just reached the bottom of the stairs when she heard a rustling noise coming from the back hall. Tightening her grip on the handrail, she froze, narrowed her eyes, and tilted her head to one side, straining to hear it again. No one else should be in the house. Everyone had left . . . hadn't they? But if everyone had left, then who or what had made the noise?

After a moment, Charlotte had just about made up her mind that her imagination was getting the best of her and that she was just spooked because of Robert's murder. Then, though it was faint, she heard the distinct creak of a door, and her heart began pounding overtime beneath her breasts as she stared at the end of the main hall, where a shorter hallway branched off toward the library.

Now what? she wondered. *Now you call the police and get out of the house.*

Chapter 14

Charlotte eased her cell phone from her apron pocket, flipped it open, and dialed 911. But as her finger hovered over the send button, a mental image of Jean the nanny popped into her head, and she suddenly remembered that not everyone had left with Sophia and the children. She'd completely forgotten about Jean being there, and she hadn't seen the nanny leave. And the bodyguards; she'd forgotten about the bodyguards.

Feeling more foolish with each passing moment, she immediately deleted the 911 number, snapped the cell phone closed, and dropped it back into the pocket of her apron.

Wouldn't that be just peachy? She could see the headlines now . . . . MAID CALLS POLICE ON BODYGUARDS AND NANNY.

Charlotte suddenly frowned as another thought occurred to her. But why would Jean or, for that matter, why would the bodyguards be in that particular part of the house? The only room in that part of the house was the library.

Immediately, the theft of the eggs came to mind, and she grew uneasy all over again. What if the person making the noise wasn't Jean or any of the bodyguards? What if the thief had returned for the rest of the eggs?

Charlotte eased down the last step and tiptoed to the front

of the parlor. Pulling aside the heavy drape that covered the window, she peered outside. Just as she'd hoped, one of the bodyguards, the one named Gus, was on the porch, and another one was standing near the front gate.

"Okay, that takes care of the front," she murmured. But what about the back?

With her ears attuned for any unusual sound, she headed for the kitchen. From the window above the sink, she spotted Gino sitting on the top step of the porch.

With two men posted at the front and one guarding the back, there was no way a thief could get past them without being detected . . . unless the thief was, in fact, one of the bodyguards. With only four accounted for, including the one driving the car for Sophia, the children, and the lawyer, there were still two men unaccounted for.

If one of the two men was the thief, then he'd have to be pretty stupid, she decided, turning away from the window. Attempting a theft now, what with the police involved and the house secure, would be asking to get caught.

Shaking her head, Charlotte slowly walked back into the center hallway. With the bodyguards more or less eliminated, that just left the nanny, and since Jean had been hired after the eggs had been stolen, there was no way she could be the thief. Besides, how would she even know about the eggs to begin with?

Shaking her head again at her own foolishness, Charlotte decided that, more than likely, Jean was the one in the library, probably doing nothing more sinister than simply searching for something to read while the children were gone. But *if* that's what Jean was after, then she was looking in the wrong place. Though the family called the room the library, there were actually very few books in it at all, and what few that were in there certainly weren't the type that anyone would read for pleasure. In fact, the library was set up more like a home office. From what she'd seen, Sophia was the only one in the family who read for pleasure, and she kept her small library of books, mostly biographies of famous people, in her room.

With thoughts of telling Jean about Sophia's stash of books, Charlotte headed for the library. But when she reached the open doorway and saw Jean, she paused. Inside the room, Jean was standing in front of the egg display, and from what Charlotte could tell from Jean's profile, the young woman was obviously enamored by the beauty of the collection.

Charlotte opened her mouth to say something, then abruptly closed it again when a feeling of déjà vu came over her and the hairs on the back of her neck stood up. There was something about Jean, something about her profile and the way she was standing there, staring at the egg collection. . . .

As if sensing that she was being watched, Jean turned toward the doorway. When she saw Charlotte, she smiled. "Oh, hi, Charlotte. I—I was looking for you when I got sidetracked." She motioned toward the display of eggs. "Those eggs are just beautiful. The detail and workmanship are unbelievable. And the stones and jewels . . . Do you think they're real—you know, diamonds, rubies, and such?"

Charlotte shrugged. "I'm not sure, but I suspect so."

"Oh, wow, and I bet that's real gold and silver too, huh?"

"Probably," Charlotte reluctantly agreed after a moment's hesitation.

"Do you get to dust them?"

Charlotte nodded.

Jean suddenly grinned, and in a conspiratorial tone barely above a whisper, she said, "Next time you dust them, do you think I could hold one? I wouldn't want to get you into any trouble though," she quickly added. "It's just that I've never seen anything like that outside of a museum."

Charlotte shook her head. "Right now, that probably wouldn't be a very good idea. In fact, it's probably not a good idea for you to be in this room, period."

Jean frowned, and then, a horrified expression came over her face. "Oh, no." She backed away from the egg display. "Was—was this where it happened, where Mr. Rossi was murdered?"

When Charlotte nodded, Jean turned and walked quickly toward the door. "Sorry," she apologized. "Oh, Charlotte, I'm so sorry. I—I didn't know."

Charlotte stepped back from the doorway and Jean joined her in the hallway.

"You won't tell Miss Sophia, will you—I mean, you won't tell her that I was in there?"

"No, of course not," Charlotte said.

Jean released a huge sigh. "Thanks. I really need this job. And speaking of the job, the reason I was looking for you—" She slid her eyes sideways toward the library then back again. "*Before* I got sidetracked. I need to run a few personal errands. For one thing, I'm almost out of toothpaste and deodorant. Anyway, I wanted to ask you if you thought it would be okay if I left now, while the children are gone? Miss Sophia said they'd be gone until after lunch, and I'd be back before then."

The girl was clearly nervous, chattering like a magpie, and though Charlotte felt sorry for her, there was something about her, something Charlotte couldn't quite put her finger on, that just didn't ring true. For one thing, Charlotte couldn't imagine her being with the children any length of time and not being aware that Robert had been murdered in the library. Charlotte felt sure that someone would have apprised her of what had happened and where it had happened when she'd been hired.

"So, what do you think?"

Jean's question jerked Charlotte from her reverie, and it took her a moment to recall just what Jean had asked her. "I think that would be okay," Charlotte finally answered. "Just as long as you're back before the children return."

After Jean left, Charlotte retrieved a new bottle of Windex from her van, but as she trudged back up the stairs to clean the rest of the bedrooms, she couldn't stop thinking about the way Jean had reacted about the eggs and the library.

In no time Charlotte finished all of the bedrooms except for the guest room that was now occupied by Jean. When she entered the room, she glanced around, and again the strange feeling she'd had about the nanny returned.

Judging from the personal belongings scattered about the room, it was evident that Jean had made herself at home. It was further evident that Jean was an LSU fan, like Robert had been. An LSU afghan was spread across the foot of the bed and a large stuffed Mike the Tiger sat on the pillows. Neither item had been there the last time Charlotte had cleaned the room.

Unlike the rest of the family's bedrooms though, Jean's room was neat as a pin. The bed was made, and, other than a pair of pajamas that had been folded and placed on top of one of the pillows, there were no signs of her dirty clothes.

In the guest bathroom the sink and the bathtub had been wiped dry, and the dirty towels and washcloths, along with what Jean had worn the previous day, had been placed in the dirty clothes hamper.

Just for good measure, Charlotte cleaned the toilet, the

bathtub, the sink, and the countertop anyway. As she wiped down the countertop though, she picked up a tube of toothpaste, set it back down, and then she picked up a spray can of deodorant and shook it.

"Now that's strange," she murmured, setting the deodorant back on the counter. Both items were more than half-full. Hadn't Jean said that she was almost out of toothpaste and deodorant?

Charlotte sighed and shrugged. Why would the nanny feel as if she had to lie about leaving for a while?

"Who knows and who cares?" she whispered, disgusted with herself for being so paranoid as she sprayed Windex on some paper towels and wiped the mirror clean.

When Charlotte returned to the bedroom, she glanced around at the furniture surfaces. Though she didn't detect any visible dust, she decided to go ahead and dust anyway, just for good measure.

With her feather duster in hand, Charlotte walked over to the dresser. But before she even got started, a small, framed photograph sitting to one side caught her eye. "Now that's odd," she murmured, reaching for the picture. But as recognition hit her, her hand froze in midair.

"But how could that be?" she whispered, once again reaching for the photograph. When she picked it up, she brought it closer and stared at each of the people in the photograph. There were three of them: a woman, a girl, and a boy. And if she wasn't mistaken, and she was sure that she wasn't, the photo was an exact duplicate of the same photograph that she'd seen on Mark's dresser when she'd cleaned the carriage house.

"Of course," she murmured. No wonder Jean had seemed so familiar when she'd been standing in the library staring at the eggs. No wonder she was sure that she'd seen Jean somewhere before. She had, in the photo on Mark's dresser.

Like Mark, Jean was much older now than when the photo had been taken, but even older, she still looked enough like the girl in the photo to be recognized.

Charlotte set the picture back down on top of the dresser, but she still continued to stare at it. She'd been surprised that the family had found a suitable, trustworthy nanny so fast, especially considering how concerned they were about security. But now she knew why. They trusted Mark, so it made perfect sense that a relative of one of their trusted bodyguards, especially if she was a sister, would be a perfect choice.

Pretty convenient, don't you think?

The moment that the pesky voice whispered the thought in her head, Charlotte squeezed her eyes closed and sighed with frustration. All of her life her imagination had been both a blessing and curse, but for the moment, she considered it a curse. Being paranoid wasn't always a bad thing, but her suspicions about Jean were getting out of hand, bordering on becoming ridiculous. The girl was probably just what she seemed to be—no more, no less.

Charlotte opened her eyes, and with one last glance around the room, she decided that everything looked just fine the way it was and didn't really need dusting after all. Besides, she still had plenty of work to do downstairs.

Before she could change her mind, she gathered her cleaning supplies and her supply carrier, and then, with purposeful steps, she headed toward the staircase.

It was almost noon by the time Charlotte finished cleaning the kitchen.

With everything that had happened the day before—

Sophia and the children's arrival, finding the bloodstained towels and washcloths, and Sophia's strange behavior—she'd completely forgotten that she'd neglected to vacuum the library. Though she was tempted to go ahead and take care of that chore as well, before lunch, the thought of having another weak spell from low blood sugar changed her mind. She really should eat first, she concluded. Afterward she'd still have plenty of time to vacuum the library and finish up in the parlor and dining room.

Maybe she'd eat on the front porch again. "Good idea," she murmured as she headed down the main hallway to retrieve her lunch from the van. Some fresh air and a bit of sunshine would be good for her.

Charlotte was almost to the front door when it abruptly opened and Gus stepped inside.

A surprised look crossed his face. "Oh, hey, Charlotte. I was just coming in to find you. The caterer is here to pick up his stuff." With his head Gus motioned behind him at the man standing in the doorway. "Is it okay for him to come in now?"

Charlotte nodded. "It's okay, Gus."

When the caterer entered through the doorway, Charlotte smiled. "I stacked it all in the dining room. And by the way, with everything that happened and not knowing when you'd be able to pick up the stuff, I went ahead and washed the tablecloth and napkins. There were some stains on some of them, and I figured that there was no use in them being ruined."

"You didn't have to have to do that," the caterer said as he followed Charlotte into the dining room. "But I appreciate it. That Ms. Rossi is a real nice lady, and I still feel bad about all of my servers coming down sick that night and putting her in a bind like that. Of course I feel bad about her being arrested and all—well, you know what I mean . . ." His voice trailed away, and it was obvious from his flushed face and the way he averted his eyes that he was embarrassed about even mentioning Emily's arrest.

"I know what you mean," Charlotte assured him, "and I'm sure that Ms. Rossi would appreciate your concern." She pointed to the large white box of linens that she'd placed on the floor in the corner. "As for the servers, at least one person showing up was better than none. We managed."

The caterer stopped, swiveled his head toward Charlotte, and frowned. "One of my servers showed up?" When Charlotte nodded, his frown deepened. "But I could have sworn they were all sick—at least that's what I was told." After a moment he shrugged. "It was probably Jody. She's pretty bad off right now—really needs the money. It'd be just like her to show up sick or not."

With a frown of her own, Charlotte shook her head. "The woman who showed up said that her name was Anna, not Jody."

The caterer slowly shook his head. "I don't have anyone named Anna working for me. Must have been someone Jake sent over. Jake—he's my partner," he added.

"Maybe so," Charlotte murmured.

After the caterer collected all of his stuff, Charlotte said, "I'll walk out with you. I need to get my lunch from my van anyway."

Charlotte followed the caterer across the porch and then down the steps, but she couldn't stop thinking about Anna Smith as she walked to the van. Once she'd retrieved her lunch from the passenger's side of the van, she closed the door and headed back for the front porch. With a nod to Gus, she climbed the steps and walked over to the two wicker chairs grouped together at the end of the porch. Once she'd settled in a chair, she emptied the contents of her lunch bag onto the small table positioned between the two chairs.

While Charlotte chewed thoughtfully on the smoked turkey sandwich she'd packed in her lunch, she became more convinced with each passing moment that she had yet another suspect to add to the list of people who could have murdered Robert. Granted, the evidence was circumstantial, and since she didn't know Anna, she had no idea what the woman's motive could be. Also, the caterer had given her a fairly reasonable explanation for the presence of Anna; then again, considering the circumstances, what else could he have said? He certainly wouldn't just come right out and admit that he'd sent a complete stranger to work for the Rossis, especially with Robert Rossi being murdered.

Charlotte finished off her sandwich and bit into the apple she'd brought. Of course, there was a way to find out if the caterer's partner, Jake, had, in fact, sent Anna Smith. A simple phone call to Jake would clear the matter up.

By the time Charlotte had finished her lunch, she'd made up her mind that just as soon as she got home that night she'd give Judith a call. In addition to the information about the towels and washcloths that she'd found in the washing machine, she'd also tell Judith about Anna Smith. And if Judith didn't want to call about Anna Smith, Charlotte decided she just might make the phone call herself.

Once Charlotte had returned her lunch bag to the van, she went back inside the house and retrieved her vacuum cleaner from the kitchen. Then she headed for the library.

The most accessible electrical outlet in the library was beside the curio cabinet. As Charlotte bent down and plugged in the vacuum cleaner though, a vision of Jean came to mind.

In spite of realizing that Jean and Mark were sister and brother, there was still something bothering her about the girl. But what? she wondered as she straightened.

With a frown, and tapping her forefinger against her lips, she peered closer at the eggs inside the case. Without thinking, Charlotte automatically counted the eggs.

Her frown deepened. "That can't be right," she whispered. But even counting a second time, then a third time didn't change the final outcome or the fact that two more eggs were missing.

Jean. Jean was the egg thief.

Charlotte didn't want to believe what she was thinking, and she tried to make excuses for the missing eggs. Someone could have come in while she was cleaning upstairs, or maybe she'd counted wrong the day before. Then, there was the fact that she hadn't actually *witnessed* Jean taking the eggs. But all of the excuses were just that: excuses. And all of them had holes large enough to drive a Mack truck through.

To gain access to the house, a person would first have to get past the bodyguards, and the only way the bodyguards would let anyone inside was if they knew the person. Charlotte was also fairly certain that there was no way that she had miscounted the eggs. And no, she hadn't actually witnessed Jean taking the eggs, but it was highly possible that the girl could have already taken them before Charlotte had discovered her in the library.

Charlotte tried to remember what Jean had been wearing. As she recalled, the nanny had on a pair of navy chinos topped by a dark pink knit pullover and a baggy navy sweater. The eggs weren't that large and could have easily fit inside Jean's pants pockets or her sweater pockets.

In Charlotte's mind she could still see Jean's profile as she had stood staring at the eggs, and Charlotte could still hear her comments . . .

Those eggs are just beautiful. The detail and workmanship are unbelievable. And the stones and jewels . . . Do you think they're real—you know, diamonds, rubies, and such?

Had it all been an act? An act to cover up the fact that she was a thief?

Sadly, Charlotte concluded that whether she wanted to believe it or not, Jean had to have taken the two missing eggs.

Charlotte figured that the nanny had ample opportunity. Even if Jean hadn't already taken them before she'd been caught in the library, she could have easily doubled back and taken the eggs once Charlotte had gone upstairs to clean.

Charlotte narrowed her eyes as another image came to mind, an image of Robert staring at the eggs with exactly the same fascination that she'd seen on Jean's face. Jean's face . . . Robert's face . . . Jean's face . . . Robert's face . . .

Suddenly, in Charlotte's mind, the profile of Robert's face superimposed itself over the profile of Jean's profile, and Charlotte felt her legs grow weak with realization.

"That's it," she whispered, still stunned by the revelation. Not only had she recognized Jean from the photo, but, in profile, she bore an uncanny resemblance to Robert Rossi as well.

No one had mentioned it, but could it be possible that Jean was also related to Robert as well as Mark? But if Jean was related to Robert, then that meant that Mark had to be a relative too. Maybe Mark and Jean were actually Robert's nephew and niece . . . or perhaps distant cousins?

With a shake of her head, and still trying to reason out her discovery, Charlotte turned on the vacuum cleaner and began vacuuming. When she vacuumed the side near the floor-to-ceiling bookcase behind the desk, she noticed that one of the photo albums on the bottom shelf was askew. With intentions of straightening the album to align it with the others, Charlotte switched off the vacuum. But when she knelt down to shove the album in line, it suddenly occurred to her that if Jean and Mark were, in fact, relatives, their pictures might be in one of the photo albums.

Should she or shouldn't she? Her hand hovered above the albums.

Snooping through a client's belongings is definitely forbidden and a just reason for immediate dismissal.

Charlotte sighed, recalling one of the many rules she had for her employees. "Yeah, yeah," she grumbled, flexing her fingers. "So who's going to know?" she whispered. Yet still she hesitated. After a moment though, her curiosity won out and she made up her mind to do it anyway. With a furtive glance over her shoulder, she pulled out the stack of albums and placed them on top of the desk. She could always claim that she was dusting the albums if anyone happened by.

Starting with what looked to be the oldest album, she thumbed through it. There were a lot of pictures in the album, but most of them were older pictures of a younger Sophia, her husband, Roberto, and their sons as children.

Closing the album, she selected another one and began scanning the pages. After the third page she suddenly realized that the woman she kept seeing in all of the pictures had to be Robert's first wife. Charlotte turned another page and her breath caught in her throat. Though quite young, the two children in the picture with the woman bore an uncanny resemblance to Mark and Jean.

Charlotte swallowed hard. Was it possible? Instead of being Robert's nephew and niece or distant cousins, were Mark and Jean Robert's children by his first marriage? If they were though, why hadn't anyone said so?

The only answer that made any sense was that no one had said so because no one knew that they were Robert's children. But how could a father not recognize his own son, or for that matter, a grandmother not recognize her grandchildren?

Maybe, just maybe, if the children were really young when they had disappeared with their mother, they would have changed enough so that no one, not even their own father or grandmother would recognize them as adults. But how young were they when they disappeared?

Charlotte closed the album and stared at the stack of the other albums. If she kept going through the photo albums, she might be able to tell at what age they had disappeared. But that would take time, time that she didn't really have.

There had to be a faster way of finding out what she needed to know. Then, suddenly, a way to find out came to her, but along with the thought, a feeling of dread settled hard in the pit of her stomach. Though she'd rather have eaten worms, Charlotte took out her cell phone and the small notebook she always kept with her. If anyone knew, it was Bitsy.

Once Charlotte located Bitsy's son's phone number in the notebook, she dialed it. After three rings, Bradley answered. "Hi, Bradley," Charlotte said. "This is Charlotte LaRue. Is Bitsy there?"

"Oh, hey there, Charlotte. Yeah, Mother's in the kitchen. So how's my favorite cleaning lady?"

Recalling the last time that she'd seen Bradley, Charlotte felt her face grow warm with embarrassment. Bradley had been visiting his mother at the time, and he'd invited Charlotte to join him and his mother for dinner. At the time, Charlotte had been a bit vulnerable, due to Louis's decision to take care of Joyce. Charlotte had mistakenly assumed that Bradley was flirting with her, only to find out that all he'd wanted was an extra woman along because Bitsy had been trying to play matchmaker by setting him up with her friend's daughter. Bradley had thought that with Charlotte along, the friend's daughter wouldn't get the wrong idea.

"If you're talking about me, then I'm just fine."

"Oh, come on, Charlotte. I did apologize."

Charlotte sighed. "Okay, sorry. But right now I need to talk to your mother."

"Is everything okay? The house?"

"The house is just fine."

"Okay, hold on a minute, and I'll get her."

Several moments passed, then finally Bitsy came to the phone. "Charlotte? Is that you?"

Certain that Bradley had told Bitsy that she was on the phone, Charlotte rolled her eyes. "Yes, Bitsy, it's me. Listen, I have a question for you. How old would Robert Rossi's children by his first wife be now?"

"My goodness, why do you want to know something like that?"

Charlotte swallowed a groan. She'd hoped she wouldn't have to explain it all, but she should have known better. Taking a deep breath and as quickly as she could, she told Bitsy about her suspicions concerning Mark and Jean, their resemblance to Robert, and the pictures she'd found. Then she gave Bitsy her best guess as to their ages now. "So, Bitsy," she said when she'd finished. "What do you think? Are Mark and Jean about the right ages? Could they be Robert's children by his first wife?"

"It certainly sounds like it," Bitsy answered. "If I remember right, the boy was around seven or eight and the girl was just barely school age, but the children's names were Ben and Kay, not Mark and Jean. At least those were the older children's names. I don't know what they named the baby—if the poor thing was ever born," she added. "You remember about those rumors I told you? Well, the one about how Robert had Linda and the baby murdered is the one I always believed. Emily once told me that the older children were away at some fancy boarding school up north, or so that's what Sophia told her. Emily said that Sophia also told her that Robert had set up a trust fund for them that covered all of their expenses." Bitsy sighed. "It's all so sad. According to what Emily said, he never saw them again or had any contact with them. Can you imagine such a thing?"

Charlotte shook her head. "No, I can't imagine such a thing. But it would definitely explain how they could come and go around the family with no one being the wiser . . . especially if—" Charlotte bit the bottom of her lip to keep from blurting out the rest of what she was thinking and immediately wished she'd kept her thoughts to herself.

"Especially since what?" Bitsy demanded.

"Er—ah, Bitsy, someone's coming," Charlotte lied. Having to ask Bitsy about Jean and Mark was bad enough, but the last thing she wanted was to give Bitsy fuel for gossip by speculating about why Mark and Jean had suddenly showed up after so many years, especially if what she suspected was true. "For now, just keep all of this to yourself, okay? I've got to hang up." Charlotte promptly disconnected the call.

All that she could do now was hope and pray that Bitsy would keep quiet. "Yeah, right," she muttered. And as she folded her cell phone and dropped it into her apron pocket, her thoughts returned to the reasons Jean and Mark or Ben and Kay—whatever their names were—had shown up. What if they suspected or even knew for a fact that their father had murdered their mother and her unborn child? And what if they had come back for the express reason of getting revenge for their mother's murder?

Chapter 15

She should call Judith immediately. Charlotte reached down in the pocket of her apron to retrieve her cell phone.

Stay out of it. Let the police handle this. Don't interfere.

Unbidden, Judith's warning popped into her head, and with a grimace, Charlotte released her grip on the phone and promptly withdrew her hand. Calling Judith about the dirty towels and washcloths and about Anna Smith was one thing. She couldn't help but feel that both were relevant to the case. But calling her with unsubstantiated speculations about Jean and Mark was another thing altogether. After all, there was no definite proof that Jean and Mark were even related to Robert Rossi. For all she knew, they could be just exactly what they seemed to be, a brother and sister trying to make a living the best way they can.

Charlotte walked over to the only window in the room. The view outside overlooked a beautiful garden, lush with evergreens and subtropical plants that encircled a large statue. The Grecian marble statue was of a woman holding a jug that also served as a water fountain with water cascading from the jug.

As Charlotte stared at the water splashing down into the fountain, she knew that what she needed was more proof, hard evidence, before calling Judith, not just mere speculations. But where could she get more proof about Mark and Jean, especially Jean?

Charlotte turned her head and stared up at the ceiling. *Jean's room.* The answer whispered through her head. Though it was true that she'd already been in the woman's room, she'd only been in there to clean it, not search it. But if she went in it for the express purpose of searching it . . .

Just the thought of going through Jean's personal belongings sent qualms of unease coursing through Charlotte. What if she got caught or someone found out? Maid-for-a-Day's reputation would be down the toilet for sure. And how could she, in all good conscience, expect her employees to comply with her rules, if she didn't set a good example and obey them herself?

Promise? Charlotte lowered her head and closed her eyes. Snooping through Jean's belongings might be the only way to keep her promise to Bitsy. If she didn't go through Jean's things, other than coming right out and asking her, she had no way of finding out the truth about her. And there was no way she could outright ask Jean something like that. Besides, snooping might be the only way to keep Emily, an innocent woman, from being convicted of a crime she didn't commit.

Like it or not, Charlotte decided that she really had no choice, at least not one she could live with and keep a clear conscience.

With her mind made up, Charlotte quickly vacuumed the rest of the library. Then, dragging the vacuum behind her, she hurried to the kitchen. But as she placed the vacuum next to her supply carrier, she hesitated. Instead of leaving the machine in the kitchen, she decided that she should take it with her upstairs. That way, if someone happened to catch her snooping, then she'd have a ready excuse for being in Jean's room.

Charlotte lugged the vacuum cleaner up the stairs, and then she headed straight for Jean's room. Once inside the room, as a precaution, she unwound the cord and plugged in the vacuum. Then, hands on her hips, she glanced around. "Where to begin?" she whispered.

The dresser, she decided. Being careful to put things back exactly like she'd found them, she started on the left side of the small dresser and searched the first drawer.

Finding nothing but bras and panties, she closed it and opened the second drawer. All she found there were several pairs of pajamas and a couple of nightgowns, all neatly folded.

Charlotte closed the second drawer and opened the last one. Inside were two stacks of folded sweaters, side by side, and nothing else.

With a sigh, she moved to the right side of the dresser. To her disappointment, each of the three drawers on that side was empty. As she closed the last drawer, a car door slammed outside.

With a frown and fully expecting to see that either Sophia and the children had returned or that Jean was back, Charlotte hurried over to the window. But the driveway was empty.

Probably just a neighbor's car, she figured as she turned away from the window. Even so, the incident was an unnerving reminder that she needed to hurry along her search if she didn't want to get caught red-handed.

"Now where would someone keep something they didn't want anyone to find?" she whispered, and as she glanced about the room, her gaze kept returning to the bed.

Recalling another time when she'd found what she'd thought was incriminating evidence under the bed of another client, she walked over and knelt down beside Jean's bed. Squinting, she peered beneath. But underneath was too dark to see anything.

"Should've brought a flashlight," she murmured.

Kneeling farther down until her cheek almost touched the rug, she stretched out her arm as far as she could reach. Scooting along from the head to the foot of the bed, she slid her hand first one way and then another along the hardwood floor. But there was nothing there but dust, and she could only stretch her arm so far.

Dusting off her hand and making a mental note that the next time she vacuumed she needed to make sure that she vacuumed beneath the bed, she crawled to the foot. Just as she was about to repeat the same searching gesture with her arm, she suddenly rolled her eyes. "Duh, the vacuum," she muttered. She could use the vacuum extension wands and get the job done just as well if not better without punishing her poor knees and getting her hand all dusty.

A few moments later, armed with the wand, she bent down and made a couple of sweeps beneath the bed. With the third sweep, the wand struck something. She figured that it was a box of some kind, and by the ease in which she was able to maneuver it from beneath the bed, she also figured that the box wasn't all that heavy.

Putting aside the wand, she placed the small cardboard box on the bed and opened it. Inside were several layers of tissue, and when Charlotte pealed away the layers, all she could do was stare with disbelief at the missing Fabergé eggs.

"One, two, three, four," she whispered. Then she lifted the tissue to find another layer of four more eggs, and beneath the second layer was yet a third layer of four eggs.

"Twelve in all," she murmured, still a bit stunned. If she remembered right, twelve was the total number that had come up missing.

An odd twinge of disappointment gripped her as she slowly shook her head from side to side. She hadn't wanted to be right about Jean, hadn't wanted to believe that she was the thief, but there was no denying the truth. And there was no denying the evidence right before her eyes.

With a heavy sigh, Charlotte finally folded the tissue back over the eggs, closed up the box, and slid it back to where she'd found it. If, as she suspected, Jean and Mark were brother and sister and because Jean had only just begun working for the Rossis, then the only logical conclusion she could come to was that Jean and Mark had been working together all along to steal the eggs.

Charlotte reached up and pinched the bridge of her nose then shook her head. Just because they were both thieves didn't necessarily mean that they had murdered Robert, did it? Not unless he'd caught them red-handed and threatened them in some way . . . or not unless they decided to up the ante and get revenge for their mother's death. Of course that was assuming that they were Robert's children and assuming that their mother had been murdered.

Even so, finding the eggs only proved that they were thieves. To prove that they were also murderers, she still needed more concrete evidence . . . but what?

Charlotte eyed the closet. *In for a penny, in for a pound.* As long as she was at it, she might as well check it out.

She searched the top shelf above the hanging clothes first. Finding nothing of interest but a couple of empty purses, she moved down to the hanging clothes.

As she searched through each piece of clothing, one by one, she couldn't help being impressed by the way that Jean had organized everything: blouses first, then slacks and jeans, a couple of skirts, a dress, and finally, a jacket and a heavy overcoat.

Though the nanny didn't own a lot of clothes and none of them was expensive or even name brands that Charlotte readily recognized, in her opinion, the girl definitely had an eye for color and style.

Once Charlotte had checked the pockets of the jacket and the overcoat, she eyed a zippered garment bag that had been shoved to the very end of the closet.

Judging by the quality of Jean's everyday clothes, Charlotte fully expected to find a nicer, more expensive garment in the bag. Reaching up, she partially unzipped the bag, and immediately wrinkled her nose. Though not as strong, the odor trapped inside the bag reminded her of how the bloodstained towel and washcloths had smelled. Growing more curious with each passing moment, she finished unzipping the bag.

At first sight, something about the garment tugged at her memory. Frowning, Charlotte unhooked the garment bag hanger from the closet rod and pulled the bag out of the closet. Once she took the garment completely out of the bag, her breath caught in her throat as she stared at the glittery costume.

Cleopatra's costume.

No wonder it seemed familiar, she thought. Jean had been Cleopatra, the mysterious guest who had disappeared before the police arrived.

And no wonder the thing smelled. If she wasn't mistaken, the spots on the costume were spots of dried blood—Robert Rossi's dried blood.

A mental image of Mark talking to Cleopatra during the party came to mind. At the time, Charlotte had thought that Mark was flirting with her. But now . . . Charlotte shuddered.

She had wanted proof, had wanted hard evidence, and as far as she was concerned, she'd found it. Even so, she still had problems believing that Jean and Mark had actually murdered Robert.

Charlotte put the costume back inside the garment bag. Had Jean and Mark set out to murder Robert, though? Or had they only intended on stealing from him, and things got out of hand?

Though Charlotte felt sure that she had found all that she was going to find, as she zipped up the bag and hung it back on the closet rod, something deep within urged her to continue searching.

The bottom of the closet contained several pairs of shoes and two suitcases. Charlotte pulled the larger one out, unzipped it, and searched it, but found that it was empty. After zipping it back up, she replaced it back inside the closet. Then she pulled out the smaller suitcase. Immediately, she could tell that there was something inside, something in the outer pocket.

She unzipped the pocket, reached down inside, and pulled out a framed picture. Just like the other picture on both Jean and Mark's dressers, there were three people in the photo; but in this one, Jean and Mark were much older and more easily recognized.

Charlotte frowned as she stared at the woman standing between Jean and Mark in the photo. If Robert had murdered their mother, who was the woman in the picture? Was it possible that Bitsy had been wrong after all? Was it possible that Robert hadn't murdered his ex-wife?

Picture in hand, Charlotte stepped over to the dresser, picked up the photo there, and held it up beside the one she'd found in the suitcase. Though the hair color and style of the two women were different, there was a slight resemblance between them. But there were more differences as well. The woman's face in the dresser photo was badly scarred and she was pitifully thin, almost anorexic looking, but the other woman's face wasn't scarred and though she wasn't exactly fat, she had a healthier look about her.

Either Jean and Mark's mother was alive and had undergone tremendous changes, including plastic surgery, or the two women were different women.

As Charlotte continued eyeing the two pictures thoughtfully, she wondered if it was possible that the two women could be sisters . . . if their mother had even had a sister.

Charlotte thought about her own sister, Madeline. At one time, when Judith and Daniel had been young and Madeline had just divorced their father, Madeline had been so distraught that she'd been incapable of taking care of them, and Charlotte had gladly stepped in and helped.

If the rumor was true about Robert murdering his first wife, and if his wife had a sister, wasn't it possible that Jean and Mark's aunt might have done the same thing for them? After all, what with Robert more or less abandoning them all those years, surely someone had been around to check on them.

Charlotte's chest grew heavy with sympathy just thinking about what Mark and Jean must have gone through, and with a shake of her head, she carried the photo back over to the suitcase. Her father had always said that there was a special place in hell for people who abused or abandoned little children, and Charlotte figured that if there was, then Robert Rossi was burning for eternity.

With one last look at the picture, Charlotte slipped it back inside the side pocket of the suitcase and zipped it closed. She had just pushed the suitcase back inside the closet, when, just outside the door, the floor creaked. Charlotte froze as a sudden wave of apprehension swept through her and panic gripped her.

Was someone out in the hallway? Had she been so caught up in trying to figure out who the woman was in the photos that she had let her guard down?

With a frown and holding her breath, she tilted her head and listened. *It's just your imagination and your guilt because you're snooping in someone else's stuff.*

Ignoring the irritating voice of her conscience, Charlotte still didn't dare move or breathe for several more moments. She *was* probably imagining things. Big old houses were always creaking and settling, especially in New Orleans where everything was below sea level anyway. Even so, and just in case there was actually someone lurking around in the hallway . . .

Gathering her courage and taking a deep breath, Charlotte marched over to the vacuum cleaner and took hold of the handle. She switched it on, and when the machine roared to life, she began vacuuming. Just in case someone was outside the door spying on her, she made sure that she vacuumed the bottom of the closet.

Then, with one last look around, she switched off the machine, and unplugged the cord. After she'd wrapped the cord around the handle, she stared at the doorway leading into the hall.

Taking a deep breath, she whispered, "Here goes nothing." With a prayer that she wouldn't run into anyone until she got all the way downstairs, she headed for the door.

To Charlotte's profound relief, the upstairs hallway was empty. Silently calling herself a silly old fool for being so jumpy and paranoid, she descended the staircase. Halfway down, the sound of voices reached her ears. Pausing, she listened until she determined that the voices belonged to Sophia and the children.

As Charlotte descended the rest of the steps, she wondered how their visit with Emily had gone. How had the children felt having to visit their mother in jail?

When she walked into the kitchen, Amanda and Brandon were seated at the kitchen table, and Sophia was slicing up large pieces of king cake at the counter.

As Charlotte placed the vacuum cleaner next to her supply carrier, she decided that if the contented expressions on the children's faces were any gauge to measure by, then the experience of seeing their mother in jail must not have been too traumatic.

"Want a piece of king cake, Charlotte?" Sophia asked. "It's from Gambino's Bakery."

Charlotte's mouth watered just thinking about the circular ring of cinnamon-flavored, yeasty coffee cake that was topped with icing and sprinkled with stripes of purple, gold, and green colored granulated sugar. But she shook her head.

"You sure? After our visit with Emily, I made Leo stop at the South Carrollton store so that we could get a fresh one."

In spite of her diabetes, Charlotte was sorely tempted, and she was truly thankful that the delicious confection was only available during Mardi Gras season, but she shook her head again. "No, but thanks anyway. I still need to clean the parlor and the dining room before I leave."

Sophia nodded as she took two saucers of king cake slices to the table and set them in front of Amanda and Brandon. Then, with a frown on her face, she turned to Charlotte. "Have you seen Jean?"

"I saw her right after you and the children left, but not since then. She said she had some errands to run, but that she'd be back before y'all returned."

Sophia's frown deepened. "I hope nothing's happened to her." Then, after a moment more, she shrugged and waved a dismissing hand. "Of course nothing's happened to her," she said. "I'm just being an old worrywart. I'm sure she'll be back any minute now."

"Mama Sophia, can I have another piece?"

Sophia turned to Brandon. "Another one so soon? My goodness, boy, you must have swallowed the one I gave you whole."

Brandon grinned but Amanda rolled her eyes. "He's a pig," Amanda said.

"Am not," Brandon retorted.

"Oink, oink, oink. Piggy, piggy."

"And you're a—"

"Now, children. That's enough."

In spite of Sophia's warning, as Charlotte picked up her supply carrier and left the kitchen, she could still hear Amanda and Brandon bickering.

In the parlor, Charlotte hurried through her chores, then moved into the dining room to clean. By the time that she had finished cleaning the dining room, and had vacuumed both rooms, Jean still hadn't returned. As she packed up her supply carrier in the kitchen, she, like Sophia, also began to wonder if something had happened to Jean.

Though she was anxious to get home so that she could phone Judith about what she'd found in Jean's room, she also wondered if she should leave Sophia alone with the children.

Charlotte had just about made up her mind that maybe it

would be best if she hung around until Jean returned, when Sophia walked into the kitchen.

"All finished?" Sophia asked.

"Yes, ma'am. Almost," Charlotte added, trying quickly to think of an excuse to stay a bit longer. She glanced around the kitchen. When she saw that the dishes the children had used for the king cake were still on the table, she said, "But I thought I would straighten up the kitchen before I left."

Sophia waved a dismissing hand. "The kitchen is fine, Charlotte. Besides, I've decided to fix my special spaghetti sauce, and it'll just get messed up again."

Now what? Charlotte wondered. "Ah, if you'd like, I can stay and help out until Jean returns."

A sly smile pulled at Sophia's lips. "That's very kind of you, but contrary to the general opinion around here, I can handle things. Besides, Joey's coming for supper, and if I know my son, he'll be here way before it's ready."

With nothing left to do but leave, Charlotte nodded and picked up her supply carrier and vacuum cleaner. "In that case then, have a good evening."

"You too, and see you tomorrow," Sophia called out as Charlotte headed for the front door.

Outside, Gus was still standing watch at the front door. "Here, let me help you with that stuff," he said. And before Charlotte could object, he pulled the vacuum cleaner out of her hand. "At least until you get down those steps," he added with a grin.

Once she had descended the steps, he handed her the vacuum. "You have a good evening, now."

Charlotte smiled. "You too, Gus. And thanks." But when she turned back toward the walkway, out of the corner of her eye she saw someone emerge from the front door of the carriage house.

Wishing for her sunglasses that she'd left in the van, Charlotte squinted against the glare of the afternoon sun. After a moment, when her eyes adjusted, she swallowed hard.

The person coming out of the carriage house was Jean. And with Jean was Mark. Within moments, both were walking briskly down the pathway toward the main house.

Charlotte quickly glanced away as an uneasy feeling shivered through her. For a moment, she could have sworn that they were both staring straight at her, and during that fleeting moment, the wild notion that they were coming after her popped into her head.

Though she tried to ignore the feelings, she hurried toward the front gate anyway. Whether she was imagining things or not, the last thing she wanted at the moment was to come face-to-face with either of them.

As she approached the gate, Gino nodded a greeting, and then walked over to unlock it. While Charlotte waited, she couldn't stop thinking about Jean. Had the nanny been inside the carriage house all along? But why? Why hadn't she returned to the main house? Surely she had to have known that Sophia and the children were home by now.

Once Gino finally opened the gate, Charlotte didn't waste time walking through it. Feeling an urgency she couldn't explain, she hurried over to the van, set down the vacuum and the supply carrier, then reached inside her apron pocket for the keys. When she pulled out the ring of keys, her hands were trembling so badly that the keys jangled. Then she fumbled and dropped the key ring.

With an impatient groan, she bent over and snatched them

up off the pavement. Sucking in a deep breath, and willing her shaky fingers to be still, she finally guided the correct key into the keyhole, unlocked the back door of the van, and opened it.

She loaded the vacuum cleaner first. When she turned to pick up the supply carrier, she saw Mark walk through the gate and headed straight for her. Charlotte's insides shriveled and her blood pounded in her ears. In Mark's hand was a gun, and he had it pointed at her.

Chapter 16

Charlotte's first instinct was to scream bloody murder and run. Only problem, her feet wouldn't do her bidding and her breath seemed to be lodged in her throat, blocking any sound. By the time she could breathe again, Mark had the barrel of the gun shoved against her side.

"No sudden moves or sounds," he warned her, his voice low and heavy with menace. "As far as anyone else is concerned, we're just having a friendly conversation."

Friendly? Yeah, right, she thought, cutting her eyes toward the gate to see if Gino was paying attention. But Gino was no longer at the gate. Instead, he, along with Gus, were standing on the porch with Jean, and both were so enthralled with whatever she was telling them that neither was paying the least bit of attention to her or her situation.

"They won't help you," Mark stated. "My sister will see to that. And make no mistake. I will shoot you if you so much as twitch wrong."

The noise she'd heard in the hallway . . . Jean must have returned to the main house and seen her snooping, then run to tell Mark.

A sinking feeling settled in Charlotte's stomach. For Jean

and Mark to risk trying to get rid of her had to mean that they had killed Robert.

Now for sure there was no doubt that Mark meant what he said. He would shoot her. But now or later, what did it matter? Either way, she'd be dead . . . unless . . . If she could bide her time and keep her wits about her, then she maybe, just maybe, she could figure a way out of it without ending up dead.

Stall . . . stall for time.

Charlotte cleared her throat. "I—I don't understand. What's this all about, Mark?"

But Mark ignored her question. "What I want you to do now is hand me the keys, then, slowly bend down, pick up that supply thing, and put it in the van. Then we're both going to get inside and you're going to drive."

"Drive where?" Charlotte asked, still trying to stall.

"Never mind where. Just do it," he demanded, emphasizing each word with a jab of the gun barrel. "Do it now."

For a moment, Charlotte wondered what would happen if she pitched the keys out into the street.

He'd shoot you.

Reluctantly, she handed Mark the keys. Then, as slowly as she could and ever mindful of the gun in her ribs, she bent down and picked up the supply carrier.

"That'a girl. Put it inside the van now."

With a rebellious glare at her captor, Charlotte did as he said.

"Now close the door."

Charlotte slammed the door shut.

"Okay, this is what we're going to do. Both of us are going to get in the van from the passenger side. You first."

Why, oh why hadn't she bought the van with the bucket

seats instead of the bench seat? she wondered as she climbed in and slid across to the driver's side. If she'd bought the bucket seats, then she wouldn't be able to slide across. She would have had to get in on the driver's side, and Mark would have had a problem keeping the gun on her while he got inside on the passenger side, which might have been enough time for her to do something. . . .

Woulda, shoulda, coulda.

As Charlotte fastened her seat belt, Mark reached across and inserted the van key into the ignition switch. "Okay, let's go," he told her.

"Which way?"

"I don't know yet. For now, just drive."

Charlotte switched on the ignition. *Stall for time . . . play dumb.* If she drove to St. Charles Avenue, she might have a better chance of attracting someone's attention. There were also several traffic lights that might help stall for time.

Once she'd checked her rearview mirror and pulled out onto the street, she glanced at Mark. "You still haven't told me what's going on—why you're doing this."

"It won't work."

"What won't work?" Charlotte asked innocently, chancing another glance at him.

"Playing dumb won't work—and keep your eyes on the road. You know exactly what's going on and why. Jean saw you snooping through her stuff."

The creaking floor. Just as she'd suspected, someone had been outside in the hallway. Jean had been in the hall. But had Jean seen her looking at the eggs or had she seen her inspecting the costume . . . or both? Hopefully, just the eggs.

"Mark, be reasonable," Charlotte argued. "All I found were the eggs." But even as she lied, a mental image of Cleopatra's costume floated through her head, and Charlotte blinked several times to make it go away. "The only reason I found the eggs to begin with was because I was vacuuming beneath the bed. Anyone could have stashed the eggs there. Just because they are under Jean's bed isn't proof that she was stealing them, and it certainly isn't reason enough to kill me. If you kill me, that's murder, not just theft."

"Just cut the crap. We both know that once the police find out about the eggs, Jean and I will be their number one suspects for murder as well as theft. Taking the rap for theft is one thing, but I'm not going down for murder, especially one I didn't commit. But that won't matter to the police or to the family. And if the police don't get us, the family will, one way or another. Besides, we can't chance drawing that kind of attention to either of us. Too many questions."

He's telling the truth, she thought as she drove across the streetcar tracks and turned left onto St. Charles. But in spite of his explanation, Charlotte felt there was more to it. For one thing, why couldn't he simply admit that he and Jean were Robert's children? Why all the secrecy, especially considering that both Sophia and Emily already knew that they existed? Unless . . . Charlotte's mind raced. There *was* another reason, another possibility.

"Who are you protecting, Mark? If you didn't kill your father, then you must know who did. Who was it?"

Jean was the most likely, she figured. Both Emily and Sophia had motives as well. Suddenly Charlotte's breath caught in her throat . . . Amanda, after she'd washed her hands . . . telling her mother, *He won't see me.* How could the girl have known unless . . . ? Was that who Mark was protecting—Amanda?

Charlotte swallowed hard. "I wouldn't tell anyone," she said. "I promise I wouldn't. Both of you could pack up and leave, and no one would ever have to know." It was a bald-face lie. Of course she'd tell, but if she could convince Mark otherwise . . .

Mark shook his head. "Can't take that chance. Now, keep going till you get to the levee."

Charlotte's insides shriveled. Beyond the levee was the *batture,* a deserted, isolated place . . . a perfect place to get rid of someone.

Growing more desperate with each passing minute, Charlotte searched frantically for something to say that would change his mind. "I still don't understand," she finally said. "Why not just come right out and admit to the family who you are? Your grandmother would be overjoyed to have you back in her life."

Mark laughed, but the cynical sound sent chills down her spine. "Yeah, right!" he retorted. "And where was my grandmother when my father gave the order to have my mother murdered? And where has she been all these years while we were stowed away in a boarding school like so much dirty laundry?"

Not Sophia, then, Charlotte decided. *And probably not Emily either, come to think of it.* Protecting Emily wasn't logical since neither he nor Jean really knew her. But if he wasn't protecting Sophia or Emily, then that left Jean and Amanda. *Try to get him talking about Amanda.*

"What about Amanda and Brandon?" she asked. "I can't help but believe that they would love having a big brother and sister back in their life. And hasn't Jean lost enough already?"

Suddenly Mark shoved the gun into Charlotte's side and fear streaked through her.

"You leave them out of it," he warned. "They have nothing to do with anything!"

Charlotte gripped the steering wheel tighter and tried not to think about the pressure of the gun against her ribs or the sinking feeling in her stomach. Jean or Amanda. He had to be protecting one of them. But which one?

The pressure against her ribs increased. "Now shut up and drive," Mark snapped.

"Okay, okay," she whispered, trying to catch her breath. Within reason, Charlotte knew that he wouldn't risk his own neck and shoot her while she was driving, at least she hoped he wouldn't. But trying to reason with him clearly wasn't working. So what now? She had to do something, and do it fast.

Up ahead the traffic light at the intersection of Louisiana and St. Charles changed from green to yellow. As Charlotte braked to slow down, a possible way out suddenly occurred to her. But there was only one way it would work. She chanced a side glance at Mark. Sure enough, he hadn't fastened his seat belt.

Charlotte watched anxiously in hopes that the vehicle in front of her would go on through the yellow light, but to her disappointment, the vehicle stopped instead.

Charlotte gripped the steering wheel tighter with frustration and stopped too. Okay, she told herself, it didn't work for this traffic light, but she still had the traffic lights at the intersections of Napoleon, Jefferson, and Broadway, before Carrollton Avenue. After Carrollton though, were Leake Avenue and the levee beyond. She'd have to do it soon, but her timing would have to be perfect for her plan to work.

The traffic light changed from red to green, and as Charlotte slowly accelerated she maneuvered around the car in front of her. Already, people were beginning to line the Avenue, setting up their ladders and lawn chairs for the evening parades.

Keeping a sharp eye on the traffic ahead, watching for pedestrians, and jockeying for the right position in the ongoing traffic, she prayed for the light at Napoleon to turn red so that she could be at the head of the line to stop. Then she added another prayer for courage to do what had to be done.

In the distance, Charlotte could see that the traffic light at Napoleon was green, and hoping that Mark wouldn't notice, she eased up on the accelerator. Keeping a wary eye on the vehicle behind her as well as the one in front of her, she slowed even more. Then, to her relief, the traffic light turned yellow.

Please go through it, she silently urged the car in front of her, and held her breath. Sure enough, the vehicle zipped right under the light before it turned red, and Charlotte braked to a stop in the neutral ground between the lanes.

Dear Lord, give me patience and courage, she silently prayed as she watched the line of vehicles to her right cross St. Charles Avenue in front of her.

There was a momentary break in the traffic. Then she spotted a large delivery truck heading for the intersection. *Wait . . . wait . . . not yet . . . now!*

Charlotte stomped the accelerator just as the truck approached the intersection, and the van lurched forward.

"Hey!" Mark yelled. "What—"

Horns blared, brakes squealed, and Charlotte braced herself for the impact. The delivery truck slammed into Mark's side of the van. The explosive sound and grinding metal rang in her ears. The jolt shook the fillings in her teeth and hurled her sideways against the driver's door. Sharp pain ripped through her left shoulder. Her head banged against the window and colors exploded in her brain. Then she tasted blood as the truck shoved the van sideways toward the streetcar tracks.

Chapter 17

When the battered van finally came to rest just shy of the streetcar tracks, the momentary silence was deafening. Was she alive or was she dead?

When Charlotte opened her eyes, she was jammed sideways against the driver's door. The first thing that she saw was the shattered windshield. The safety glass had held together, but it was crumpled like an accordion.

She was alive, she decided, tasting something salty and gritty. Blood and possibly bits of glass, she decided. But how badly was she injured? Could she move? The seat belt had kept her from being propelled forward into the steering wheel, but it hadn't kept her from being thrown sideways into the door. Trying to keep from swallowing the gritty stuff in her mouth, ever so slowly she pulled away from the door until she was upright. Except for the dull throbbing in her head and the ache in her left shoulder, so far, so good, she thought. Now if only her arms worked. . . .

As she lifted her right arm, she slowly became aware of sounds from outside the van: brakes squealing, car doors slamming, and voices shouting.

"What happened?" someone yelled.

"Some crazy fool ran a red light," someone else answered.

"Alive or dead?" a third voice asked.

"I saw movement. Someone's alive."

Charlotte ignored the outside sounds for the moment. When she felt the tender knot on the side of her head, she winced. Using her fingers, she gingerly explored her face. No gashes anywhere, but her bottom lip was bleeding. She must have bit her lip. With her forefinger she carefully swabbed the inside of her mouth to rid herself of the bits of glass.

Still testing for injuries, she turned her head, first to the left and then to the right. But when she saw Mark, she forgot all about the dull throbbing in her head and her busted lip.

Mark was slumped over double at an unnatural angle, the side of his head resting on the mangled dash. His eyes were closed and his face was awash in blood. As best as she could tell, there were several minor cuts on the side of his head and one really deep-looking one on his forehead where he'd hit the windshield. Though he was unconscious and his breathing was shallow, at least he was alive . . . for now. But he needed help. And from the sounds of things, help was coming.

"Someone call the police!" a voice shouted.

"Call for an ambulance too," another voice yelled.

"Let's get the door open!"

Suddenly the driver's door was jerked open. "Hey, lady, are you okay in there?"

Charlotte forced herself to turn away from Mark. "I—I think so," she answered in a shaky voice as she stared at a man hunkered down near the door. "But he—" She motioned toward Mark. "He needs help."

"Just take it easy now. The police have been called and help is on the way."

* * *

From the moment the paramedics and police arrived, everything became a blur. Because of the scheduled parade, the police and paramedics worked quickly to clear the intersection.

Though Charlotte kept saying that she was okay, the EMT who examined her insisted that she needed to have a doctor check her out. In spite of Charlotte's objections, she was loaded into an ambulance and taken to the nearest hospital. Once there, an ER doctor who looked way too young to be a doctor in the first place examined her.

"The busted lip will heal on its own," he told her after a nurse had cleaned it and he'd poked and prodded around the lip, her head, and her shoulder. "But I want X-rays of that bump on the head and your shoulder."

An hour later, the same doctor returned to give her the news that nothing was cracked or broken. "A mild concussion is always possible with head injuries," he said. "But in this case, I don't think that's something you have to worry about. You're going to be sore, but Tylenol should help." He turned to the nurse. "Go ahead and give her a couple of Tylenol. And give her some sterile gauze for that lip too."

With a nod at Charlotte, the doctor turned to leave. "Ah, excuse me," Charlotte said. "Could you wait up a second?" When the doctor paused then faced her again, she continued. "I was wondering if you could tell me about Mark—Mark Jones, the man who was in the van with me? And what about the driver of the other vehicle? Are they okay?"

The doctor sighed then frowned. "Mr. Jones is seriously injured. He's in surgery. The other one just has a few scrapes and cuts."

"Thanks," Charlotte told him.

When the doctor left, Charlotte hurriedly dressed, but all she could think about was calling Judith to let her know what she'd discovered about Jean and Mark. She figured that once she'd put in a call to Judith, she'd hang around a while until she knew, one way or the other, if Mark was going to make it.

Just as Charlotte finished dressing, the nurse returned with the Tylenol and gauze. Charlotte obediently swallowed the pills, tucked the gauze into her pants pocket, and then left the small examination room.

The first person she saw when she stepped out into the hallway was a policeman. The minute the patrolman saw her, he stepped in front of her. "Ms. LaRue?" he asked. "Ms. Charlotte LaRue?"

Charlotte swallowed hard and nodded. "Yes?"

"I'm going to need to ask you some questions about your accident."

Suddenly Charlotte's nerves tensed, and words like *careless* and *reckless endangerment* popped into her head. She should have known better, but with everything that had happened, she'd never once considered that there might be legal repercussions when she'd purposely caused the wreck. All she'd thought about was trying to stay alive.

"Yes, of course," she finally answered. "But would it be okay if I just made one quick phone call to my family first, just to let them know that I'm all right? I'm also going to need a ride home." It wasn't exactly a lie, she reassured herself. She would reassure Judith that she was unharmed, just as soon as she told her about the accident. And she would need a ride home since she'd trashed her van. Then an idea occurred to her. Under normal circumstances, Charlotte never name-dropped, but she figured this was far from a normal circumstance. Maybe, just maybe, if he knew that her niece was a detective . . . "In fact, my niece is Detective Judith Monroe. She's with the sixth precinct."

The patrolman narrowed his eyes suspiciously, and for a moment, Charlotte was afraid that she'd gone too far, that she shouldn't have mentioned Judith.

"You can make your call," he finally said, "but I still have to question you."

Relief washed through Charlotte and, before she thought about it, she smiled. But her smile quickly turned into a wince of pain. "Ouch," she complained, and quickly pulled out the wad of gauze from her pocket and blotted her lip. Sure enough, it had started bleeding again.

Genuine concern crossed the patrolman's face. "You okay?" he asked.

Charlotte nodded. "Okay," she mumbled through stiff lips. "Just need to remember not to smile." Once she was sure that her lip had stopped oozing, she motioned toward the ER waiting room. "I'll call in there."

With the patrolman a few steps behind her, Charlotte headed for the waiting room. Ever conscious of the policeman's ominous presence, she walked over to an unoccupied corner of the room. To her profound relief, the policeman didn't follow her, but stationed himself at the door.

Charlotte eyed an empty chair, but decided she was far too nervous to sit. She took out her cell phone and tapped in Judith's phone number. Judith answered on the third ring.

"Judith Monroe, here."

"Judith, this is Aunt Charlotte, honey. I've been in an accident and need a ride home."

"An accident! What kind of accident? Are you okay? What happened?"

"I'm just fine, but that's not the only reason I'm calling and I don't have a lot of time, so listen up." Charlotte turned to face the corner of the room and lowered her voice. "I know who's been stealing those Fabergé eggs. Jean, the Rossis' new nanny, and her brother, Mark—he's one of the Rossis' bodyguards—they're the thieves. I found the eggs beneath the nanny's bed. But Mark and Jean aren't really who they say they are. They're really Robert Rossi's children by his first marriage. Their real names are Ben and Kay Rossi, and I'm pretty sure that both of them also had something to do with Robert Rossi's murder."

"Whoa, slow down, Auntie. Back up a minute. Are you sure you didn't get a lick on the head in that accident? You're not making a lot of sense."

"Well, I did get my head banged, but the doctor said I'm just fine, and if I'm not making sense, it's because I'm trying to hurry through this."

"Why don't you start from the beginning?"

"There's no time for that now." Charlotte turned to see if the policeman was still standing by the door. "There's a policeman here and any minute he's probably going to arrest me for reckless endangerment or some such thing. You need to have Jean—I mean Kay—picked up right away before she finds out what's happened—"

"Aunt Charley, I can't just go out and arrest someone on your say-so, not without knowing—"

"Judith, that Kay person and her brother tried to kill me."

"What!"

Again, Charlotte turned to check out the whereabouts of the patrolman. When she saw that he was walking toward her, she said, "Just hurry up and get here. That policeman is coming now."

"Auntie, don't you dare hang up! For one thing, you haven't told me where you're at."

"The emergency room at Memorial."

"Don't hang up, Aunt Charley!" Judith demanded again. "Let me talk to the patrolman."

"Okay." Charlotte swallowed hard and held out her cell phone. "My niece wants to talk to you."

Frowning, the patrolman took the phone. "Yeah, hello." After a moment, he said, "Roberts—Jack Roberts, with the second." A moment more passed. "She ran a traffic light at Napoleon and St. Charles." After several moments in which he mostly listened and shot daggers at Charlotte with his eyes, he finally said, "Yeah, I understand." He closed the flip phone and handed it back to Charlotte.

"She hung up," he told Charlotte, "but said to tell you that she's on her way."

Charlotte dropped the phone back inside her pocket.

"She also said for you to wait here," he added, and motioned toward a chair. "Sit."

Her nerves still jumping, Charlotte sat in the chair he'd indicated, and silently prepared herself to explain her actions. Then, to her utter amazement, the patrolman said, "I'm going outside to have a smoke. Once your niece gets here, then you can go over what all happened with both of us."

Without another word, he pivoted and marched out of the waiting room.

As Charlotte watched the patrolman disappear through the doorway, her mind raced, mostly with thoughts of Mark and his sister. Mark had tried to kill her, but that didn't mean that she wished him dead.

Charlotte lowered her head and stared at the tile floor. Unbidden, memories of another man who had tried to kill her came to mind and she shivered. It had been almost a year since the incident had happened, and the man had died. He'd died because of something she'd done while trying to protect herself. Logically, she knew that what had happened wasn't totally her fault, that time or this time. But the last thing she wanted was for the same thing to happen again, for another man to die because of her.

There was no way that she could just sit and wait. She needed to know what Mark's condition was. Glancing around to make sure that the patrolman was nowhere in sight, Charlotte stood and walked purposefully toward the door. If she happened to run into the patrolman on her way out, she figured she could always claim that she needed to use the rest room.

Once in the hallway, there was still no sight of the policeman, so she walked quickly toward the reception desk.

"Excuse me," she said to the woman behind the desk. "Where did they take Mr. Mark Jones for surgery? He was just brought in a little over an hour ago—an accident victim."

The woman turned to the computer monitor, typed in something on the keyboard, then scanned down the screen. "He's in surgery on the third floor," she said.

"Thanks," Charlotte whispered, and headed for the bank of elevators.

When she reached the third floor, she finally found the waiting room for surgery, and again headed for the information desk. Two older women, both wearing badges identifying them as hospital volunteers, were seated behind the desk.

"May I help you?" the one on her left asked with a smile.

"Oh, I hope so," Charlotte told her. "I'm trying to find out about Mark Jones. We were in an accident, and downstairs they told me that he was in surgery."

The woman smiled again. "Like I just told his mother, he's still in surgery, but he's doing well. Shouldn't be too much longer now."

"Oh, wonderful, I'm so glad that he's . . ." Charlotte's words died in her throat as the rest of what the woman had said sank in, and she frowned. "Did you say his *mother?* His mother is here?"

"Yes, of course. She's right over there getting a cup of coffee."

When the volunteer motioned toward the coffee station, Charlotte turned to where she had pointed. There was only one woman at the coffee station, and she had her back to Charlotte.

Charlotte took a step toward her. But as Charlotte took another step, the woman turned around. When Charlotte saw who the woman was, she froze with disbelief as she watched the woman seat herself and take a sip of the coffee.

Chapter 18

Suddenly all the pieces of the deadly puzzle fell together. "Of course," Charlotte whispered. How could she have not known? The resemblance was there all along. Just barely, but it was there. The heavy-framed glasses were missing, and her dark hair was styled differently, but there was no mistaking that she was the same woman in all three photos Charlotte had seen.

Afraid that the woman would see her, Charlotte tucked her head and eased over to a group of chairs on the opposite side of the room. She picked up a magazine on a nearby table, then chose a chair that was facing the opposite direction, seated herself, and pretended to be reading the magazine.

Thinking back, Charlotte figured that the photo in the family album where the children were really young had to have been taken right before Linda Rossi had disappeared. And the other one, the one in which her face was scarred, must have been taken after she had disappeared. She could have been in a terrible accident of some kind, Charlotte decided.

Yeah, right. More like an accident on purpose.

Charlotte shivered. If, as Bitsy believed, Robert had tried to kill his first wife, but she'd somehow survived, the scar could have been the results of the attempted murder. And later she could have had plastic surgery to repair her face, which would explain the photo tucked away in Jean's suitcase.

Now it all made perfect sense, Charlotte thought as she dared a quick look at the woman.

. . . we can't chance drawing that kind of attention to either of us. Too many questions.

Mark's words rang in Charlotte's head. Mark hadn't been trying to protect his sister, Jean, or his half sister, Amanda. He'd been protecting his mother, the woman who now called herself Anna Smith, the same woman who had showed up on the night of the party and claimed to work for Big Easy Catering Company, and the same woman that the family thought was dead.

Not everyone thought she was dead, though. Charlotte tucked her head and stared with unseeing eyes at the magazine. *. . . that sweet Linda came back to make sure Robert paid for what he did to them. . . . And I helped too.*

Sophia had known, Charlotte realized. The old lady had recognized that Anna was really Robert's first wife, Linda.

Charlotte bit off a groan and squeezed her eyes shut as she recalled the blood on the towel and washcloths that belonged in Sophia's bathroom. Sophia had not only recognized Robert's first wife, but the crafty old lady had probably helped her ex-daughter-in-law cover up her crime by creating a diversion so that Anna would have time to clean herself up without anyone being the wiser.

Now what? Charlotte wondered. After a moment she sighed deeply, opened her eyes, lifted her head, and stared straight at the woman she now knew was Linda Rossi, the same woman who she was convinced had been responsible for Robert Rossi's murder.

As if Linda Rossi sensed someone was watching her, she

looked up and glanced around the room. Then her gaze clashed with Charlotte's. Even from across the room, Charlotte could tell from Linda's startled expression the exact moment the woman recognized her. When Linda shifted her gaze toward the door, for a second, Charlotte was afraid that she might run.

Before she had time to talk herself out of it, and praying that Linda wouldn't run, Charlotte dropped the magazine, stood, and with determined steps, hurried across the room to where Linda Rossi was seated.

Linda didn't run though, and by the time Charlotte reached her, Linda had regained her composure and had pasted a fake smile on her face.

"Hey, Charlotte. Fancy seeing you here." She motioned toward Charlotte's busted lip. "My goodness, what happened to you?"

As if you didn't know, thought Charlotte. Aloud she said, "The lady at the desk said that Mark was going to be okay." Without waiting for an invitation, Charlotte sat down in a chair directly across from Linda.

"Mark?"

Charlotte nodded, crossed her arms against her breasts, and leveled a no-nonsense look at Linda. "Yes, Mark, aka Ben—your son," she said bluntly. "That is why you're here, isn't it? And by the way, how did you know he was here?"

"Why would you think that? I—"

"Don't!" Charlotte shot back. "Don't even try denying it."

For long tension-filled seconds, a kaleidoscope of emotions played across Linda's face. Then a lone tear trickled down her cheek and her face collapsed into utter desolation. "He—he has an emergency contact card in—in his wallet."

Deciding to go for broke, Charlotte pressed her momentary advantage. "You do know that the reason your son is in there, fighting for his life, is because he was trying to protect you. Unless you tell the truth, not only will he be charged with attempted murder on me, but there's a good chance that both he and your daughter could be charged with murdering their father as well."

Tears streamed down Linda's cheeks, and hugging herself, she rocked back and forth as suppressed sobs shook her body and heart-wrenching mewling noises escaped her lips.

Sympathy welled up within Charlotte, and it was all she could do to keep from rushing over to Linda's side and comforting her in some way. But she kept reminding herself that an innocent woman's life was at stake—Emily's life.

"Look, we both know that Ben and Kay didn't do it," Charlotte said as gently as she could. "And we both know who did do it. You did it." She paused, then added, "Didn't you, Linda?" When Linda still didn't say anything, Charlotte searched for something to say, some way to get Linda to admit what she'd done. Then, out of nowhere, she recalled a particular episode of *NYPD Blue* that she'd watched in which Andy Sipowicz had been interrogating a suspect. Granted, *NYPD Blue* was just a television show, but . . .

"Maybe you didn't set out to kill him," Charlotte suggested. "Maybe things just got out of hand. Maybe he walked in on Ben or Kay stealing the eggs, and . . ." Charlotte purposely left the sentence unfinished in hopes that the stratagem would work and that Linda would explain.

Linda reached up and covered her face with her hands. "You're right," she sobbed.

Charlotte hardly dared to breathe as she waited while Linda drew in a deep, shaky breath, scrubbed at her eyes, and sniffed as she tried to compose herself. Spotting a box of tissues on a table nearby, Charlotte got up and retrieved the box.

Pulling several tissues free from the box, she offered them to Linda. “Here,” she said. “Blow your nose.”

“Thanks,” Linda whispered. After she blew her nose, she motioned toward the empty chair beside her. “Please, sit here. I’d just as soon not attract any more attention than I already have.”

With a nod, Charlotte sat down. Then she reached out and squeezed Linda’s shoulder. “Why don’t you start from the beginning,” she suggested gently.

Linda nodded, sucked in a deep, shaky breath, and in a soft voice laced with pain and regret, she began. “I was really young and naive when I married Robert,” she told Charlotte. “You’ve heard the phrase, ‘Too stupid to live’? That was me. But by the time I realized just who and what Robert was—what I’d married into—it was too late. By then I had two little children to take care of.”

Linda squeezed her eyes closed and shook her head. “He was a monster.” When she opened her eyes, they sparkled with anger and a tinge of fear. “A horrible, sadistic monster who took pleasure in other people’s pain. Believe me, I have the scars to prove it.” She paused, and after a moment, a faraway look filled with sadness came into her eyes.

“Then one day I met Luke. Robert had gone on one of his rampages, and as a result, I ended up in the ER with a broken arm. Luke was the ER doctor who took care of me, and he was one of the kindest, most considerate men I had ever met. He was everything that my husband wasn’t, and I fell in love with him. Then, after a time, to my amazement, I discovered that he loved me too, and he loved my children.”

Abruptly, Linda shook her head as if to rid herself of the bittersweet memory. “Anyway, to make a long story short, I got pregnant, and like an idiot, instead of just leaving, I told Robert

I was divorcing him. It didn't take him or his hounds long to sniff out the truth, and he gave the order to—to—" Linda's voice broke. "To have Luke and me killed," she whispered, her eyes filling with more tears.

Charlotte immediately reached over and took Linda's hands in her own. After a moment Linda squeezed Charlotte's hands and haltingly continued. "He-he had Luke murdered first. Even show-showed me the article in the newspaper. Then he-he had one of his flunkies drive me to-to-a swamp on the Westbank." She shook her head. "I-I tried to get away, tried to run, but he-he caught me. Shot me in the stomach to kill my baby, then shot me in the head. He-he killed my-my sweet baby," she sobbed, no longer caring that the people seated around them had begun to stare.

Tears of sympathy sprang into Charlotte's eyes. She reached out and wrapped her arms around Linda and held her until she stopped crying again.

When Linda finally pulled away, she continued her terrifying story. "After he shot-shot me, I-I pretended to be dead, and he-he started burying me."

At even the thought of being buried alive, Charlotte shivered.

"Before he finished, though," Linda went on, "he took off. I must have passed out, because when I woke up, I was in a hospital. Later I learned that a hunter had heard the gunshots. When the hunter went to investigate, he found me and took me to the hospital."

Suddenly Linda stiffened and defiant fire danced in her eyes. "But I survived," she told Charlotte. "My baby was dead and my face was a mess, everyone that I loved had been taken from me, but I survived. The one thing—the only thing—that kept me going was my children, Kay and Ben. All I could think about was finding them, finding them and making sure that they didn't grow up with Robert as a father. It took me two years to find them, then another year to figure out how to kidnap them from that school where he'd dumped them. Then there were the countless surgeries to repair my face."

"What did you live on? How—"

"Even before I met Luke, I knew there would come a day when I'd have to leave Robert, so for a long time I'd been saving every penny I could get my hands on. Later, when the money ran out, I worked at odd jobs just to keep food on the table and a roof over our heads. But I did it."

As a single mother, Charlotte could sympathize, and though she'd had her own tragedies in her life, her tragedies paled in comparison to what Linda had gone through.

"Why didn't you go to the police?" Charlotte asked. "Or the FBI? Someone?"

Linda laughed harshly. "Which ones? Robert bragged that he had them all on his payroll."

As if the mention of police had conjured one up, out of the corner of her eye Charlotte spotted Judith walk in through the waiting room door. Charlotte panicked, afraid that Linda might try to run once she learned that Judith was a detective.

"Not every policeman is on the take," Charlotte said quickly as Judith headed toward her. "In fact, I can vouch for one detective in particular who is squeaky clean."

"I can't afford to trust any of them," Linda retorted, and she was still shaking her head when Judith approached Charlotte.

"Aunt Charley, I've been looking all over the hospital for you. You were supposed to wait for me downstairs."

Charlotte nodded. "I know, hon, and I'm sorry." Charlotte turned to Linda. "Linda, I want you to meet my niece." Charlotte glared at Judith, hoping that she wouldn't jump to conclusions. "Judith, this is Linda Rossi." Charlotte turned back to Linda. "Judith happens to be that squeaky-clean detective I told you about."

When Linda stiffened and her eyes darted back and forth between Charlotte and Judith, Charlotte knew that she had to say something and say it quickly.

"Linda, please," Charlotte begged. "I promise you that my niece is one of the good guys, one you can trust with your life. And once she knows what all you've been through, I also promise she'll help you."

Though Judith gave Charlotte a narrow-eyed, suspicious look, to Charlotte's relief she seemed to sense that she should keep quiet for the moment and let Charlotte do all of the talking.

"I want you to continue your story," Charlotte told Linda. "And I want Judith to hear it. I'll fill her in later on what you've told me so far, but she needs to hear the rest. And you need to tell the rest," she added meaningfully.

Charlotte was afraid to move or even breathe as she watched the play of emotions on Linda's face. Then, to her relief, Linda finally nodded, and Charlotte was able to breathe again.

"Are you who I think you are?" Judith asked as she sat across from Charlotte and Linda. "Are you Robert Rossi's first wife?"

Linda nodded, then with a shudder of revulsion, she said, "Legally, I guess I'm still his wife since there was never a divorce."

When Judith frowned, Charlotte spoke up. "I'll explain that part later." She turned to Linda. "Tell Judith what happened the night that Robert was killed."

"I will," she whispered. "But first you have to understand that no one set out to murder him. From the time that Ben and Kay were old enough to understand about their father and what he'd tried to do, all they wanted was revenge. Not murder. Just revenge. They only wanted some way to make him pay for what he'd done. Don't ask me how, because I don't know, but some way Ben got hired on as one of the bodyguards, and at first it was all about stealing the eggs, or so I thought. Then, just a couple of nights before the party, I overheard him and Kay making plans to break into Robert's safe in the library. There was no talking them out of it, and believe me, I tried. Anyway, when Ben came in complaining about having to help serve because the people Emily hired were sick, I figured that was my chance to keep an eye on them, just in case things went wrong."

Charlotte nodded. "I thought something was fishy when I introduced you to Mark—I mean Ben—that night. But weren't you taking an awful chance that Robert would recognize you?"

Linda shrugged. "Why would he? He thought I was dead. Besides, I avoided him as much as possible, and I don't exactly look like I did back then."

Sophia's epiphany. "But Sophia recognized you," Charlotte said. "And she helped you."

Instead of answering Charlotte, Linda turned to Judith. "I killed Robert," she said in an even voice. "But I want you to know it was self-defense."

"Explain," Judith told her bluntly.

"Just before midnight I realized that I hadn't seen Kay in a while, and I went looking for her. The library door was cracked open enough for me to see that Robert was holding a gun on Kay, and I realized that he must have caught her trying to break into the safe. Then I heard him tell her that he was going to make an example out of her so that no one else would think they could steal from him and get away with it. Once I realized that he intended to kill her, I panicked. I grabbed the knife hanging on the wall and I stabbed him."

A faraway look came into Linda's eyes. "One thing about Robert, he kept all of his weapons in tip-top condition," she whispered. "That knife was razor-sharp."

A moment more passed and Linda finally shook her head. "Kay was in shock. I was trying to drag her out of the library and we were almost to the door when Amanda suddenly appeared. Before I could get Kay out and shut the door, Amanda saw Robert. I tell you it was the strangest thing I've ever seen. That child didn't scream or even cry. She walked right past us as if we weren't even there. When she got to Robert, she just stood there staring at him for what seemed like forever. Then she reached down, dipped her fingertips in his blood, and smeared it over his eyes."

Cold shivers chased down Charlotte's spine as she listened to the harrowing account.

"It was as if she were in a some kind of a trance or something," Linda whispered. "Then, just like that"—Linda snapped her fingers—"she came out of it, and from the way she acted you'd have never guessed that anything had happened. She looked me straight in the eye and said that I shouldn't worry, that she wouldn't tell. And she said that she was glad that her father wouldn't be able to hurt her mother anymore." Linda shook her head. "Even more strange, before she left the library, she hugged us both. After that, she headed for the kitchen."

"So that's how the blood got on the costume," Charlotte murmured. But both Linda and Judith ignored her.

"I'm telling you," Linda continued, "by that time, I was almost a basket case. I sent Kay to find Ben, and he made sure that Kay got out. They wanted me to go with them, but I told them that it would look too suspicious if we all disappeared. Besides, Robert couldn't hurt me any longer.

"Anyway, I needed to clean up and was able to slip up the stairs without anyone noticing. Or so I thought." Linda looked directly at Charlotte. "A while ago, you asked about Sophia. Sophia followed me up the stairs and helped me get cleaned up. But I honestly think that the old lady thought I was a ghost or something."

Linda turned to Judith. "I swear I never meant for Emily to take the blame," she vowed. "I'd already made up my mind to turn myself in, then"—"she motioned toward Charlotte—"all this other stuff happened."

It was well past dark by the time that Judith was finally able to take Charlotte home. As Judith pulled into the driveway on Charlotte's side of the double, Charlotte was relieved to see that Louis's car was parked in the other driveway. With Louis home, at least she wouldn't have to worry about Joyce.

"Get some rest, Auntie," Judith told her as she slipped the gear into park.

"I intend to," Charlotte told her. The Tylenol she'd been given in the ER had long ago worn off, and though she'd expected to be a bit stiff and sore from the wreck, she felt as if every muscle in her body had rebelled. "Right after I take a long hot bath," she added.

"If you'd like, tomorrow I can take you to see about your van."

"Thanks, hon, but right now I'm too tired to even think about it."

"Just give me a call then when you're ready. And another

thing, Auntie. Just so you know, you did good today." Before Charlotte even had a chance to savor the rare compliment, Judith added. "Just don't ever do something like that again."

Charlotte could have argued with Judith that she certainly hadn't set out to get involved with the mob or with a murder investigation, but she was just too bone tired. Instead she said, "Do me a favor, please. I don't really feel up to getting the third degree from Hank tonight. Wait until tomorrow before you tell him about my little accident." Then, without waiting for Judith's answer, Charlotte opened the car door and climbed out. "Love you, hon. Good night, and thanks again for the ride home."

Charlotte had slept until almost eight on Tuesday. She was in the kitchen having her first cup of coffee and had just begun skimming the headlines on the front page of the *Times-Picayune* when someone knocked on her front door.

"Probably Hank," she grumbled as she went into the living room. But when she peeped out of the front window, she saw Louis instead.

"Just a minute," she called out as she hurried to the bedroom to get her housecoat. On her way back to the door, she slipped the housecoat on and tied the belt. Then she opened the door.

"Where's your van?" Louis asked, his gaze taking in her disheveled appearance and honing in on her busted lip. "What in the devil's going on?"

As if it's any of your business. Charlotte sighed. He was going to find out eventually, one way or another, so she might as well get it over with.

"And a good morning to you too." She motioned for him to come inside. "It's a long story, so you might as well come in."

Once inside, Charlotte motioned for him to follow her. "And you might as well have a cup of coffee." Without waiting for an answer, she headed for the kitchen and Louis followed her. Once she'd poured him a cup of coffee and seated herself at the table, she said, "I had a wreck yesterday."

"Guess that explains the missing van and busted lip." Suddenly he reached for the newspaper, thumbed through several pages, then pointed at a particular article. "But what about this?" He slid the paper in front of Charlotte.

When Charlotte saw the headline, she felt as if someone had punched her in the stomach. "A CLEAN GETAWAY FOR LOCAL MAID."

Without giving her time to read the article beneath the headline, Louis slid the paper away and said, "I assume that you're the maid it's talking about?"

Charlotte snatched the newspaper back, and only after she'd skimmed the article did she dare to breathe again. The article was an account of her harrowing escape after being kidnapped because of the information she had about the murder of Robert Rossi. "At least they didn't mention me by name," she murmured. "I wonder how that happened."

"So it was you." Louis slapped the top of the table. "I knew it! I leave for a couple of days and all hell breaks loose. And they didn't mention your name because you're going to have to testify when it goes to trial. What in the devil were you thinking?"

Charlotte felt her temper rising. "What was I thinking?" She glared at him. "Well, duh, let's see now. How about I was thinking that I didn't want to end up with a bullet in my head?"

Louis held up a hand. "Okay, okay, just calm down. All I'm saying is—"

"All you're saying is I told you so," Charlotte retorted. "And a fat lot of good that does now."

Louis shrugged. "Well, I did tell you—"

"I don't want to hear it, so just put a lid on it."

For long moments, the air between them crackled with tension, then, as quickly as it had erupted, Charlotte's temper abated. "Drink your coffee before it gets cold." She shoved out of her chair. "I need to check my blood sugar and eat a bite of breakfast. Should I fix enough for you too?"

Louis shook his head. "Thanks, but I ate earlier with Joyce."

Charlotte paused. "So how is Joyce this morning?"

"About the same. And contrary to what you think, I also came over to thank you for what you did for her while I was gone." A grin pulled at Louis's lips. "She told me all about how you bullied her into going to the beauty shop."

Charlotte smiled then winced from the pain in her busted lip. "Just chalk it up to therapy," she said as she gingerly felt her lip to make sure it wasn't bleeding again. "If a woman looks good, she feels good."

"Whatever, it seems to have worked. Her spirits are up, and she's even talking about having Amy come over and spend the afternoon."

Score one for the good guys, Charlotte thought. "That's wonderful and exactly what she needs." A warm glow filled Charlotte, and thoughts of her own grandbaby-to-be made her want to smile again, until she remembered that she shouldn't because of her lip. "Speaking of grandchildren, did I tell you that Carol is pregnant?"

Louis shook his head and grinned. "Hey, that's great. Congratulations, Grandma."

"Thanks, *Grandpa,*" Charlotte shot back. But the moment

the words left her mouth, Charlotte felt her face grow warm, and she quickly turned away and walked over to the cabinet. Not only was she embarrassed by the implied relationship, but she was also ashamed. Once again she had to remind herself that she was not just sitting around waiting for Joyce Thibodeaux to die so that she and Louis could resume some kind of a relationship.

Since there was no telling who else might show up on her doorstep after Louis left, Charlotte decided that she might as well get dressed. Besides, she thought, at some point she had to see about renting a car, at least until she found out the fate of her van.

In between phone calls from Hank, Madeline, Daniel, and Judith, Charlotte tried to rest, but relaxing proved to be impossible, especially when her thoughts kept returning to earlier that morning when Louis had dropped in.

Charlotte put down the latest mystery novel she'd been reading and stared at Sweety Boy who was busy pecking at the cuttle bone in his cage. "Maybe I need a hobby of some kind. What do you think, Boy?"

Realizing that he had Charlotte's attention, the little bird began squawking and chirping, then, sidled over to the cage door.

"No, I'm not letting you out right now," Charlotte told him. With a groan she pushed herself up off the sofa and went into the kitchen for something to drink. But the more she thought about it, the more she decided that a hobby might not be such a bad idea. At least it would be something to occupy her mind besides work and family . . . and Louis Thibodeaux.

Charlotte filled a glass full of water. "Humph!" she grunted. "At the rate I'm going, maybe I should take karate or some kind of martial arts class, or at least a self-defense course. Now wouldn't that be a hoot?" Charlotte drank the glass of water. But as she sat the glass on the counter, the sound of a horn beeping out front made her frown. When the horn continued beeping, her frown grew deeper.

"What on earth?" she complained as she went back into the living room. Unable to stem her curiosity, she walked to the front window. Outside, sitting in her driveway was an unfamiliar van.

"Now what?" she muttered as she opened her front door. The moment that she stepped out onto the porch, the irritating beeping abruptly stopped, and the door to Louis's side of the double swung open.

"What's going on?" Louis asked as he joined Charlotte on the porch.

"I haven't the foggiest," Charlotte answered.

Suddenly the van door opened, and to Charlotte's utter amazement, Emily Rossi stepped out.

"Hey, Charlotte," Emily called out. "Could you come here a minute?"

Charlotte was both overjoyed to see that Emily was out of jail and puzzled, wondering why on earth Emily was even there. Charlotte turned to Louis. "It's okay. It's just Emily Rossi."

But instead of going back inside the house, Louis's mouth took on an unpleasant twist as if he'd just bit into a lemon. "Maybe I'll just wait here until you see what she wants," he said, and then he walked over to the swing and sat down.

Though Charlotte told him, "Suit yourself," secretly she was relieved to know that he was staying.

As Charlotte descended the stairs and approached Emily, a black Lincoln Town Car slowed in front of her house then pulled into her driveway behind the van. Charlotte immediately recognized Gus as the driver.

Emily glared at the Town Car. "I told him to give me an hour or so," she said, clearly displeased that the bodyguard had shown up so soon.

"Emily, what's going on? And by the way, I'm so glad they released you."

"Me too," Emily said with feeling. Then she reached out and patted the side of the van. "But how do you like my new van?"

Charlotte frowned as a sneaking suspicion began to form in the back of her mind. "The van is just fine."

"Don't you want to check out the inside? It's top of the line and has every imaginable gadget there is."

The suspicion in the back of Charlotte's mind began to grow. "Emily, what's this all about?"

"Here." Emily held out a key ring. When Charlotte began to shake her head, Emily picked up Charlotte's hand and dropped the key ring into her palm. Then she folded Charlotte's hand over the key ring. "It's yours," Emily told her. "The van is all yours."

Again Charlotte shook her head and tried to give the keys back to Emily. "I can't possibly—"

"Yes, you can," Emily said sternly. "It's my way of saying thank you. After all, it's because of me that your van got totaled."

"That's not exactly true, but how did *you* know it was totaled? I only just found out myself a few hours ago."

Emily's lips curved into a sly smile. "Oh, I have my ways. But never mind that for now. Could we go inside and at least talk about it? Besides, there are a few other things I need to talk to you about."

Feeling more uncomfortable with each passing moment, Charlotte finally nodded. "We can go inside, but there's no way I can accept that van." Again she tried to give Emily back the keys, and again Emily refused.

As they both climbed the steps to the porch, Emily asked, "Who's your friend in the swing?"

"That's Louis Thibodeaux, my tenant," Charlotte told her.

"Funny. He kind of reminds me of my bodyguards."

Charlotte glanced at Louis then rolled her eyes. "Just ignore him," she told Emily.

Once inside, Charlotte motioned for Emily to be seated on the sofa. Then she dropped the van keys on the coffee table. "Can I get you something to drink? Coffee? Iced tea?"

Emily smiled. "No thanks," she said as she glanced around the living room. "Nice place," she said.

Charlotte nodded and seated herself in the overstuffed chair across from the sofa. "I like it. Now—about that van."

"Let's not talk about that just yet. I just thought you might like to know that I've been cleared of all charges, thanks to you and thanks to poor Linda. When I think of all that she's gone through, all that Robert put her and those kids through, I get so mad I can hardly see straight. Which brings me to another reason I'm here. I'm hoping to persuade you not to hold what Mark—I mean Ben—did against him. None of this is his fault, you know. And he was only trying to protect his mother, something any good son would do."

"What's the latest on his condition?" Even as Charlotte asked the question, it began to dawn on her that the whole deal about the van was, in all likelihood, actually a bribe, a bribe cleverly disguised as a thank-you gift.

Emily smiled. "Oh, Mark—I mean Ben—I swear I don't think I'll ever get used to calling him Ben. Anyway, he's going to be just fine. The minute I heard about what happened, I instructed Leo to fly in the best neurosurgeon in the country for him. With some recovery time and some physical therapy, Ben will be as good as new in no time." She paused and her smile faded. "Of course when he does recover, he'll probably end up in prison, unless . . ."

"Unless I refuse to testify against him," Charlotte said bluntly, finishing the sentence for her. "But why, Emily? Why do you care what happens to Ben or Linda, or even Kay?"

Emily smiled. "Didn't fool you for a moment, did I?"

"If you're talking about the van, then no."

Emily sighed and her expression grew serious. "Leo has informed me that up until Robert died, Linda was legally still his wife. And since Robert was so arrogant that he never made out a will, the estate could be tied up forever. I could fight it, but that could take years. Besides, Linda and I have already discussed it all and have come to an agreement. I've instructed Leo to represent all three of them, and Leo seems to think that he can get them off. He's pleading self-defense on Linda's behalf, and of course neither Sophia nor I will press charges against Kay for stealing the eggs. But everything else hinges on whether you will refuse to testify against Ben.

"I know how all of that sounds." Emily grimaced. "It may not seem like it, but believe it or not, I do care what happens to all of them, even in spite of all that other stuff."

After a moment, Charlotte said, "I believe you." And she meant it. Though she'd only known Emily for a short period of time, she'd known Bitsy for many years. If Bitsy believed in Emily and said Emily was a good person, then she was.

At the thought of Bitsy, Charlotte's insides twisted into knots. All day she'd put off calling the old lady. Suddenly an idea came to Charlotte. "Tell you what, Emily. I'll make you a deal. I'll refuse to testify against Ben if you do two things for me. No—make that three things." Charlotte held up her index finger. "Number one. Take the van back. There's no way I can accept an out-and-out bribe. And we both know that's what it would be." She added her middle finger. "Number two. *You* call Bitsy and explain everything that's happened. I love her dearly, but trying to explain all of this gives me a headache just thinking about it. And last but not least, number three." She added her ring finger. "Simply pay me for the hours I've already worked and we'll call it even."

A slow smile pulled at Emily's lips. "You drive a hard bargain, Charlotte LaRue, especially the part about calling Bitsy." She giggled. "Bless her old heart, Bitsy means well and has a heart of gold, but she can be a pill sometimes. As for the pay I owe you"—Emily reached inside her purse and pulled out a fat envelope—"I believe this should cover it." She placed the envelope on the coffee table. "But are you sure about the van?"

Charlotte stared at the money she'd earned and thought about the van. Never in her entire life had anyone given her a car. She'd had to scrimp and save and work hard for every vehicle she'd ever owned.

Her mind wandered back to the conversation she had with her insurance adjuster earlier that day. The van was totaled, and because of its age, the Bluebook value would be barely enough to cover a down payment on a new van, which made Emily's offer oh-so-tempting. Fighting the temptation, Charlotte nodded. "I'm sorry, but I'm sure. I just can't accept the van."

"Okay, then I guess we have a deal," Emily said with a sly smile. "I'll call Bitsy. And now"—she stood—"I really have to go. I've got about a million things to take care of." She walked briskly to the front door. "I'll see myself out. Now you take care, Charlotte LaRue, and if you ever need a permanent job, just give me a call. I owe you big-time."

With that, Emily flounced out the door, closing it behind her.

After a moment, Charlotte sighed. "Well, Sweety, I had my chance." Her gaze landed on the envelope of money, and when she reached down and picked it up, only then did she realize that beneath the envelope were the keys to the van.

"Why, that little sneak," she muttered. Snatching up the keys, she rushed over to the door. But she was already too late. Gone were the Town Car and Emily, and still parked in her driveway was the van.

"Deal, my hind foot," Charlotte grumbled as she closed the door. Deciding she'd better check inside the envelope to see if Emily left any other surprises for her, she opened the flap and pulled out the wad of bills.

Folded neatly on top of the stack was the title to the van. Charlotte thumbed through the money, and did some quick calculations in her head. Give or take a couple of dollars, she figured the total was correct.

But what was she going to do about the ding-dang van? With a deep sigh, Charlotte walked over to the sofa and sat down.

What goes 'round, comes 'round, and people get paid back for the things they do in this life.

As the saying swirled in Charlotte's head, she wondered if it meant that people got paid back for the good things that they did in life as well as the bad things. Or did it mean that if she accepted the van, then she would get paid back for taking a bribe?

"Not a bribe," she whispered. It wasn't a bribe if she'd already decided to refuse to testify against Ben *before* Emily offered the van . . . was it?

Only time would tell, she finally decided. Only time would tell.

A Cleaning Tip from Charlotte

To get rid of those unsightly water rings that are left on wooden furniture after the grandchildren or careless guests leave, try rubbing them—the water rings, not the grandchildren or guests—with a generous dollop of regular mayonnaise. Leave the mayonnaise on for several hours, then wipe off with a clean cloth. Of course, to avoid this type of mishap to begin with, always have plenty of coasters scattered around.

A Special Dedication to the Citizens of New Orleans

On August 29, 2005 Hurricane Katrina struck the Gulf Coast, and New Orleans, Louisiana received a deadly blow resulting in the loss of lives, the loss of a way of life, and the loss of a great historical city that will never be the same again. When writing *Married to the Mop*, I never once dreamed that such a terrible disaster could happen to the great city that I've grown to love and appreciate. It is my sincere hope that the New Orleans depicted in this book will in some small way remind my readers of what a wonderful and unique city it was, and with God's help, will be again.

Barbara Colley, September 2005